The Incredible
True Story of
the Making
of the Eve of
Destruction

Also by Amy Brashear

No Saints in Kansas

The Incredible True Story of the Making of the Eve of Destruction

AMY BRASHEAR

Published in the United States by Soho Teen
an imprint of
Soho Press, Inc.
853 Broadway
New York, NY 10003

Library of Congress Cataloging-in-Publication Data
Brashear, Amy, author.
The incredible true story of the making of the Eve of destruction / Amy Brashear.
ISBN 978-1-61695-903-6
eISBN 978-1-61695-904-3
1. Motion pictures—Production and direction—Fiction.
2. Nuclear accidents—Fiction. I. Title.
PZ7.1.B75154 In 2018 | DDC [Fic]—dc23 2018027722

Interior design by Janine Agro, Soho Press, Inc.

Printed in the United States of America

10 9 8 7 6 5 4 3 2 1

To all my new friends joining me in the Fallout Shelter
Welcome Mixer is at 8:00.

In nuclear war, all men are cremated equal.
—Dexter Gordon

Though the events of December 1984 are factually accurate, some names might have been changed to protect the families of the victims and those who risked their lives to provide testimony about their ordeal in the making of the film *Eve of Destruction*. This is their story.

Comment from Laura

It's safe to assume that people will believe what they want to believe. But everything within the pages of this black-and-white composition notebook is factual: a black-and-white accounting of what happened to the best of my knowledge. I didn't exaggerate. Nothing is made up. I hope to see it stacked in non-fiction sections (under Ratliff, comma, Laura*) in bookstores and libraries around the world. It's a true story.* My *true story. And it all begins with me, Laura. Also, it is my sworn duty to keep a record in case my mutant children want to know why they have a tail. I can tell them it's all Hollywood's fault.*

When There's a Flash, Duck and Cover!

by HARLEY JONES
Film Reporter

EXCLUSIVE: After completing the highly anticipated sequel to last year's box office smash *The Year That Never Was*, Norman Edman will bring *Eve of Destruction*, based on the cult classic by Boudreaux Beauchamp, to the big screen. Eddie Payne (*Crime Lieutenant*) will adapt.

Flash. Bang. Roar. An atomic bomb can spoil your whole day. The novel has been compared to *Dr. Strangelove or: How I Learned to Stop Worrying and Love the Bomb*, released in 1964 and directed by Stanley Kubrick, based on the novel *Red Alert* by Peter Bryant. *Eve of Destruction* takes a comedic look at a small town's ultimate fate after coming face-to-face with an atomic bomb. In the novella, the Federal Civil Defense Administration estimates that 12 million will "die" in the mock drill, but what they don't expect is that those 12 million "dead" would soon be casualties in the first nuclear attack on American soil.

Set in June 1954, it tells the story of four teenagers who face the smoldering ruin of the life they once knew. All different stereotypes—a troublemaker jock, the beautiful popular girl, the attractive popular boy, and the shy girl—come together and share their untreated first-degree burns and memories of friends and family members disintegrating by flash. As they watch as total social collapse mixes with slow-motion starvation, they discover how they have a lot more in common than they once believed. Starring Owen Douglas (*Room 472B*), Freddy White (*The Harlem Project*), Astrid Ogilvie (*The Delightful Miss Dunne*), and Peony Roth (*The Temptation of Christine*), as Hank, James, Martha, and Helen, respectively.

With the box office smash of *WarGames* and *The Outsiders*, BC-AD Productions is looking to capitalize on the teenage trend that seems to be popular with the moviegoing public. Abbott & Davidson Publishers is looking to release a special-edition copy of the novella when the movie is released in theaters next summer.

Chapter One

It was one minute to noon, and I was standing in the lunch line at school—it was chicken and noodles day, which meant I'd find a bone, and it would ruin my meal like it always did. The cafeteria was buzzing about that week's game, Griffin Flat versus Hollow Court. Go, Shiners! The season was a bust—zero to eight, with two games left to play. Seemed pretty damned pointless to be slaving away on a game when your players already knew that the only winning move was not to play. *Rah-rah.* It was hard to cheer for losers.

I grabbed a carton of milk from the crate, even though chocolate milk and chicken and noodles were a lengthy bathroom situation in the making. Then I reached into my pocket for lunch money borrowed from my stepbrother, who was still getting used to me as his "sister" and not the dorky girl who took over the "man room" down the hall.

Shhhh. The siren across the street from the school blended with the other four in town. Louder, more intense, its wavelike tones mixed with the voices of the cafeteria on that Thursday. No one paid attention. Once a week the town did some kind of siren test just to make sure we were used to ignoring it in case of an actual emergency. Two minutes and the sirens went off, but no one noticed because ever since FEMA[1] implemented the weekly occurrence, it had blended in to our mundane lives.

"Can those sirens shut the hell up?" Kevin Barnes asked, messing with the dial of his boom box.

Kevin was a senior and all-around badass. He sat across the room with the pack-a-dayers, next to a door that led to the trash cans where everyone went for a smoke. I sat across the room next to the pay phones. So when one of them had to make a phone call, we listened in on their conversations. My friend Max had been known to blackmail many of them.

"Thank God," Kevin yelled once the sirens died down. He turned up the volume on his boom box and tapped his shoe to the beat of "99 Red Balloons" by Nena[2] as he sat on the tabletop. (Ms. Little, the librarian and cafeteria monitor, had told him hundreds of times not to sit where he ate, but he didn't listen.)

"Everyone, shut the hell up!" Kevin screamed. A man's voice got louder with each turn of the volume dial.

"Now's your once-in-a-lifetime chance—all you have to do is be caller nine. Caller nine. That's it."

"Language, Mr. Barnes, language," Ms. Little said with her index finger to her lips.

But people actually shut up. We stared at Kevin's boom box while the radio station went back to playing music—"Every Breath You Take."[3]

"What's going on?" I asked Max, but he just shrugged. He

---

1 FEMA stands for Federal Emergency Management Agency, which is an anagram for a joke.

2 Nena, "99 Luftballons," Epic, 1983. Originally a German song that was rereleased in English as "99 Red Balloons." It's a protest song. I personally prefer the German version even though I have no idea what she is singing.

3 The Police, *Synchronicity*, A&M, 1983. It's the perfect song, actually. It's a song about stalking, or how Big Brother is always watching you.

was into the comic book[1] that I let him borrow a week ago. At first, I thought everyone was looking at me. But they weren't. It was the phone bank behind me. I watched them like a science experiment. (I'm into science—don't hate.)

Background: Everyone was listening to the radio. But the music stopped. Everyone got real quiet.

Objective: To find out why everyone was staring at me.

Results: Pending.

Limitations: They stared back.

Conclusions: Pending.

I got all A's in science. I was popular in science class. Everyone wanted to be my partner because I got all A's.

Kathy was sitting across from me. She was tapping her fingers on the tabletop and repeating seven digits. "444-2323."

I started repeating them too. *444-2323.*

All around the cafeteria, legs were being swung over the bench seats. I glanced at the phone booth behind me, then at my classmates running toward me. A mad dash to the phones. I stood up, grabbed a receiver, dug a quarter out of my pocket, and dialed the number. 444-2323.

And waited.

It was ringing.

There was no busy signal.

I was caller number nine.

"Hello. Caller number nine? Are you there? This is DJ Crazy Bob in the morning. Who's this?"

"Um. Laura," I said.

"Oh, shit on a cracker," Dana said as my voice echoed in the cafeteria.

"Turn it down. Turn the volume down," Ms. Little snapped at Kevin.

---

1 *The Fury of Firestorm: The End of His Rope!* Issue #28, October 1984.

He turned it down. My voice wasn't so loud. It also wasn't how I thought I sounded in my head.

"Congratulations, Laura. You're the ninth caller, and that means if you correctly answer these three questions, you'll be the winner of the ultimate star treatment prize package."

"I will?" I asked.

"Yes, you will. You and a guest will get the star treatment on the set of *Eve of Destruction*. Can you believe it?"

"No."

"Well, you better start believing."

That's where DJ Crazy Bob stopped talking and Journey[1] started playing.

I waited on the line until the song ended and DJ Crazy Bob was back on the air.

"Just three questions. Three easy-peasy questions. You got that?"

"I think so."

"And since the prize is a walk-on role of the film, we're basing the questions on the Big One—the Big Bomb—okay? Got that?"

"I think so."

"Ready, Laura?"

"I think so."

"Okay. Laura, a girl of few words, here is question number one. Who is considered to be the father of the atom bomb?"

"Dr. Robert Oppenheimer."

"Correct."

"Go, Laura, go!!!!" Dana said, clapping her hands and jumping up and down behind me.

"Question number two: A thermonuclear weapon is made up of two isotopes. What are they? Wait, these questions are hard. Who made these up? Laura, why don't you hold on a sec? Let me talk to someone about this—"

"No, wait—I can answer that," I said, turning to face my classmates, who were staring at me.

---

1 Journey, "Don't Stop Believin'" *Escape*, Columbia, 1981.

"Really? You can answer that?"

"Yes."

"Okay, go on. Try to answer."

"Uranium-235 and plutonium-239."

"Um. That's correct. Are you pulling my chain, Laura? Are you even in high school?"

"Um, yeah, I'm in high school."

The room was silent like it was witnessing something magical.

"Well, okay, then. Last question, Laura, and it's a doozy— well, to me it's a doozy. To you, it's probably what happens when you mix the colors blue and yellow together—"

"Green."

"Correct. But not the question. This is the question. And if you get this right, you'll win the role of a lifetime."

Everyone around me was quiet. Even Dana, and she had never been quiet a day in her life. All eyes were on me. I didn't want to make a fool of myself. I had to get this question right.

"Last question—since the plot of *Eve of Destruction* takes place in 1954, and MAD was a product of the United States doctrine during the height of the Cold War, and our current relations with Russia today are, in a word, icy, what does MAD stand for?"

Dana flipped her thumb up and down—a way to ask if I got this, and I nodded and smiled. I had this. "Mutually Assured Destruction. It's like if we push the button, they'll push the button, and we'll all die."

"Morbid," Kevin said, crossing his arms over his chest.

"Congratulations, Laura. You're the winner of the ultimate star treatment prize package. I can't wait to see you on the big screen. I'm DJ Crazy Bob, and I'll be back after these words from our sponsors—playing the hits of today and tomorrow—if there is a tomorrow."

Some lady took my contact information and gave me the spill about how no one in my family could be an employee with the radio station, and if they were, my winning the ultimate star treatment prize package would become null and void.

"You're going to be a movie star?" Dana said, slowly and in a whisper.

"No, I don't think I will be."

"Have you been living under a rock?" Her eyes practically rolled out of her head as she gave me the lowdown—the 411—as if I didn't know—on the movie that was set to shoot here, well, near here in two weeks.

Okay, for those reading at home—or literally living under a rock—it started with a rumor, then an announcement, and then finally scouts, a promise, and a movie.

But a major motion picture in the land of (insert lyrics to *The Beverly Hillbillies*[1]) or at the base of the Ozark Mountains. All the alphabet soup was here. News crews set up shop. They were invited by the governor. Perfect photo op. "Blah blah blah, welcome to Arkansas, blah blah blah. Home of diamonds, Tyson chicken, Walmart, and the Razorbacks, blah blah blah." The papers and TV ate it up. Governor Clinton[2]—charisma was his middle name.

Now, of course total-destruction-due-to-total-world-war movies had been done before in prime time, but this wasn't some movie of the week that would make the president twitch with a tinge of guilt over annihilation of the planet; this was actually a good idea. Hell, if the Russians were aiming their weapons at us, we would do the same. We had Star Wars to lean on if things got dicey. (No—I'm not talking about the greatest movie ever made. I have a crush on Han Solo.)

---

1 A television show that aired on CBS from 1962 to 1971 (I was a toddler when it was on TV). But the premise was this: Jed Clampett hits it oil rich and moves his family (Granny, Elly May, Jethro Bodine) to California, hijinks ensue. Though the show never technically clarified where the Clampetts were from, we as Arkansans claim the Clampetts as our own.

2 William Jefferson Clinton, born in Hope, Arkansas. At the age of 32, he is the youngest governor to ever take office. He was governor from 1979 to 1981, then lost and won again in 1983. His wife is named Hillary, and they have a three-year-old daughter named Chelsea.

No—this was different. This had movie stars. Real movie stars. Not the TV kind. Owen Douglas, Astrid Ogilvie, Peony Roth, and Freddy White (who was black). Max had a crush on Astrid, but she was British from cheery old England and had an accent that didn't sound like something like molasses being poured out of a mason jar. She was attached to this year's mega-star who made somewhat of a splash at the MTV Video Music Awards[1] (the same MTV Video Music Awards where Madonna got down with her bad self in a wedding dress), Drake Cooper.

"Just in time for Thanksgiving break," Dana said.

"Nothing says Thanksgiving like death and destruction," I said.

"Exactly. Are you with your mom and Dennis or your dad this year?"

"Mom and Dennis. Dad's stuck on base."

"What about Terrence? Is he going to be there too?"

"Still working the custody issues."

"It's still crazy to think that your brother is Terrence Jennings."

"Step—"

"What?"

"He's my stepbrother."

"Whatever. Same difference."

"My mother still says a prayer for your family during Sunday morning services," Kathy said, blowing her nose with her napkin.

"That's nice," I said.

"Well, yeah, that's why she does it," Kathy said, stuffing the last bite of chicken and noodles into her mouth. Then she carried her tray over to the cleaning station, leaving Dana and me alone.

---

1 They were held on Friday, September 14, 1984, at Radio City Music Hall in New York City. On that night, it was dubbed Video City Music Hall. Dan Aykroyd and Bette Midler hosted. It's well known for the uncomfortable sitting with your parents as you watched Madonna roll around on the stage to "Like a Virgin." I know Terrence and I haven't fully recovered.

"She's weird but popular, so it cancels out the weird," Dana said. "But honestly, your family situation is weird."

My family situation. That was a small word for what it really was—dysfunctional. Messy. Scandalous. We were *The Brady Bunch*,[1] minus four kids and a maid—and the whiteness.

"Don't be so ashamed you're Terrence's stepsister. His dad had sex with your mom while still married to your dad."

"Thanks for that recap."

"Don't mention it."

"Yeah, don't mention it again, please."

"Oh, come on. You have a story. It will be awesome in the tabloids. White woman screws black man—"

"Breaks up two families. Screws not just each other but us as well," I said finishing it for her.

Talk about small-town gossip.

---

1 I've watched reruns in syndication. It's about a blended family: Mike Brady and his three sons—Greg, Peter, and Bobby—Carol Martin Brady and her three daughters—Marcia, Jan, and Cindy—and their live-in house-keeper, Alice. It's cheesy.

Chapter Two

Mr. Truitt paid—I totally just wrote *paid* and most definitely had to scratch that out. Mr. Truitt totally did not pay us with the opposite sex. Duh—sorry, *paired* us with the opposite sex, though I saw right through his veiled attempts at equality by his pairing me with an athlete, boosting his academic grade point average. That week's new charity case was Rodney Romero. C-student, starting center for the Griffin Flat varsity basketball team, and my stepbrother's best friend.

We were working on half-life pesticides, which somehow morphed into talking about radiation, which led into a discussion on nuclear weapons. As usual.

"Arkansas has a thirty-six percent chance of being annihilated. A high probability that if the blast doesn't get us, the fire will," Max said behind me. "You know there're eighteen silos in this state. That's eighteen potential death traps. There's one twenty-five miles from here."

"Calm down, man," Rodney said, pouring a beaker of bleach into a beaker of vinegar. I grabbed it out of his hand

and threw it in the sink before he decided to wage chemical warfare on us. I didn't need Max's doom and gloom to become a reality.

"Leave it," Mr. Truitt said. "I don't want y'all cutting yourself on the shards of glass."

"Was I not supposed to do that?" Rodney asked as if he were stupid. But he wasn't. He was just stupid at science.

But that was Mr. Truitt's plan all along. I did the work, and Rodney got the credit—an A credit for his transcript that made premier schools with powerhouse athletic programs look at him as much more than a 2.5-GPA basketball star.

Mr. Truitt placed a new rack of beakers on the workstation in front of us.

"I'll do it," I said, knowing full well that I was being taken advantage of—again.

"It takes approximately thirty minutes for our Titan II intercontinental ballistic missile to hit Moscow. It takes approximately thirty minutes for their R-36M—known by NATO as SS-18 Satan—to hit our target, which, for all purposes, could be Blackwell or Hattieville, or what happened at Damascus could happen at one of those," I said.

Damascus, Arkansas, was a little shit-hole town home to nothing except for the Little Rock Air Force Launch Complex. Fifty-some miles from Little Rock. Thirty-some miles from here was a secret thing that everyone here always knew was in the ground. That became a government cover-up.

My dad spent a lot of time in the bunker there, and then he spent a lot of time in the bunkers at the other nine missile silos around us. There were eighteen missile silos around Arkansas total. I didn't see Dad a lot anymore. Mom was too preoccupied with Dennis to worry about my psyche, so I focused on school. It was the only thing that made any sense in my life.

On our first day in class, Mr. Truitt laid down the rules:

1. No eating or drinking.
2. No long sleeves.

3. Tie back hair.
4. Wear protective glasses.
5. Wear protective apron.
6. Wear closed-toe shoes.
7. Don't smell the chemicals.
8. Don't play around.
9. Wash your hands.
10. Do not pull the safety shower string.

If someone pulled the safety shower string, water would flood the room. Everything would get wet, and the person responsible would see the principal and be doing worksheets for the rest of the term.

While others thought about it or pretended to pull said string, I never did—but now that string was freedom.

I got up from my stool, leaving Rodney on his own, and went over to the shower and pulled. And it rained. It rained hard.

I had done it. I did the one thing that made the vein on the right side of Mr. Truitt's neck pulsate. Oh boy, was he mad.

Talk of suspension. Talk of calling my mom. I was looking at hard time—

But I would pull that string again.

I was done with partners and raising the GPA of my fellow classmate. They wouldn't use me anymore. No longer a tool for some trophy. Laura Ratliff was free of the oppressive regime of Griffin Flat athletics. Worksheets, lots of worksheets, would be in my future.

"Laura Ratliff, principal's office. Now," Mr. Truitt screamed, his finger pointed at me and then the door.

Oohs and *aahs* followed me out.

"Dead girl walking!" Max said, giving me a thumbs-up. He was trying to suppress his laughter and failing.

I sat in front of the principal. He stared at me through his glasses, the lenses so thick his eyeballs were magnified, and then at my permanent file, which was also thick. Thick with accolades, not demerits.

"Laura—" Principal Parker started, leaning back in his chair. His tie sat on his belly, and his mustache still had crumbs from this morning's breakfast. "I'm disappointed in you," he said, tapping his left hand's fingers like he was playing a piano. The faint spot on his finger where a wedding ring once sat was hardly visible now. His wife had died. She didn't leave him like my mom left my dad. "Truly disappointed."

Disappointed was something my mom would say.

Principal Parker looked at me and shook his head. And it wasn't meant in a sarcastic way.

"I'm sorry," I said, lying through my teeth. But I knew that was what he as the principal wanted to hear.

The principal's office was one place not to talk back—even if you knew deep down in your heart that you did the right thing, not just for your sanity but for the athletes in this school to finally do their own work. Fight the power—oh, whatever, it didn't matter. Principal Parker was talking suspension. A day. Worth it.

But then he brought up Mrs. Martin, and I felt my heart sink as I slumped into the chair.

Mrs. Martin was the supposed confidante for all students at Griffin Flat High School, but she was the one in danger of having a nervous breakdown. And according to Principal Parker, pulling the safety shower string that resulted in gallons of $H2O$ being sent down in a waterfall and flooding a portion—a tiny portion, I may state as fact—of the chemistry lab classroom meant that I, Laura Ratliff, was on the verge of going full-on cuckoo, as in *One Flew Over the Cuckoo's Nest*[1] cuckoo. And I guessed liability issues deemed that I needed to see Mrs. Martin. Now, she had seen me in her tiny closet of an office before, ever since that Monday after

---

1 It's a 1962 novel by Ken Kesey and a major motion picture starring Jack Nicholson. It takes place in a mental institution.

the town found out about the dissolution of my parents' marriage by way of a third party.

Mrs. Martin always talked in questions. "How does it make you feel?" was a given, but "What are you going to do about it, Laura?" was one of her favorites.

We'd talk about my parents' marriage and how I wished it would have been. I wanted parents like Jennifer and Jonathan Hart. I wanted parents who loved each other. I wanted a grandfather like Max. I wanted a dog like Freeway. I guess I wanted to be Laura Hart, not Laura Ratliff. But like *Hart to Hart*,[1] my family was canceled prematurely.

I moved from Principal Parker's office to down the hall to see Mrs. Martin and sat in front of her, trying to figure out what her angle was going to be this session. I didn't think anyone forced me to sit there. I mean, not really. I was not obligated at all to be here. Yes, the administration had to get permission from my parents. But I had the right to say no. Well, at least I thought I could. Though I never tried.

"Laura Ratliff," she said, taking my file out of her filing cabinet and laying it on her desk. Then she pulled out a new yellow notepad from her bottom drawer.

I grabbed a Snickers from her bowl of candy, tore it open, and popped it in my mouth.

"Congratulations," she said, sitting at her desk and finding an ink pen that actually worked.

She collected pens, especially ones that held no ink.

"Thank you," I said. "It was my finest moment. Honestly, I probably should have pulled it sooner."

"No, on being caller number nine," she said, shaking her head. "You shouldn't have pulled the string to the safety shower."

---

1 It premiered in 1979 and stars Robert Wagner as Jonathan Hart, CEO of Hart Industries, and Stefanie Powers as Jennifer Hart, a freelance journalist. They jet-set around the world solving crimes. I wanted to be part of that family. I would have gladly walked Freeway.

"Shouldn't have, *but—*"

Mrs. Martin knew of my tendency to be a smart-ass. "You know better than that."

I grabbed another Snickers.

"Laura, where should we start?" she asked.

She started the discussion. I went back to eating another Snickers. When I didn't answer her question, she took away the Snickers bowl.

"You pulled the safety shower. Does it have anything to do with being caller number nine?" she asked.

"No," I said.

"I need you to talk to me," she said.

I twisted my scrunchie around my wrist.

"Remember, *The Day After*[1] was only a movie," she said,

---

1 On November 20, 1983, 100 million people dropped everything to watch *The Day After* on ABC, a TV movie about the nuclear annihilation of Kansas City and the aftermath in Lawrence, Kansas. Prior to the TV movie airing, there was a special viewers guide sent in the mail. We were supposed to watch *The Day After* and then have a discussion, but if we needed to talk to someone, there was 1-800-NUCLEAR, a special counseling hotline. If we needed to talk to someone because it got too much too fast, they were there. Seriously, as a nation we had homework. And we were warned, *DON'T WATCH IT ALONE!* Local affiliates even went so far to advise parents not to let kids watch it at all. Mom and Dennis didn't listen. They let me watch it. I curled up on the couch and watched the end of the world happen with no commercial breaks!

Terrence said he watched half of it at his mom's house before he got bored and did homework instead. He missed the mushroom cloud, the firestorms, the wind, the skeletonized people, the buildings exploding, people vaporized, the slow deaths of hundreds of thousands, the radiation poisonings, the panic, the savaging, the pillaging, the government not knowing how much to dig in the irradiated farmland, the possibility of deformed infants, no medicine, no cures, no hope, only despair. We don't even know who shot first. But as John Lithgow said in the movie, it doesn't matter.

After the movie they said it would be much worse than what we saw—there would be vomiting with acute diarrhea, and much, much more.

Max's parents confined him to his bedroom and checked on him to make sure he wasn't watching it. He had little to add to the conversation the next day at school. The movie was scary. It left me feeling nothing. I was hollow inside. I was afraid. I still am.

repeating the one line that she told me after I came in crying last November. The time when I broke out in a cold, shivering sweat, followed by weeks of depression and anxiety.

It's only a movie. Just like it's only a game.

"Do you believe everything they tell you?" I asked.

"Laura—"

I sighed, reaching for the bowl of Snickers, but then realized she took that away, just like the politicians were doing with my hopes and dreams.

"No, it has nothing to do with that—though that subject appears nightly in my nightmares," I said.

"Laura, how does that make you feel?"

That dreaded question that people who get psychology degrees and decide to head-shrink for a living ask.

How does the fear that adults with the power to flip a switch are going to mess it up before I got my chance sound to you? Not good. We were living in a nuclear soap opera.

"How does it make me feel?" I said, repeating her question.

"I asked you," she said.

"It makes me feel—"

There were two camps: the *holy beep, we all could die* and the *maybe things won't be so bad*. I fell into the first camp. The camp that knew it had fifteen minutes to accomplish everything it wanted to before it died. That did weigh on your psyche.

Last November, after watching *The Day After*, I called 1-800-NUCLEAR with the rest of the poor saps. I was afraid that my parents would be killed and I would survive. I was afraid that I would die and my parents would survive. I once had to make Mrs. Martin a list of everything I was afraid of:

My parents will die
I'll get sick
I'll die
Bad grades
People won't like me

I'm not pretty
I won't ever have a boyfriend
Nuclear war

Whenever I tried to talk about my feelings on nuclear war, what actually happened was silence. I couldn't. If I talked about it, then that meant it was on the horizon. A nuclear payload heading down on us, down on me.

Yeah, we did drills where we hid under our desks. You know, those were some badass desks. Immune to an ICBM, or what you probably would see in your underpants right after. And we had a fallout shelter in our basement at school, but it was locked after too many students found that to be the perfect make-out spot.

On a scale of one—does not bother me—to five—very disturbing—I was on a ten going on eleven.

Mrs. Martin looked at her watch. "We should continue this conversation," she said. "I'll schedule you in for a weekly session."

I was defeated. But nodded anyway.

"Does this count as my punishment for pulling the safety shower in chemistry?" I asked.

She shook her head and smiled. "No, you're suspended for one day. You got off easy."

Worth it.

I leaned over the desk to grab a handful of Snickers from the bowl she purposely put out of reach. I took a glance at my folder, which was flipped open, and died a little inside.

Laura Ratliff is afraid of not having a future. She is afraid of dying in a nuclear blast. She comes from a broken family, which isn't that uncommon, but it was done in such a way that it became town gossip.

Mrs. Martin, I thought, *you're going to miss me when I'm gone.*

Chapter Three

I was sent home—and by home I mean the Flat Inn. My mom was the general manager of the only decent (or so she claimed) hotel in the town. Helping was my after-school job. Folding towels, emptying the trash, stocking the sweets shop. That afternoon, I grabbed an orange soda from the cooler, found a comfy seat in the lobby and watched as my mom dealt with crisis after crisis.

"What's leaking from the ceiling from the fourth floor?" a guest asked.

Um. Rain? I didn't say it out loud. That would be rude to the guests. End of the world to some of these people. The customer *wasn't* always right. Sometimes they were downright stupid.

"I'm sorry, sir. Let me see if we have any available rooms I can move you to," Mom said.

The phone didn't stop ringing, and Mom didn't stop trying to explain why they were sold out. She hung up the phone. "Why don't you take your little hammer and nails and build you one," she said to no one as the phone rang again. "Flat Inn, this is Edna. How may I help you? No, I'm sorry. We are all sold out for that week. What's going on? Well, ma'am, they're shooting a movie—"

Some of the crew and a few of the actors were staying here, and Mom was going insane. Some of the older actors were renting houses. I guess they were too old for the hotel lifestyle. I didn't blame them. After the "secret" came out about my mom and Terrence's dad, Mom and I pretty much moved into room 104. Next to the kitchen. Noisy. And you could smell the free continental breakfast at five-thirty in the morning. Dad escaped to Little Rock Air Force Base's barracks.

"Welcome to Flat Inn. Checking in?" she asked a man with a suitcase.

Paula walked over and sat down a stack of brown and green folders and a stack of paper. "Put a copy of this letter in each one."

The letter. Mom worked hard on that letter. The owner, Paul Passoni, wanted to make sure he had all his bases covered when it came to the possibility of a nuke attack. I mean, Griffin Flat might be smallish, a little over eight thousand people, but we were on the nukemap.[1] There were eighteen possible targets, not to mention the Little Rock Air Force Base, and Nuclear One.[2] We were pretty much right smack dab in the vicinity of a ground zero situation.

"Your mom wants this done ASAP," Paula said.

"And let me guess: She wanted you to do it?"

Paula always was a slow learner. She was hired because she was the owner's sister. Nepotism and all. She blew her gum into

---

1 A list of "top Soviet nuclear targets" all over the United States of America.

2 A pressurized water reactor nuclear power plant on Lake Dardanelle in Russellville, Arkansas. There is only one power plant in Arkansas, and we also have a silo. That means we're a military target—a *primary* target—as in one that gets picked even in a "limited" nuclear war.

a bubble and walked away. No matter how incompetent, you didn't fire family.

I started stuffing and occasionally reading the letter.

Dear Guest,

I hope your stay will be comfortable and enjoyable.

As you may know, our country is in tense relations with the Soviet Union. We may have to face the threat of rising tensions, which may escalate to a full-out nuclear strike.

Whilst Arkansas has not yet been affected, we request that you follow the instructions below, should there be an air raid in the vicinity of the hotel.

1. If you hear a siren while in the hotel, please go down the staircase to the lobby, which is the lowest floor of the hotel.

2. Please do not use the elevators.

3. Disabled guests or guests who might have difficulties reaching the lobby are requested to inform our front desk at check-in.

4. Staff will direct you to the shelter area.

5. Please stay in the designated area until it is safe to leave.

For any other assistance, please feel free to contact the Front Desk or the Manager on Duty.

I am sure you will join me in hoping a quick end to the Cold War.

Sincerely,
Edna Jennings
General Manager

No matter how insane—I mean *insane*—this thing was, I felt like I was living in a movie. We were on the eve of destruction. (Laugh-out-loud funny here. I get the title of the movie. What do they say? Roll credits.)

When Mom had a moment's peace, she came over and sat

down at my small table in the breakfast area. "You shouldn't have to do that," she said.

"Paula—"

"But thank you."

Before she could lecture me about my one-day suspension, I told her about the radio contest and how I won. "They were chanting my name in the locker room." I raised my right arm and started chanting, "Laura! Laura! Laura!"

"And then—"

"And then I get to bring a friend with me to the set."

She smiled, sort of. "So I guess you're going to be bringing"— she sighed—"Dana."

Dana. The bane of her existence. I am not going to use the word *hate* because that might not be the type of word Mom would use. No, slash that. She hated Dana. A lot of parents did. Dana was the type of friend who would barge into family situations without asking. One time she just showed up after Mom was going to take me on a special trip to Little Rock and thought she was going, too. Once my dad sent me flowers to my school for Valentine's Day, and *she* got mad. Her mom did too. (Her dad didn't send her any.) Her mom called my mom at work and complained. Like, who did that? I wasn't exactly friends with Dana. Never really had been. She was just there. And I told Mom that repeatedly, but she didn't believe me.

"What about Max?"

"Um, maybe."

Max at a movie lot? Oh dear, he would probably go on a tangent about something and get us kicked off the set. He was really smart but had a problem focusing. We had been friends since kindergarten. Max Randall and Laura Ratliff. Let's just say we were destined to be by each other's side alphabetically until graduation. But he was my friend, and even though he was super smart, he didn't make me feel super dumb. He was on the maybe list.

"Or what about—no. No . . . I'm not going to push it, but

why don't you just think about—no, no . . . I'm not going to be that mom. Laura, how about—"

She was trying to say Terrence. My stepbrother. The boy who I shared a bond with now. Both our lives had changed. If I did pick Terrence to go with me, I would make Mom happy, and also Dennis, and of course Terrence, if he was into that kind of thing. I would have so many brownie points with my mother. I could have gotten away with anything with her. And if I could have gotten away with that suspension, I would have said yes. Instead I said I'd think about it. How did I know that was the ticket? She smiled. Patted my knee and said "thank you" in a whisper.

She grabbed her smokes and her lighter, the reason why she came this way in the first place. "So about that suspension," she said.

"It's all good," I said, just thinking about the easy work it was going to be compared with the incompetence of GFHS athletes. (Not all were dumb. I probably should make that clear. Rob Turner went to Vandy, the Harvard of the South, just last year.)

"It'll be on your permanent record."

"It won't."

"It might. And colleges don't take too kindly to rebels."

Oh, the college talk. Planning for the future when we were on the eve of destruction. (There I go again. I'll probably do it a couple more times. Don't hold it against me, my fine reader.)

"Don't worry about it, Mom."

"I'm your mom. I'm supposed to worry."

I rolled my eyes and she did too.

"Well, Dennis should be home, so if you want to leave, you can," she said, going outside to smoke.

Home. That was a four-letter word. I hadn't had a "home" since my mom's illicit affair spread like a forest fire.

Chapter Four

Dennis was simultaneously cooking dinner and fixing the broken disposal. Dad never fixed things before. Grandpa would come over and try to fix things, but usually he couldn't. If Dennis had one good quality, it would be that he was a good handyman. He owned Jennings's Hardware down on Sixth Street, next to Rudy's Diner and across the street from Gus's Garage. We liked our businesses in Griffin Flat to be named by someone. Names were important. Now back to Dennis and his exceptional talent of burning a chicken noodle casserole. "Your mom called and said she's going to be late, so we should start without her when Terrence gets home."

Home. That was a funny word. Next to *family.* That was an equally funny word. I was not bitter—not bitter at all. Dennis tried, and I guess I did too, but it wasn't exactly an ideal situation. It was ours, though. Part of the problem was how it all went down. And the gossiping. Oh dear God, the gossiping. I was at Brenda Leigh's Beauty Parlor getting a perm when Terrence's mom came bursting through the door, calling my mom a tramp, a whore, a bitch, a downright home-wrecker—and then proceeded to tell the entire salon the story in dramatic detail. She had seen Dennis's truck (it had a logo on the side for goodness' sake) at the Flat Inn. She'd marched right through the front doors and into the lobby. Scared Paula to death. She demanded to see her husband. Demanded the room number and a key. Poor Paula probably almost peed her pants. She said over and over again, "Ma'am, I'm sorry, but I cannot do that without a supervisor's approval." Mrs. Dianne Wilcox-Jennings, now Ms. Dianne Wilcox. She reverted back to her maiden name after she caught her husband tugging on his belt rounding the corner with my mom, who was clipping an earring on her right ear, an earring that Dad gave her for their anniversary.

"Oh, hell, no," Ms. Wilcox had said, waving her finger in his face.

"I was just fixing an issue in one of the rooms," Dennis had said.

But Ms. Wilcox wasn't buying any of what he was selling. Her attention had moved to my mom.

"Edna, this lady wants a key to a room. She says her husband is staying here—oh." Paula had stopped talking and backed all the way into the back room and laughed.

Ms. Wilcox knew who I was. She bent down and grabbed my hands and said, "I don't blame you, child. Your mother made her bed, and she's going to have to lie in it."

"With your husband," Charlene said, sitting under a hair dryer. (Charlene, a twin who was kind of the queen of gossip land. Her twin, Darlene, was next in line for the throne.)

Ms. Wilcox glared. "Well, I just thought y'all should know what kind of hussy this town has."

Ms. Wilcox left, and no one could stop talking about what happened. Brenda Leigh was in so much shock my hair ended up extra frizzy since she was distracted and added too much ammonium thioglycolate.

I went home to discover my dad and mom fighting. Apparently, Brenda Leigh's wasn't the first stop for Ms. Wilcox. Dad moved out that night and a week later to the base. My parents were officially divorced two months later. A month after that, I walked down the aisle as maid of honor at Dennis and Mom's wedding. Terrence was the best man. Once they were pronounced man and wife, we were officially a dysfunctional family.

"Terrence's in front of the TV," Dennis stated. It wasn't very clear that he wanted me to go join Terrence until he said, "Go on."

Terrence and I didn't exactly have a lot in common. We were not in the same social circle. He's black and I'm white. (I'm stating this as fact in case Hollywood wants to make a movie later on.) The only thing we did have in common was our parents, and I guessed that was better than nothing.

"Hey," I said, sitting beside him on the living room floor.

TV looked better from down here.

"Hey, what's up?" he said, looking up and then down trying to do geometry, read a chapter of *1984*,[1] and watching MTV[2] all at the same time. "Oh, yeah, congrats on winning the contest. You totally kicked ass."

"Thanks," I said.

---

1 It was published in 1949 by George Orwell. He's an English writer. We're reading it in English class. We have to write our opinions on it every day. I'm having a hard time with it. Before what happened with my parents, I don't think I cared if Big Brother was watching, but now—with the tiny town of Griffin Flat commenting on my family situation, I guess I'm more on the side of Winston Smith. Dana's all, "I don't get what the big deal is. Who wouldn't want to be watched all the time? What do people have to hide?" But me? I think I don't want people watching me, making me think a certain way. The rewriting history part? Well, that doesn't sound half bad, given what's happened to the Ratliff/Jennings family.

2 MTV stands for Music Television, which shows music videos. It launched in 1981. Trivia: "Video Killed the Radio Star" by the Buggles was the first music video ever shown.

"Who you taking? Dana? Max?" He said *Dana* the same way Mom did at the hotel.

"I don't know yet. It's a pretty big decision."

"Very."

I couldn't tell if he was sarcastic or not. I chose to believe or not.

He went back to his studying and watching MTV, but every so often he'd look up and ask another question about what I thought it would be like and if I would have to miss school, or say that if I was invited to any raging parties, he wanted to go and protect me. And something about Astrid Ogilvie's number. He was clearly delusional.

For the next thirty minutes I helped him analyze a chapter in *1984*. It was poignant. We were living in the age of Big Brother.

"You know you're going to take Dana," he said.

"I'm not so sure."

"You know she'll make your life miserable if you don't."

"She'll make it about herself, like she won the contest, and I kind of want it to be my own thing."

"I get you. I get you."

Mom came in, threw her coat on the coatrack and her purse on top of that, took a seat on the pink chair (the only item of furniture we brought from our house), and closed her eyes as the "Thriller"[1] music video played in the background on TV.

"Dinner's ready," Dennis yelled from the kitchen.

"Feed me," Mom said.

Dennis and Mom were gross. So lovey-dovey. Terrence and I rolled our eyes and gagged.

Dennis placed the chicken noodle casserole on two pot holders in the middle of the table. Terrence and I had eaten it for lunch, but at least Dennis's meal actually tastes like chicken. Mom passed around plates. Terrence grabbed me a Tab from the fridge and a Coke for himself. I took four forks from the silverware tray.

---

1 Michael Jackson, *Thriller*, Epic, 1982. Zombies literally come to life.

We said a quick prayer thanking God for the food and hoping no one died anytime soon with the impending threat of world war. You know, the usual.

The conversation lagged a bit until Dennis asked about our day. Mom started complaining about the idiotic guests who stayed in the many rooms at the Flat Inn. "Honestly, some people shouldn't be allowed to travel."

Dennis was next. "It's very busy. The film crew has been at the store every hour on the hour buying supplies. Sales are most definitely up. They should film a movie here every year. It's definitely good for business."

Terrence didn't talk much. Like me, he wasn't quite used to this new family dynamic. When we first moved in, he spent every moment in his room. He only came out for food but usually brought it back to his room. We rarely made eye contact. We were, like, living in a dream world. Our parents had done this to us, my dad, his mom. I just hoped it was worth it. The secrets. The extramarital affair. The sex. I hope it was worth it in the end. (I can't believe I wrote *sex*. Pray for me, dear reader. Please.)

I didn't tell what my day was like. Mom did that. She was the one who brought up the shower. And everyone laughed. "It was probably a scene out of *Carrie*,[1] right?" she asked.

"Well, yeah, water instead of blood," I said.

"And you got suspended?" Dennis asked.

"For one day. I wouldn't even call that a suspension."

Terrence scooped mashed potatoes onto his plate. "Rodney was pissed," he said.

"Why?" I asked.

"Because you were his partner, and now he has to do the work."

---

1 A horror novel written by Stephen King. It was published in 1974. Seriously, it's about high school and the struggles we girls go through and the revenge scenarios some of us imagine. Pretty smart for a guy who was writing about girls.

I laughed. "I'm going to enjoy doing worksheets for the rest of the semester. I regret nothing."

Mom choked back a laugh.

"Does this suspension mean I'm grounded?" I asked.

"No. I can't watch you." Mom handed me a piece of buttered bread, and I set it on my plate. "So have you decided on who you're going to take?"

"No—"

"It's a big decision."

"I can't tell if you're being sarcastic or serious."

"Dead serious."

"If I don't take Dana, she'll kill me."

"With friends like Dana, you certainly don't need enemies," Dennis said.

"You know that's right," Terrence said, chugging his Coke.

"Or Max," Mom said.

"He'd be correcting everyone on the set. That would be annoying," I said.

"Do you have any other friends?" Dennis asked.

Mom whacked him on the arm. "Dear, she has friends."

"I have friends. I have friends," I said.

"Of course you do, Laura. I didn't mean it how it came out," Dennis said, apologizing.

The truth was, I didn't have a lot of friends. I had a lot of adversaries—but those certainly didn't count as friends.

"Well, take someone who won't overshadow you. Who will let you have your day in the spotlight."

"And that certainly wouldn't be Dana," Mom said, clearly giving her opinion on Dana.

And I got it. Dana was annoying.

Terrence scooped himself a third helping of casserole while trying not to laugh. No one ever gave him hell for his friends. Dim-witted as they might have been.

"What about Terrence?" Dennis asked.

"Dad, don't," he said, shaking his head.

"Everyone wants you to pick them. Just like in *Willy Wonka and the Chocolate Factory*,[1] everyone is going to want your Golden Ticket. It might as well be Terrence."

"Yeah, honey, don't pressure her," Mom said, patting his hand.

"No pressuring, just thought this would be an awesome bonding time for them."

"Laura, you don't have to," Terrence said, getting up to grab another Coke for himself. "Want another Tab?"

I nodded as sirens blared in the distance. *Woooooooweeeeewooooo.* The crew was testing the sirens for the fifth night in a row.

---

1 It's a movie that came out in 1971 and starred Gene Wilder. It's also a book but has a slightly different title, *Charlie and the Chocolate Factory.* That's by Roald Dahl and was published in 1964.

Chapter Five

Terrence's grandmother, whom I called Grandma Jennings (she wanted me to call her that), left a tin of homemade fudge on the back steps. Dennis took a handful, melted them, and poured it all over some homemade vanilla ice cream (homemade—it said so right on the label). I grabbed a bowl and a spoon and headed to the enclosed porch to eat in peace, but Terrence was already out there, reading the liner notes to *Purple Rain*.[1] He collected tapes like I collected comic books. (Those selection sheets from Columbia House[2] were always filled out. Eight tapes for a penny. I called it a scam. He said it wasn't. But he was also known as Terry with a *Y* and Terri with an *I* on those forms. So who was scamming whom?) I sat down with *Alpha Flight*, volume one, issue sixteen. It wasn't out until Friday, but Dewayne Smith, owner of the local bookstore, liked to hook me up early with my favorites, which included X-Men, the Flash, and Firestorm. Especially Firestorm.

---

1 Prince and the Revolution, Warner Bros, 1984.

2 It's a mail-order music club.

"Who do you think would win in a fight, Batman or Superman?" Terrence asked me, picking up another tape from his overflowing tape deck.

"Superman—wait—Batman—wait—Christopher Reeve or Adam West—or are we going by comic and—"

"Wow. You are a geek."

"Geeks will inherit the earth," I said with a mouth full of fudge ice cream.

"Yeah, they will," he said, placing Run-DMC's[1] self-titled album in the tape player and then pressing PLAY. (They're a lot more aggressive with their rhymes than the Sugarhill Gang[2] or Kurtis Blow[3] or Grandmaster Flash and the Furious Five.[4])

"Hard Times"[5] started, and he nodded and tapped his foot to the beat. "I finally got it," he said, handing me a cassette tape.

"No way," I said. "It was your white whale."

"I know. It came on the radio, and—boom—it was mine," he said, taking the cassette tape back and replacing the Run-DMC in the boom box. Somehow he'd pressed the RECORD button just at the right time, praying to the radio gods that the DJ didn't talk just as the song started. It was a lot of work to record a song off the radio.

He turned the volume to full blast and looked at me and smiled.

---

1 Hip-hop group from Queens, New York, consisting of Joseph Simmons, Darryl McDaniels, and Jason Mizell.

2 Hip-hop group from New Jersey consisting of Michael "Wonder Mike" Wright, Henry "Big Bank Hank" Jackson, and Guy "Master Gee" O'Brien. They are known for their 1979 hit "Rapper's Delight," which is one of my favorites.

3 Hip-hop artist from Harlem, New York.

4 Hip-hop group consisting of DJ Grandmaster Flash and five rappers, Melle Mel, the Kidd Creole, Keith Cowboy, Mr. Ness/Scorpio, and Rahiem.

5 A song by Run-DMC. It was released in 1983 as a cassette single under Profile records. It was originally recorded by Kurtis Blow in 1980 for his self-titled debut album.

Not many would admit that Joni Mitchell was one of your favorites. But Terrence wasn't like most people. His musical faves were eclectic. They ranged from Johnny Cash to Billy Joel.

I wasn't exactly a connoisseur when it came to music. Whatever MTV deemed to be in the top twenty, I listened to—and Madonna. But when Terrence was at his mom's, I'd been known to come in here and listen to his music. He had cassettes full of different musical stylings. CCR, The Band, Queen, Bob Dylan, Leonard Cohen, even a little John Denver, seriously . . .

When I was done, I tried to put everything back in the order Terrence left them. Though he hadn't explicitly come out and said it, I didn't think he wanted me touching his things.

I'd never had a brother and he'd never had a sister—we were only children in our broken homes—so boundaries had been set, though never really explained.

Joni Mitchell's "Big Yellow Taxi" ended, and he sorted through his collection of mass chaos on the floor in between picking up and putting down cassette tape after cassette tape.

He stopped, took the cassette out of the case, slid it into the boom box slot, and pressed PLAY.

The sound of a bass filled the room.

Terrence didn't say anything as "Rapper's Delight" by the Sugarhill Gang filled the room.

My left foot tapped against the floor, keeping the beat, and my head nodded, and I started talking real fast and in rhymes. I liked hip-hop. No one knew that. I tried to keep up with the song, but mouthing the lyrics was hard. Especially when they rhymed.

I could feel Terrence's eyes on me. I stopped mouthing the words and froze.

He knocked his shoulder into me, smiled, and we both as a duet finished the rap. "Say what?"

The song ended and Terrence went searching for a new one. He had dozens of tapes with only a couple of songs recorded on them. The outside was written with the title of whatever he'd crudely recorded off the radio.

While he was distracted, I tried to think how to approach the subject. Maybe Mom and Dennis were right. Maybe I did need to give Terrence a chance. He was not going anywhere unless the bomb dropped.

"So," I started.

"So what?" he asked, knocking over a stack of tapes.

"I was thinking about the movie—"

"How awesome it's going to be? Yeah, you're going to be hanging out with Astrid Ogilvie, Freddy White, Peony Roth, and Owen Douglas. Pretty damn cool."

"Pretty damn cool," I repeated.

"I just hope Dana won't ruin it for you."

"I'm not going to take Dana," I said.

"Really? Well, that's good."

"Yeah?"

"But you know she won't be happy," he said.

"Yeah, I know."

"Just so you know."

I nodded. "But I don't think I can take it. I have a line, and she'll probably weasel her way into saying it."

"You know that's right."

"So I was thinking," I said, twisting my scrunchie around my wrist. "Do you want to be my guest?"

"What? Are you serious?" he asked, nearly dropping his bowl to the floor.

"Yeah, I'm serious," I said.

"Really? Do you know what you're asking?"

"I do."

He got this big smile on his face and said, "Yes," with so many exclamation points.

I'd made his day, year, life.

He put in a new tape, turned the volume to the max, and rapped (badly) to "Friends"[1] as we finished our hot fudge ice cream.

---

1 Whodini, *Escape*, Jive Records, 1984.

Chapter Six

I was one hundred percent sure that Terrence was going to tell everyone at school how he was going to be my guest for the contest, and I would have to deal with the fallout from that concerning Dana. The Doomsday Clock[1] was ticking. Mom was right—I probably shouldn't have smiled at her when it was my turn to pass out the milk cartons in kindergarten.

Dennis had already left to open the hardware store when I made my first walk through the house. Terrence was trying to finish his homework while downing a bowl of cereal, and Mom was putting on her makeup over the toaster, waiting for what I assumed was a strawberry Pop-Tart.

"Good morning, sleepyhead," Mom said. "I'm glad you're up. I didn't want you to sleep all day."

---

1 The metaphorical clock is maintained by the Bulletin of the Atomic Scientists. It all started back in 1947 as a way to predict how close the world is to global destruction. The original setting was seven minutes to midnight. Today it's three minutes to midnight.

"I would," Terrence said.

"This is supposed to be punishment, not a vacation."

"Mom, don't worry. I have tons to do," I said.

"Tons?"

"I do have a plan."

"A plan to stay in your pj's all day?"

"How'd you know?" I asked, reaching inside the freezer for the box of frozen waffles.

"Laura—"

"Mom—"

"Maybe you should go to the hotel with me."

"Um. No. Those people make me want to bang my head into a wall."

"Those people?"

"The guests."

She shrugged. "Yeah, but you don't. You have to have self-control."

"Self-control?"

She nodded. "That's why you don't reach across the desk and slap them silly."

Shortly after Mom and Terrence left, I had a second breakfast in front of the TV with Hope and Bo.

"Like sands through the hourglass, so are the days of our lives"[1]: Mom had started to record the show. It was legal now. The Supreme Court ruled that we were not going to jail if we recorded a TV show with our VCR.

My day of fun started off right. I had a list of things I wanted to do, and I crossed each thing off once I'd accomplished said item.

Read the paper—check

Take quiz about nuclear war from the paper—check

I was planning to drop the quiz off at one of the many locations it suggested once I went out for the day. My day. *Laura's Day Off.*

---

1 The tagline for *Days of Our Lives,* a soap opera on NBC.

But then an advertisement for an antinuclear meeting at Arkansas Tech that morning caught my eye. The advertisement was halfway down the page—a good three-by-five box.

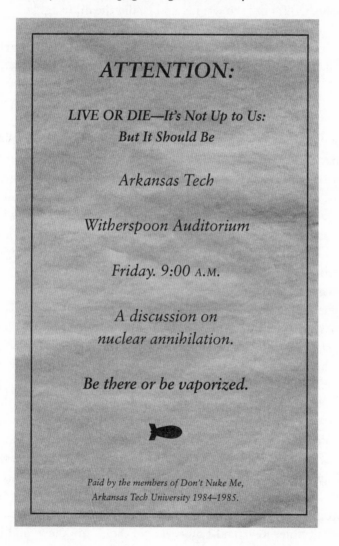

ATTENTION:

LIVE OR DIE—*It's Not Up to Us: But It Should Be*

Arkansas Tech

Witherspoon Auditorium

Friday. 9:00 A.M.

A discussion on nuclear annihilation.

Be there or be vaporized.

Paid by the members of Don't Nuke Me, Arkansas Tech University 1984–1985.

My idea of a fun, relaxing morning changed. The phone rang. It was Mom making sure that I hadn't gone back to bed. I promised her I was indeed up. I was stuffing my backpack with some essentials, two comics, and a spiral notebook. I promised Max I would make some progress. We were writing our own comic book. I did the writing and he did the drawing.

"So what's your plan?" Mom asked.

"I think I'm going to go see Granny." I left out the part about going to Tech.

Mom sighed heavily over the phone. Granny and my mom didn't get along at all. Granny sided with Dad when the marriage went down the drain. And Granny's my mom's mom. That was what made it so surprising. Granny didn't go to the wedding. Didn't offer congratulations. Even though my mom was her daughter, she was no longer welcome in Granny's home. I was. But we didn't talk about Mom. I obeyed her wishes. I went to her house every Sunday to watch *Murder, She Wrote*,[1] where we assumed Jessica Fletcher, aka J.B. Fletcher, was a serial killer who lived in Cabot Cove, Maine—population dwindling by the episode.

Granny didn't have much. In fact, she moved into our old home (the home where Mom, Dad, and I spent many happy years) when she gave her life savings to Reverend Floyd Lowry at *The Gospel Hour*. Thousands of dollars went into the pocket of the televangelist. A year ago, he went on his TV show and asked the congregation sitting at home to bless him. He asked the people for $4.5 million. He pleaded for them to send anything and everything they had. Reverend Lowry believed that God wanted him to raise the money to "erect a church that would bring the nonbelievers to the feet of Jesus." It was controversial. It was a scam disguised as a fund-raising drive. Reverend Lowry was adamant that if the church did not reach its goal, then God "would call him home." As in, if he didn't raise the money by a certain time, Reverend Lowry would die. Who knew God had the same tactics as the mob? His tears were used to swindle

---

1 A show on CBS that premiered this year.

people out of money. He hid behind his faith and took everything that my Granny had. I begged her to not give him a single dime, to see if he would die. But she felt she had to. He was testing her faith just like God was testing Reverend Lowry. Reverend Lowry met his deadline and ended up raising $6.2 million.

My dad felt sorry for her. My mom was embarrassed for her. Great-Aunt LouLou, my papaw's sister, always said, "A minister can praise you with one hand and reach for your pocketbook with the other." And she always would add with so much bitter disgust, "If my dear brother had gone to the doctor for care instead of the mailbox to send a check to Brother Lowry, he'd be alive today," and after she said that, she would spit each time.

When Dad moved to the base, Granny moved in. Dad started footing the bill. He got the house in the divorce settlement. And though Mom wouldn't admit it, she was thankful that she didn't have to deal with Granny.

"Be nice," I told Mom over the phone.

"I am," she said.

"Mom—"

"Yes, ma'am, check-in is at three P.M. I'm sorry, no exceptions," my mom said, not meaning me. "Okay, Laura, I've got to go. Someone stopped up their toilet. I've got to go unclog it."

"Gross," I said, imagining the smell.

"Laura, be careful. Look both ways when crossing the street with your bike. And go with the flow of traffic. Love you."

"Do you want me to tell Granny hey for you?" I asked.

"I guess," she said, then hung up the phone.

I grabbed my backpack and headed for the garage, hopped on my bike, and headed south across the railroad track, down the road from Ellis Grocery, and across the way from the Raines' chicken houses.

"My baby girl," Granny said, dragging out the words *baby girl* in her southern twang. "Come here. Give your dear granny a hug."

I obliged. I even told her that Mom said hey, which she

believed. "I've been praying that your mama would talk to me, and Jesus did fulfill his promises."

"Yeah—"

"Now, come on inside, and I'll make you a grilled cheese."

"Granny, I'm not really hungry. I just came to borrow Dad's motorbike."

"Oh, baby girl, I don't want you to get hurt on that busted old thing."

"I won't. I'll be careful. I promise."

She nodded. "Your mom knows, right?"

"Sure," I said, lying through my teeth.

"Baby girl, I can tell you're lying."

"And how much did you send Reverend Lowry this week?" I asked, smiling.

"I see what you did there. I see what you did there. Where are you going with that old thing?" she asked.

"I'm on my way to Tech," I said.

"Baby girl, I hate to break it to you, but that's in the opposite direction."

"I know. I just need something with an engine."

"Does your mom know?"

"Sure," I lied again.

"What's so important that you'd risk your mother's wrath?"

I sat on the front porch and said, "The end of the world."

"The Rapture," she said. "Making sure you're right with the Lord, you are, aren't you?"

"Granny, it's not that—it's the *real* end of the world. Don't you know there's probably going to be a nuclear war?"

"God won't let man be wiped out by a nuclear holocaust," she said, patting my knee.

"Granny—"

"No, baby girl, God protected us once. He'll do it again," she said.

That was how she told me a story about how my grandfather

was a volunteer Civil Defense[1] watcher. He watched the sky for Soviet planes. Then she told me about my mom. Stuff I did not know. How my mom was a wreck at school, afraid the missiles would blow up the whole world while she was in math class. She even had an assignment that she had to turn in: "What do you want to be when you grow up?" She turned it in blank.

"When the sirens blared for a false alarm one day, your momma got to building shelves, two-by-four pine shelves with her daddy. She stocked canned goods in the garage. And she got the neighbors to give us three seats in their fallout shelter. One day—I don't remember which one; it's been a long time—while I was waiting for your momma to get home from school, there was a loud boom and then a mushroom cloud in the sky. But it was nothing. I never told your momma about that. She would have been in the bunker for years, and you probably wouldn't have been born."

"Why don't I know this?" I asked. My mom and I were a lot alike.

"Why talk about something that will never happen?" she said.

"Granny, it's a matter of when it will happen."

"Who says? The news? Poppycock."

"Granny, I've got to go," I said, standing up.

"Baby girl, I wish I could tell you that it will be all right," she said, wiping her hands on her apron. "Us grown-ups have got this covered. Have faith."

I twisted my scrunchie on my wrist.

"I blame this movie. Everyone is on edge—even your dad is worried."

---

1 An older government program that helped citizens in times of possible Soviet attack. They were responsible for the creation of duck-and-cover drills and the Bert the Turtle mascot, because you know when you see the flash, you're supposed to duck and cover. My mom was told to hide under their desks in case of atomic attack, but today? We're pretty much told not to bother. It was replaced by FEMA in 1979.

"Dad? My dad?"

"He called the other day."

He called her? We hadn't spoken in over a month.

"He was checking up on me. I called him when I saw a lot of military men in their fatigues carrying shortwave radios and Geiger counters," she said.

"Granny, now you have me worried. Are you sure you saw what you saw? Maybe it was on TV?"

"Baby girl, don't worry. We're fine," she said, leaning over to rub both her knees.

"Are you okay, Granny?"

"It's my fibromyalgia," she said. "It acts up every now and then."

I helped her inside the house. She sat on her recliner and pulled the lever to put her feet up. "Don't worry about the things you can't do anything about," she said. "Like Reverend Lowry says, we won't suffer a nuclear war, because God would simply not allow it."

I rolled my eyes. She gave that man her life savings in the hopes that he wouldn't die. I would not trust in the words he said about what God would or would not allow.

"I've got to go. I don't want to be late," I said.

"Okay, okay. Be careful, baby girl. Granny loves you."

"I love you too," I told her.

I found the motorbike in the back of the garage, along with a pair of goggles, and one good kick got it started. The dirt flew up as I took it across the countryside. Each hill felt like a roller coaster and made my stomach flip. Faster and faster I went. I even ran a stop sign. Going fast really cleared the head.

It was out of my way, but I wanted to see Dad.

PRIVATE PROPERTY
NO TRESPASSING

WARNING/RESTRICTED AREA

IT IS UNLAWFUL TO ENTER THIS AREA WITHOUT PERMIS-
SION OF THE INSTALLATION COMMANDER

-------------- ------------------------ ------------------------

WHILE ON THIS INSTALLATION ALL PERSONNEL AND THE
PROPERTY UNDER THEIR CONTROL ARE SUBJECT TO SEARCH

USE OF DEADLY FORCE AUTHORIZED

I had done this hundreds of times. I'd ride Dad's old motorbike
to a few miles north of Damascus to the Titan II Launch Complex 374-7. One of eighteen around the state. Fifty-four around
the country. A six-thousand-mile range and a thirty to thirty-five-
minute flight time. It was invincible. It had been activated in 1963
and deactivated in 1980. Now I ride to the ones close by, which
included Blackwell, Hattieville, and Plummerville.

I was hoping to catch Dad out there on the site. A wave,
anything. Sometimes I would. I'd disobey the WARNING sign and
walk up to the eight-foot-tall chain-link fence that protected just
two acres across, where a couple of antennas stuck out of a
concrete silo lid, the only marker of Armageddon, and stand
and talk to Dad. We'd talk until someone would walk by and
yell that I didn't belong, and I'd run. This wasn't a safe place.
Nowhere was a safe place.

I wanted to be asleep when the big one happened. I would die.
We all would die. Griffin Flat was only minutes away from any
silo. We were close enough to a major military installation. We'd
be killed almost instantly if the Soviets attacked. No amount of
preparation was going to protect me from a nuclear blast that
close. I wouldn't have to worry about how to survive anarchy or
whatnot. I wouldn't be there to see it. It sounded defeatist, but it
was the truth. I thought about it all the time. I looked up at the
sky, at every contrail, thinking that this was it—this could be an
incoming warhead.

I turned the motorbike around so fast that it blew dirt and dust up into my face. It covered the tears falling down my cheeks. I wanted my dad, but he needed to be here in case of a red warning attack.

Thirty miles in the opposite direction, I parked the motorbike with the other motorbikes and followed the signs pointing toward the Witherspoon Auditorium.

"Is this the meeting for—" I started, but a boy with black-rimmed glasses and curly hair that went down to his shoulders finished my sentence.

"Don't Nuke Me? Yes, if you're here for that, then you're in the right place."

"I guess I am," I said.

He tilted his head and sized me up before he blew past me when he saw someone more important walk in.

I found an empty seat by the window and listened to people's conversations. Two boys discussed the limitations on an actual deterrent to having a nuclear war. And two girls discussed the qualifications for the group leader while also discussing the degree of hotness of the boy next to the signup sheet.

No one questioned why a high school student was here. (Though I didn't relay that information.) I was one more body for the cause. And there were a lot of bodies here for the cause. By the time the meeting got started, it was standing room only. Some people were even two to a seat.

"Great turnout," said a girl at the podium. She had buttons up and down her vest. Anti this, anti that:

Together We Can Stop the Bomb
Freeze Voter '84
Better Active Today than Radioactive Tomorrow!
Women Are Disarming the World

You can't cuddle children with Nuclear Arms.
She was fired up, angry.

"This is a war against war," she said. "We must be prepared for when the day comes—Don't Nuke Me, Mr. President."

A few boys sat in the back blowing up red balloons that spread out among the feet. A few girls were tying ribbons to the ends. A few balloons popped, and it made us all jump, but the boys went back to blowing up the balloons as replacements.

The girl moved out of the way while the crowd chanted, "We don't want a nuclear war in 1984—"

A boy stood at the podium, the president of the Don't Nuke Me organization, and talked about donations. I eyed a T-shirt he was selling. It was a single-file line of apes that had evolved into humans, but then—Flash. Boom. Blast. Mushroom Cloud.—and back to apes.

"We have a responsibility," he said, "to make sure that this movie will not be one that will soon be forgotten in the minds of the viewers. We don't need to wait until *Eve of Destruction*. Hollywood is filming a nuclear movie here. We don't need this to become another Hollywood scare tactic that sends people to push the button first, like in a game of chase. A group of teenagers will be threatened by a bomb attack. They will be forever changed. We don't need to make whatever happens on a script page reality."

Chant: "We don't want a nuclear war in 1984."

"We'll be extras because it will be fun to say we're in a movie. But let's not forget—if we don't have a nuclear freeze, there won't be any movies for a very long time, at least not in our lifetime. We'll be in the dark ages—medieval."

Chant: "We don't want a nuclear war in 1984!"

A man with a bushy gray beard stepped up, leaned on the podium, and then laid into us like it was a Sunday morning fire-and-brimstone sermon. "Don't want to live through nuclear war? Wouldn't want to be around after it's all over? Think that it will be easier to just let yourself be vaporized? Sorry, but you won't have that option. Only the politicians can save you. Sadly, there's a good chance that you will be killed in an instant even if you're in a fallout shelter, but if somehow you survive it certainly won't be painless."

I swallowed hard and twisted my scrunchie on my wrist as others nodded and, in a way that resembled a Sunday morning service, screamed, "Amen." This was a come-to-Jesus meeting to the tenth degree.

"If you stare at the flash, you will be blinded if you're lucky. If not, your eyes will literally melt out of your skull. And that's just before—or the eve of the destruction, if we're thinking thematically. Looting will occur after. Rape and pillage will be the norm . . ."

He described in great detail what would happen to the body. I was queasy.

"Some believe that being prepared for a nuclear war would make the event more likely. Apparently if we were adequately prepared, we would no longer fear such a war as much. We need a nuclear freeze. You there," the man said, pointing at a girl in the front row. "Tell me, why are you here?"

"All I want to do is grow up, not blow up," she said.

Chant: "We don't want a nuclear war in 1984."

He asked a few more people, and they responded in the same manner, though with slightly different words. I thought about what I would say if he pointed at me. I wanted to live. Grownups were the ones who created the bombs, but maybe we kids should be the ones to speak up and say enough was enough.

"No more nukes," a boy said. "If I've got fifteen minutes, I don't want to think about what I could have done."

The crowd cheered, clapped, and nodded.

"We don't want Ronald Raygun to put Pershing II and Tomahawk missiles in Europe. We need a nuclear freeze. We need to make a statement to show the politicians in this country that we don't want a nuclear war in 1984," said another guy.

Everyone got a red balloon. We walked quietly out of the

building and onto the lawn. We stood on the grass that had turned brown for the winter. Loudspeakers played "99 Red Balloons" by Nena, first in English and then in German. But it no longer felt like an upbeat dance tune; it had an eeriness to it.

The leader of the Don't Nuke Me group on campus raised his arm in the air and counted down with his fingers. Five. Four. Three. Two. One. And as a group we released every single red balloon into the sky. Red filled that blue sky. A symbolic act— because every single red balloon could be a missile.

"We don't want a nuclear war in 1984 . . ."

Though I felt sick to my stomach, it still growled. I pulled into McDonald's. I ordered a chocolate milkshake and a large fry. If the bombs had gone off, that would have been my last meal.

"Laura, is that you?" a man asked from a corner booth.

"Pops!" I said, picking up my tray from the counter.

"Scoot over for my grandchild," he said, gesturing to the man at the end of the booth.

I sat and began unwrapping the straw and sticking it in my milkshake.

"What do you have there?" Pops asked.

"Milkshake and fries, the lunch of champions."

"Why aren't you in school?"

"I got suspended."

"What did my grandchild do to get suspended?"

I wasn't really his grandchild. Not biologically. Pops was Dennis's dad. Terrence's grandfather. But even though I wasn't blood, Pops called me his grandchild. His new granddaughter by marriage. His only granddaughter.

"Long story. Let's just say it was totally worth it."

He laughed and so did his buddies. They all tipped their hats with an introduction. Pops would come here every weekday and sit in this booth and drink his coffee with sugar and talk to his friends. They would stay until the lunch crowd arrived, which was now. I think they stayed later because I was here. But they were in deep discussion about the movie *Eve of Destruction*. One of Pop's buddies was lending his barn to the film and another was lending his law office, though the location director wasn't sure if they would need them or not.

"I'm going to be in it," I said, smiling.

"Well, ain't that a thing."

I took the top off my milkshake and started dunking my French fries. "I get to invite a guest, and I asked Terrence if he wanted to go with me. He said yes."

"I'm glad you two are finding solid ground. You're making your pops proud."

When Terrence's dad and my mom got married, it was Pops who helped me feel welcome. I didn't have a grandfather who was alive, so he filled that role. It felt weird having a grandparent who was nice and didn't have a flaw—like giving hundreds to thousands of dollars to a testiphony.

"You and Terrence will have a lot of fun. You'll remember this time for the rest of y'all's lives," Pops said, grabbing a fry and dipping it in my milkshake. "Yum. Next time I'll have to get one for myself."

With the last fry on my tray eaten, the men grabbed their coats, straightened their hats, and said their goodbyes.

"Fair warning," Pops said. "Watch out for the speed trap down on Hunt Road—that hill toward the Piggly Wiggly. There was a cop hiding by a bunch of overgrown bushes." He turned to me. "That's where I got my umpteenth speeding ticket—by not paying attention to gravity."

"Love you, Pops."

"I love you too, Laura."

WANTED: EXTRAS FOR
EVE OF DESTRUCTION FILM

Little Rock, Ark.—Curious about the end of the world? Here's your chance to take part in the apocalypse. In *Eve of Destruction*, it's 1954, and a Red Warning is looming over the country. A nationwide drill is set for 10 A.M. across North America. What happens to an American city when the unthinkable happens . . . FOR REAL?

All ages welcome. Locals with pre-1954 vehicles are needed. Dates: November 26–December 6.

Refreshments and snacks provided.

READER POLL: WAR AND PEACE

Headed your way to a movie theater near you is *Eve of Destruction*, the story of a world on the brink of annihilation. The nation fears a Red Warning, so to be prepared for the worst, the United States declares the first nationwide Civil Defense drill. Set in Arkansas in June 1954, the story follows four teenagers as the town of Pikesville stages a mock attack.

Even in 1984, people have nuclear war on their minds. Do you think there will be a nuclear war in your lifetime? Do you think if there is a nuclear war, you will survive? Do you favor a nuclear freeze? Please answer honestly. Once done, drop off your surveys at any of the following locations: Ellis Grocery, the post office on Main Street, the town hall (the local FEMA location) on Hatcher.

Results will be published in an upcoming issue of the *Arkansas Telegram*.

1. What are the chances of a nuclear war?
☐ High
☐ Low

2. Do you think a nuclear freeze will happen in your lifetime?
☐ Yes
☐ No

3. How often do you think about a nuclear war happening?
☐ Several times a day
☐ About once a day
☐ Almost once a month
☐ Almost never

4. Given that the state is a prime target, how prepared do you believe we are in case of attack?
1 2 3 4 5 6 7 8 9 10

5. If a nuclear war occurs, do you believe one side will emerge as a "winner"?
☐ Yes
☐ No

6. What are your chances of surviving a nuclear war?
☐ None
☐ Poor
☐ Good
☐ Excellent

Your Age
☐ 15 or under
☐ 16 to 21
☐ 22 to 30
☐ 31 to 45
☐ 46 to 60
☐ 61 or above

Your Sex
☐ Male
☐ Female

Chapter Seven

Mom dragged Dennis to the hotel to fix a few issues that had been plaguing the staff of the Flat Inn, Terrence was at a pickup basketball game down at the Y, and I was at Max's house trying to decipher my handwriting. Max's room was the natural place for the creative process, strewn with his own drawings, action figures, and costumes from Halloweens past. Last year we went as Batman and Robin. I was Robin, of course. I never got to play the lead.

"I think we need a female lead," I told Max.

"Why?" he asked.

"Because they keep canceling the ones that have one, like *She-Hulk*."[1]

He didn't answer. I got to work on the origin story of my girl while Max got to drawing.

---

1 She-Hulk had her own comic books, but they were canceled in 1982. She became a minor character in other comics, including the Incredible Hulk. Two years ago, she was a member of the Avengers, and this year, she appeared in the April issue as a member of the Fantastic Four.

"I want her to be strong and independent and speak her mind but not be too bossy," I said.

"Okay, how about a name?" he asked.

"Penny," I answered, my eyes on my notebook. "Penny Star."

"Is that too on the nose?" he asked, sharpening his pencil.

"Really? Too on the nose? Like Flash or Firestorm—"

"Okay, I get your point," he said.

"Thank you very much."

"Well, does it not sound like a stripper?"

"Uh, fine, I'll change the name."

A loud, piercing sound came from the living room. Max's older sister, Erica, was home from college, watching soap operas. When she was done screaming—it didn't last long—she turned down the volume. She was thoughtful that way. "I only want to hear that tone blaring in the end-times," I said, pulling my knees to my chest.

"Like now?" Max said.

"They're doing more tests lately, aren't they? Should we be worried?" I asked.

"We're just getting our origin story."

"I went to a meeting yesterday at Tech about the end of Star Wars," I said.

"The movie?"

"No—nuclear arms race," I said. "We set off ninety-nine red balloons in protest."

"When did you get political?" he asked.

"I'm not."

"You do know red balloons are not great for the environment."

"Do you think there's going to be a nuclear war?" I asked.

"No. No one is that stupid," he said. "What does your dad say?"

"My dad?" I asked.

"You know, your dad knows all about this nuclear weapons business?"

"He doesn't talk about it."

"You mean, he can't talk about it."

"Yeah, can't."

It was a lie. Dad once talked about it.

My dad was a member of the 374th Strategic Missile Squadron, the United States Air Force unit that was assigned to the 308th Strategic Missile Wing, stationed at Little Rock Air Force Base. The 374th Strategic Missile Squadron was equipped with the LGM-25C Titan II Intercontinental ballistic missile (ICBM), with a mission of nuclear deterrence. The squadron was responsible for nine missile sites. Well, eight now. The ninth was at 374-4 at the underground missile launch facility near Damascus, Arkansas, population three hundred.

The missile they were "guarding" until they got the orders to "deploy" was a silo-based, liquid-propellant ballistic missile. It was the largest ICBM ever deployed by the US Air Force. It carried a W-53 9.0 MT nuclear warhead. The missile had a diameter of 3.05 meters, a length of 31.30 meters, and a launch weight of 149,700 kilograms. The missiles had a two-stage liquid propellant design and reached a speed of twenty-five times the speed of sound by the time the engines cut off. Meaning kaboom rather quickly. After the "incident," it was found later in a ditch. On that day three years ago, the Damascus site became decommissioned and disassembled. Now there were nine ICBMs[1] that Dad's unit was responsible for.

Dad lived on base now, full-time since the divorce, and he couldn't really call, so he wrote. The government liked to leave me with my imagination running wild, since there were a lot

---

1 374-1 Blackwell, 347-2 Plummerville, 347-3 Hattieville, 374-4 Springfield, 374-5 Wooster, 374-6 Guy, 374-7 Damascus,* 374-8 Quitman, and 374-9 Pearson.

*On September 18–19, 1980, a Broken Arrow happened.

of black marks on his letters. Once he said he had been at the site at Damascus, and the United States government messed up one time and blacked out Arkansas instead. One time he let it slip after too many beers (this was after Mom's illicit affair with Dennis was found out) that when (he said *when*, not *if*) a nuclear war happened, he would be in the bunker. He was the one who typed in the codes and turned the key to annihilation. The next morning, he asked if he'd said anything incriminating. I lied because I didn't want my dad to get in trouble, but he could tell I was lying. I didn't want my dad to be transferred because he couldn't keep a secret.

And I could. I knew the secret eight-digit code.

"Can you imagine the big red button sitting on the president's desk, ready to be pushed?" Max asked.

I glanced up from my notebook and scowled at him. "I don't think it's a big red button, and it's certainly not on the president's desk."

He winced dramatically, as if he'd just been slapped. "I know . . . but it's funny to imagine." He laughed.

"It's just keys and codes."

"How do *you* know?"

"Um, the beginning of *WarGames*.[1] You remember the beginning of *WarGames*," I said, changing the subject.

"Yeah, the beginning of *WarGames*."

"So—our script," I said, hoping he'd finally take the hint.

I couldn't tell Max what my dad had said while piss drunk. My dad could have been tried for treason. It was an accident, what happened at Damascus. A socket fell in the silo and hit

---

1 A 1983 major motion picture starring Matthew Broderick. David Lightman hacks War Operation Plan Response with the help of Jennifer, played by Ally Sheedy, and we as planet Earth almost went to DEFCON 1 and World War III.

the side of the missile, causing a major leak of flammable rocket fuel, and it *nearly* went BOOM. He didn't die, but he could have. He still worked on the ICBMs. And the ICBM was six hundred times more powerful than the bomb that destroyed Hiroshima. My dad didn't have anything directly to do with the "accident," but he was on location with the ICBM at the time. And he still worked on them. If he had *everything* to do with it, they wouldn't keep him on, right? Right?

"What if the government is hiding something from us?" Max asked out of nowhere. Well, not out of nowhere. He was smart.

"Like before?" I asked.

"Didn't your dad get into trouble?"

"It was an accident," I said.

"Accident? I'm sure it was the Russians," he said with a wink.

"It *was* an accident."

"Sure it was, Laura. How many times have we accepted these 'accidents'?" he asked, using finger quotes. "We should be a part of the resistance, not a part of the propaganda machine."

Max went back to drawing but left me thinking about the plot to our comic, which we were calling *Big Sister*. He wouldn't allow me to see his drawings. Only when they were perfect, but according to him, they never would be.

After each drawing, he'd crumple it up into a ball and drop it into the waste bucket he kept beside him. He would take the trash bag home when he left after each work session—or what Max's mother would describe as a playdate. He was a budding tortured artist.

"One little peek?" I would ask.

And he would say no and then get defensive. I would only see what he'd drawn when it hit the comic bookshelves at Dewayne's.

"So you want to change the main character from a boy to a girl superhero?" he asked.

"Or a villain?" I said.

"Or a villain."

Our script was about done. (And by "done," I mean we'd started over a few times. But our first line remained the same: *And with a big, loud bang, everything was gone.* Max and Laura's untitled comic had fun promising the apocalypse.) Also, our plot was simple: A few teens got trapped in the cellar of Old Barnaby's Farm in a small town called Seaside during a nuclear exchange between two opposing foes. (Max and I were afraid to say who the two opposing foes were; we didn't want our sales to be compromised, and if we kissed and made up with the USSR, then we'd be screwed financially.) Some went mad, some tried to escape, some fell in love. But all got superpowers. When they emerged, they saw a changed world. It was overrun by an organization called Big Sister. Big Sister keeps order in the wasteland that it created. Chocolate was distributed for radiation sickness. We couldn't decide if our characters were going to be superheroes or supervillains in the new world order.

"Godzilla was created because of nuclear radiation, and he's a monster, and yet our superheroes are created nearly the same, and they're not," he said.

"It's like they see nuclear fallout quite differently than we do," I said.

"You think?"

"I was being sarcastic."

"Me too."

"You know, if we were born one year later, we would have had completely different sets of friends at school and be completely different people."

"I think about that a lot."

Chapter Eight

According to Tom Brokaw, the Doomsday Clock was set at three minutes to midnight. 11:57. They might as well have moved the hands to midnight because that was what it was like at church that Sunday morning.

Mom skipped church. She still had a mile-long list of stuff to do, and a big crew was showing up on Monday. Terrence was with his mom, so I went with Dennis to church. We were late and sat in the front pew in the sanctuary. After the service we went to the fellowship hall and waited for the potluck.

I watched as Dana approached, homing in like a missile homing in on its primary target—Moscow, or Leningrad, or . . . Laura.

"Dana Cobb, daughter of Nathaniel and Melanie Cobb, sister to David Cobb and Daniel Cobb, friend to everyone except you," she said.

"Why are you talking in the third person?" I asked.

"No, Dana has once again decreed that the friendship with Laura Ratliff is over."

"Dana—"

"How dare you speak her name!" she cried.

Now I was confused. *Whose name?*

"The end is near," she said in the silence.

"You mean . . . the world?"

"No, our friendship."

"Near, or over?" I asked. I was grumpy and hungry. I wanted clarity. I wanted to end the conversation.

Her eyes turned to slits. "Laura, I never want to speak to you again. I have written it down. I have commanded it."

Fine. Is that it? I didn't say the words out loud, but I came close.

She opened her Bible and flipped straight to Exodus. Commandment eleven. Added fresh in blue ink. (It had smeared.) *Thou Shall Not Be A Friend, Acquaintance, Adversary, or Confidante. Laura Ratliff Will Be Dead To Me—As Judas Was To Jesus—Now And Forever, Amen.*

I frowned. "Jesus *forgave* Judas."

She rolled her eyes. "A misjudgment on his part."

"Wow," I said. Looking up, I tried to reclaim my place in the food line. Old people usually go first, leaving only the Jell-O that looks like mold, the green bean casserole, and the cold macaroni salad. No deviled eggs, no fried chicken, no homemade yeast rolls. But today the trays of decent foods still held out hope . . .

"Wow what?" she asked.

"Wow, I might actually get fried chicken this time, if I pay attention."

She snapped the Bible shut. "You are not a nice person!" she hissed. "And I'm glad we're not friends anymore."

"My mom will be glad too," I said as she walked away.

She froze, then spun in place. "I just have to know," she snapped, folding her arms across her chest.

"Have to know what?" I groaned.

"How could you do that to me?" She pouted. "I thought you were going to choose me. I'm the one who wants to be a star!"

"Exactly."

"But you chose Terrence."

"Well, yeah. He's . . . around. Also, because you would make it about yourself," I said.

"How dare *you* make it about *yourself*," she retorted. "It's not the Christian thing to do."

"But I'm the one who won the contest."

She drew close. "I hope your character dies in a nuclear explosion."

I shrugged. Whatever. The truth was that I didn't know a thing about my character. I didn't even know if I had one. At least one beyond *Teenage Girl Extra*. My eyes drifted toward the steaming tray of fried chicken. "Are you in line or not?" I asked.

"Laura—you, you . . ." she sputtered. "I'm leaving. Like I said before, we're no longer friends. I'm warning you: don't you dare say my name ever again."

With that, she stormed out of the hall. She didn't come back a third time. She'd said her peace, and I said mine.

Dennis and I stopped by the hotel on our way home with a plate of food. Somehow Dennis got decent food from the clutches of the senior citizens. When I told Mom what happened at church with Dana, she literally did a little dance behind the front desk.

"Thank the Lord, he's finally answered my prayers," she said as the phone rang. She left it ringing, breaking the number one rule at the Flat Inn. It was a miracle, and she had to praise God for his righteousness (or whatever she was saying), acting like she'd witnessed a real live miracle, not the end of a friendship. Was it a friendship? I wasn't even sure. Our relationship? No, that sounds romantic. Our thing was over.

And before *you* even think it, or flip the pages to see if we made up—let me say it clearly—this isn't going to be one of those stories where we become friends later, defying adversity and all. No, our thing was dead.

Chapter Nine

Mayor Curtis Hershott, a man who was long-winded when he talked, usually about his own endeavors, straightened his bow tie when he got annoyed, tapped his fingers one at a time on the podium when he got bored, and was so proud of Griffin Flat that he had been elected mayor for five consecutive elections. (No one else wanted the job. He had run unopposed every four years.) Mayor Hershott was also the man (with help from Governor Clinton) who got *Eve of Destruction* to be filmed here in the first place. "This will finally give some recognition to our town. Don't you all want to be put on the map?" he asked with so much excitement that we all agreed, even though it was a disaster from the start. Permits. Agreements. Complaints. The only one who wasn't upset and regretting the decision was Mayor Hershott. He was still so excited about Hollywood coming. In fact, he had a walk-on role—and he had lines. (He probably had it written into the contract.)

This was like any other town hall meeting. There were three

items on the agenda, and they had everything to do with *Eve of Destruction*.

1. Party

The "Welcome to Town" party, also known as the "suck up to the celebrities at the red barn in the middle of town" party. Welcome to Griffin Flat, or Pikesville for the next few weeks.

"Remember the three *F*s—Fun, Food, Fellowship," Mayor Hershott said.

"Fun, Food, Fornication," Max said beside me in a whisper, mimicking the mayor's voice.

I laughed.

"Laura," Mayor Hershott said, leaning on his podium, "come." He waved me forward.

I stood next to him at the podium, looking out at the townspeople.

"Laura and *I*"—he smiled—"will be on the set as we will both be in the film. We will represent Griffin Flat with class." He messed with my side ponytail and had me sit back down.

2. Christmas decorations

"Please hold off putting up Christmas decorations until after the movie ends filming. The movie is set in June 1954, so it doesn't make much sense to have Santa Claus on one's lawn, does it?" Mayor Hershott asked.

3. Dirt

"The production team has asked Dutton's Dirt Carriers to supply tons and tons and tons of dirt to be brought in and dumped on Sunset Drive. It will be dumped and blocked during filming."

"Excuse me. I live on Sunset Drive—how am I supposed to get to work?" Mr. Jones asked.

"It is best you make other arrangements."

"You've got to be kidding. I can't make other arrangements. I can't—"

"Would someone be willing to pick up Mr. Jones for work and drop him off after?" Mayor Hershott asked.

Someone in the back raised their hand, and we moved on.

"We're going to make this the best film ever made in the state of Arkansas," Mayor Hershott said as the food group set up sign-up sheets on clipboards and hung them on nails around the room.

Debbie Hendricks walked to the front of the room and started talking about food. A lot of people were still talking about the dirt on Sunset Drive and paid no attention to her.

This was it! Griffin Flat would be nuked. We'd beat out hundreds of other small towns across the United States for the once-in-a-lifetime experience of being in a fake nuclear war. (It probably hadn't hurt that Governor Clinton had been on board from the start.) A clap of thunder boomed. People jumped, including me. Max did too. He hit me on the arm, as if I was the one responsible for him jumping, then laughed.

"It's the bomb," Kevin Barnes yelled.

"Don't joke," someone responded. "It could—"

"Mayor Hershott, what about the sirens? Should we be worried?" Brenda Leigh asked.

"Yeah, there's been a lot of them lately," Mr. Romero, local car salesman, and Rodney's dad, said. "Is the country planning for an attack? Should we be prepared?"

"You should always be prepared," Mayor Hershott said, which did not help ease the thoughts of the worried people in the room.

"The end is near, my fellow citizens, the end is near," Max whispered.

"FEMA has agreed to participate. They've dropped off a pamphlet for each household. You can pick yours up after the meeting," Mayor Hershott said.

Mr. Romero gasped. "A pamphlet?"

"A real nuclear blast could only improve Griffin Flat," Max whispered in my ear, back in his normal voice.

"Please," Mayor Hershott implored. "This is a wonderful opportunity for our town. We need to think about how we act during the filming of the movie. They're from California; we're going to show them southern hospitality—"

"Southern hospitality, but leave your white robes at home," Max whispered again.

By now the crowd was murmuring so loudly that the mayor had to slam his fist on the lectern. "Hollywood knows what it's doing!" the mayor cried.

Everyone fell silent.

But that was all. Mayor Hershott had nothing more to add. Meeting adjourned.

Chapter Ten

Monday afternoon I was sitting in chemistry doing worksheets. I was proud of my life choice of pulling the safety shower string. Mr. Truitt was pulling out his hair trying to make sure he didn't get a talking-to by the athletic director. Max, the only other person in class with a decent passing grade, was paired up with Rodney. Like I'd been a few days ago. And like always, Max was doing all the work.

"Did you see the Hog game on Saturday? It was def," Rodney said, trying to make small talk while watching Max do the experiment.

"Excuse me?" Max said. "I can't hear you . . ."

Rodney sniffed. "Def. DEF."

Max shook his head, biting his lip to keep from smiling. "I have a hearing problem."

"What?"

I started laughing. I couldn't help it. *Max, you jerk.* Mr. Truitt flinched at the outburst. He pointed at the door and sent me straight back to the principal's office. Wonderful.

I was being treated just like Victory—our main character's name in *Big Sister*. Maybe that's what Max had intended all along.

"Ms. Ratliff," Principal Parker said, standing at his office door.

Oh crap. The *Ms. Ratliff*. That was as bad as the "Laura Beth" I got at home.

The chair in front of Principal Parker's desk was still warm from the butt before. Kevin Barnes decided at lunch to not go out to the smokers' corner. Instead, half the school watched as he lit one up right at the table over his tater tots. I could still smell the stale cigarette smoke and fried potatoes.

"Why are you here again?" Principal Parker asked. My permanent file on his desk.

"I laughed at a joke in Mr. Truitt's class."

"Uh-huh."

"And Mr. Truitt didn't think it was funny enough to laugh at."

"Uh-huh."

"But it was Max—"

"Stop right there."

Max had a reputation.

Principal Parker took a deep breath. "I get it, I really do, but you have to show respect to the teachers. We're not here to test your intelligence."

I blinked at him. "Then what are you here to test for?" I asked.

"Honestly?" he muttered. "Start with my patience."

I made it back to class just in time for the school sirens to go off. It was a drill—another drill.

We made our way into the hallway and sat in front of the lockers. Terrence sat beside me, and Rodney was on the other side. Max was across the hall making faces. Not exactly following the rules, but certainly testing Principal Parker's patience, had he been there.

"Chuck, sit down now," Coach Brooks shouted.

We all cringed, waiting for him to blow his whistle.

Coach Brooks was the assistant varsity football coach and civics teacher. He wore his whistle everywhere he went. I once saw him at an afternoon showing of *E.T. the Extra-Terrestrial*.[1] He blew the whistle when two adults started having a conversation during the scene when Elliot thought that E.T. had died.

Sure enough, there it was: a piercing screech.

"Coach, I can't," Chuck groaned. He stood against the cold metal of his locker with Dana and Kathy. They supported him as if they were adoring cheerleaders without brains, which they were. But they also had a reason to support him: Chuck had a broken leg.

"Chuck, get your ass down now before a nuke takes you out," Coach Brooks yelled.

In case of nuclear attack, I'd decided I wanted the pointy end of the bomb to fall right above my head—I'd be skeletonized.

Chuck shook his head. "Coach, listen, it hurts. I won't be able to get back up."

Dana's and Kathy's indignation on Chuck's behalf was too much for them to bear. They ran down the hall. Coach Brooks wasn't happy. He called out their names but once he saw Chuck sliding down the lockers and falling to the floor, he smiled and spat his whistle from his mouth. He knew that Dana and Kathy had made the right decision. Chuck lay flat on the floor, turned on his stomach. His head in the middle of the hallway. His leg touching the wall.

His face was creased in agony as he writhed on the cold linoleum. He wasn't faking. I felt bad for him. "Cover your head

---

1 A sci-fi movie directed by Steven Spielberg. It came out in 1982. It's basically about a boy who befriends an alien and tries to get him home before the government kills them.

now, Chuck," Coach Brooks ordered, and Chuck obeyed, even though he was in DEFCON 1^1 in pain.

"You're all going to die—so kiss your asses goodbye," Chuck said.

Is this appropriate? I wondered. I would have asked it out loud if another teacher had been present. Where was Principal Parker during these drills?

The sirens seemed to go on longer than usual. I felt queasy. Like something was looming on the horizon. And it wasn't good. It could be Thanksgiving—in three days—with just Mom and Dennis. Terrence would be with his mom for the holiday. The sirens went on and on. These days those lilting doomsday whistles seemed to erupt more frequently—sour and out of sync and coming from every direction. I always pictured a chorus of limp-winged fallen angels, booted out of heaven for singing like crap. Stripped of their harps. Wailing for our attention while we marched toward the apocalypse. (But maybe that was because I was still bitter that Mom made me try out for chorus in ninth grade; when I didn't pass the audition, it ruined extracurricular activities for me for good.) Still, the world continued not to end. Our butts continued to remain firmly glued to the dirty hallway floor.

And then: blessed silence.

A collective sigh of relief. We all stood. Well, all of us except for Chuck.

"Can someone help me up?" Chuck asked, raising his right arm in the air and waving his hand for anyone with strength to grab it.

I took a step forward.

"No, don't help the dead person," Coach Brooks commanded, laughing.

---

1 DEFCON 5: Normal Readiness. DEFCON 4: Above Normal Readiness. DEFCON 3: Air Force Ready to Mobilize in 15 Minutes. DEFCON 2: Armed Forces Ready to Deploy and Engage in Less than 6 Hours. DEFCON 1: Maximum Readiness.

I couldn't tell if Coach really meant what he was saying. I wasn't sure what to do. So I froze in place, staring as Chuck clumsily tried to get himself into a standing position.

Orwell was right. All you have to do is keep people scared.

FEMA

FEMA was created to ensure that the United States government survives a nuclear attack. In a nuclear attack, most people will be killed instantly, due to the blast, heat, or the initial radiation that follows.

BE PREPARED

This is in no way meant to frighten you; however, in a State of National Emergency declared by the President of the United States, it is best to be prepared because there will be casualties.

WARNING

An attack warning signal will be heard. An attack warning signal means that an actual attack against the United States has been detected—and protective action is necessary. An enemy attack on the United States is possible in these rising global tensions. In the event of an attack you will receive a warning. To be prepared, know there are Alert Signals: a 3 to 5 minute steady blast of sirens. In the event of a real attack, there is an Attack Warning Signal: a 3 to 5 minute wavering sound on sirens. Please familiarize yourself with the distinction of each.

EVACUATION

In the event of an attack on the United States, if you live in a target area, it is best to be prepared to evacuate to a safer location. In the event of an attack, locations in your area have been designated as safe places to go. These locations have been marked with a sign—black-and-yellow with three upside down triangles with the words FALLOUT SHELTER clearly visible. Please locate and be familiar with the nearest shelter. You will live in the shelter for fourteen days. There are things you can do in order to survive. Make sure that all windows are blocked in the room. Possible items of use: bricks, concrete, building blocks, sand, books, dirt; furniture can also be used in an emergency. Sanitation arrangements need to be made because there will be no water or toilets. See your local FEMA office for more instructions.

SUPPLIES

A list of suggested items to have in your shelter:

Water
Milk and/or formula
Food—canned or dried
Bottle and can opener
Eating utensils
Plastic and paper bags
Battery-operated (transistor) radios
Extra batteries
Candles and matches
Soap
Sanitary napkins or tampons
Diapers
Towels and washcloths
Garbage can
Toilet paper
Emergency toilet (bucket and plastic bags)
First aid kit
Toothbrush and toothpaste
Powder
Work gloves
Extra clothing
Coats
Rain gear
Extra shoes
Extra socks

Sleeping bags and blankets
Pickax
Shovel
Saw
Hammer
Broom
Nails and screws
Screwdriver
Roll of wire

HEAT AND BLAST

The temperature of the heat and blast will be hotter than the sun. It will destroy surroundings up to many miles from ground zero. To protect your shelter from the heat blast, it is recommended that you paint your interior walls with antiflash white. It is the brightest white paint color. It will reflect thermal radiation. Contact your local FEMA office for more information.

FALLOUT

Fallout is dust that is sucked up from the explosion. The radiation from the dust is dangerous. Exposure can lead to sickness and/or death. Contact your local FEMA office for more information.

ELECTROMAGNETIC PULSE (EMP)

During a nuclear explosion, an electromagnetic pulse, or EMP, will occur. In the event of one, most electronic equipment will be ineffective. An EMP will cripple infrastructure and make it nearly impossible to retaliate against a possible attack. Contact your local FEMA office for more information.

The main goal is to survive a nuclear attack. Please follow your local authorities' instructions.

Chapter Eleven

By five o'clock, Jennings's Hardware was officially out of white paint. God help you if you painted your house any color other than white.

"Did you at least save any for us?" Mom asked.

"Of course. But we don't really need it. There's not going to be a nuclear war," Dennis said.

"But what if there is?" I asked.

"We'll just do what the government tells us."

Right. Of course, the government wouldn't lie to us. That only happened in books like *1984*.

"Seriously, what if it does happen?" I asked again.

"We'll survive," he said.

Adult reassurances ranked even higher on the bullshit-o-meter than those of the US government.

"Why don't we just paint ourselves white?" Mom asked. "To deflect the blast, do you think?"

"Government wants us racist even in death," I said, mostly to myself.

"Harharhar," Dennis said dryly. But then he started laughing for real.

"So, Dennis, who's going to paint these interior walls?" I asked cautiously, knowing full well that Terrence and I would be stuck with the rest of the town anti-flashing the inside of our homes so white we'd need to wear sunglasses just to sit in our living rooms.

"Oh, you know who," Dennis said with a wink.

Terrence was still at his mom's and would be until Monday. So it was just Dennis, Mom, and me for the night, making brownies for the Welcome to Griffin Flat party. Nothing says "southern hospitality" like hundreds of calories. Dennis and I were taking turns licking the bowls. That was, until I got a call from Max telling me to get to his land, or the Woods. (Everyone in town called that area on Crow Mountain the Woods. Max, though, called it his land.) There had been an invasion.

Mom was against my going.

"No, today is family time," she said, pouring brownie batter in an 8x8 glass pan.

"Family time? Terrence is with his mom. Can't you just pretend I'm with Dad?"

Mom laughed. "When's the last time you were with *your* dad?"

"Edna," Dennis warned in a gentle voice.

Mom sighed. She opened the oven, put the brownies in, and set the timer for twenty minutes. And she sighed again, cracking eggs over the bowl to mix another batch of brownies. And she sighed again, wiping her hands on a rag. We were a family—Mom and I and Granny—we were a family that sighed when angry.

"Dad would let me go," I said, unable to keep from poking the bear with a stick.

"Of course your dad would. He would want to be the good guy."

"Dad *is* the good guy."

She whirled to face me and opened her mouth, but Dennis touched her lower back before she could start talking. I had to hand it to the guy: he was like some sort of pacifist puppeteer when it came to my mother.

She could have taken my comment in many awful directions, all of which probably would have been true. But the immutable facts remained: she was the one who cheated. And she was the one who wanted the marriage to end. She was the one who filed divorce papers. She was the one who married Dennis not long after the papers were signed. She was the bad guy in my eyes. But I couldn't say that. I would have been the bad guy for pointing it out.

"Terrence is probably at the party," I pointed out, for all our sakes. "His mom probably let him go," I added unfairly, licking the leftover batter in the mixing bowl with my finger.

"Don't start—"

"Start what?" I feigned innocence and went for another dip. That did the trick. "Go . . . go to your party," Mom grunted. She stomped over to her purse and dug for her keys. "Here," she said, throwing them at me.

I smiled as I changed into some black leggings, an oversized light-pink sweater, and a pair of hot-pink Keds. I kept smiling as I put my hair in a side ponytail and grabbed my black backpack. I was smiling still as I waltzed out the door, waving to Mom and Dennis.

They looked like they felt sorry for me more than anything else.

Now, Max's land was really his grandfather's land. Of course, Max gets his grandfather's land when his grandfather dies, but that's another story. The place was up on Crow Mountain. It was too far to ride my bike. People had been coming out here since the 1960s. Meaning people like my mom, which was kind of weird if you thought about it—since there was a ton of drinking and sex. Lots of unplanned pregnancies were conceived here. Probably followed by vomiting and dry heaving. Ahh . . . memories.

Max's grandfather was a bootlegger. During Prohibition he was the area's biggest supplier of moonshine. (Commonly overlooked bit of Griffin Flat trivia: moonshine is the reason why our high school mascot is called the Shiners.) He made it in this cave on his land. It was dry and open. But the cave was like a small factory. He had this huge distiller. Even after Prohibition he continued making moonshine. Max's dad continued the family tradition, even though it was *so* illegal. Max's grandfather made the best illegal but tasty stuff. Max's dad kept it in an underground shelter that his parents built during the brink of the Cold War. Back during the Cuban missile crisis. Back when we were almost annihilated by the Russians. *Again.* But everyone bought from him, even my grandfather, and Pops. There were quite a bit of "accidents" that occurred around here. When caught, a lot of men *and* a few women decided to make a break for it and run. And within a hundred feet of the cave is a drop. Watch your step, 'cause it will be your last.

Everyone from high school was here.

It wasn't really saying a lot: Griffin Flat High School wasn't that big, and neither was my class. I pulled up right behind Kevin Barnes's beat-up old truck, got out of my car, locked it. An unlocked car equaled the perfect place to do the nasty. Many parties ago, after an incident that happened that one does not speak of, someone created a sign and nailed it on an old oak tree.

WHAT YOU SEE HERE
WHAT YOU DO HERE
WHAT YOU HEAR HERE
WHEN YOU LEAVE HERE
LET IT STAY HERE

"Laura," Max yelled, running toward me, "I have been waiting for you."

"Are you drunk?" I asked.

"Nooooooo, honestly, I'm not. It's soda."

"Max—Max—Max—Max—Max—Max—Max . . ." the crowd chanted.

Max turned to the crowd, raised his cup in the air, and then proceeded to chug.

"Max—Max—Max—Max—Max—Max—Max . . ." the crowd chanted again.

Max stuck out his tongue, shook his head, crushed his cup with his left hand, and threw it to the ground. "Yeah, boy."

The crowd cheered and went back to their drinks.

"What?" I asked, laughing.

"We all just formed a cult—and I'm their leader. Does this mean I should go to the store and pick up some Kool-Aid?"

"Don't drink the Kool-Aid. Wait—" I said. "You're the leader?"

"I know, I know. Last week they didn't know my name. This week, damn, I'm—Max!" He yelled his name and everyone in unison proceeded to chant, "Max—Max—Max—Max."

"I am a god," he whispered in my ear.

I laughed.

"You'll never guess who's here," he said.

"Who?"

"Come—you've got to see." He grabbed my arm and dragged me to the cave. Sitting on a crate of dried apple slices was one celebrity—Astrid Ogilvie. Her blonde hair was so big. And her curls were permed, by the way; I can spot a perm a mile away thanks to Brenda Leigh's Beauty Parlor. Plus, I get perms. Astrid kept moving her curly hair out of her face, blowing it back, but eventually asking some random girl at my high school for a scrunchie. There's something about our weather down here that makes our hair rise to the occasion. Some say it's the humidity, others say it's to be closer to God, either way. No one knows the struggle of having to iron your hair just to get through a day.

No one in the cave was talking—they were just staring at her like we had just seen three seconds of unscrambled Cinemax or something.

Max grabbed my arm and pulled me toward her.

"What do you think you're doing?" I asked, trying to get him to let me go.

"You have to meet her. She's just a person. Just like us."

"No. She's famous. We're not." Hearing my words in my head, I realized I sounded like Dana. Now I wanted to puke, and I hadn't even had a single sip of beer.

"Come on."

"If this isn't rock bottom, then I don't know what is," Astrid said, clearly to us, but pretending as if she were just talking out loud to herself. Her eyes caught mine.

"Something I can help you with, miss?"

"I was just coming over here to say hi, that's all."

"Well, hi," she imitated, emphasizing the southern drawl that was apparently my speaking voice.

I turned to walk away.

Max grabbed both my arms and said, "This is my friend Laura. She's going to be in the movie too. She won the radio contest."

Astrid flashed a big, fake smile. "Congratulations." She sipped her beer with a straw. "I bet you'll do great playing a hick."

"Why don't you reach down with both hands, firmly grasp the stick, and pull it out of your anus," Max replied.

I laughed.

Her straw fell from her mouth. "Excuse me?"

"Take that stick, ya hear?" Max used the same exaggerated cowpoke lilt she'd just used with me. "Out. Of. Your. An-u-u-s."

"You can't talk to me like that," Astrid snapped.

People were staring now.

"Do you know who I am? Because you can't talk to me like that. Who invited you to this *party*, anyway?"

"It's my land. Who invited you?"

She didn't look the least bit apologetic. "Kathy Baker."

Of course. Kathy Baker: spoiled, stuck-up, and pretentious. The problem was that Max might not have been afraid of celebrities, but he was afraid of Kathy.

He grabbed my arm and pulled me away.

"I think I need a new pair of underpants," he said once we were outside the cave.

"I can't wait to see Astrid's character die as a fireball engulfs her as she runs across Main Street searching for shelter," I said.

My Lord. I really am Dana.

"Where's Peony?" I asked Max.

Max put his index finger to the side of his nose and sharply inhaled.

"Oh," I said, nodding. "Rehab."

"Fifth time's the charm," he said.

Members of the football team were trying to pump the keg. I opted for a can of Coke. I nearly bumped heads with Kathy Baker as she grabbed a Diet Coke from the ice chest and shook the can to remove the excess ice. She would regret that later when she popped the tab.

"How'd you get Astrid to come?" Unlike Max, I felt only pity toward Kathy.

"I, like, asked her," Kathy said under her breath. (As if talking to me would infect her with radiation poisoning.) "My dad was refilling a prescription for her. I, like, asked, and she came."

I can just imagine how that conversation went:

"The Woods, it's like where we party, and, like, we get drunk and hang. Making out is optional. [Insert laugh.] Please come and meet us there. You'll, like, have lots of fun. It's up the mountain and, like, go half a mile and turn right and you'll see a big oak with a sign nailed on it—WHAT YOU SEE HERE WHAT YOU DO HERE WHAT YOU HEAR HERE WHEN YOU LEAVE HERE

LET IT STAY HERE and, like, around the corner is a cave, and that's where we'll be. There'll be, like, beer and moonshine—tasty, trust me. See ya!"

Kathy said "like" a lot. To the point that it made you want to throw yourself off a cliff. That was her scariest quality. All at once, I spotted Dana behind her. *(Speak of the . . . Devil. No. Speak of the Divine? The Ditzy? Whatever.)* At Kathy's heel—like a dog. If you're keeping track at home, Dana hadn't said one word to me all day, which was fine, but I was kind of worried about what she would do. Like with a bomb of the nuclear variety being dropped, I was waiting for the fallout.

"What are you doing?" Dana whispered.

I thought, *To me?*

"Be nice," Kathy whispered back, and smiled.

I didn't understand why they whispered. I could hear them just fine. They were drunk.

"I still can't get over the fact that you get to go to the set and hang out with her for real," Kathy said.

"It's really not that big a deal. You can hang out with her too. She's in the cave."

"Oh, Lauren, she's a celebrity," Kathy grumbled.

I rolled my eyes. "It's Laura."

"Lauren, I have to ask . . . I mean, I know why you didn't choose me." She was now speaking too loudly, slurring her words a little. Her face was sweaty. "I mean, I, like, have major talent that would, like, outshine you tremendously. But have to ask, why didn't you choose your best friend here?" She reached back and grabbed Dana's hand.

"She's not my best friend," I said, my eyes on Dana.

"The feeling is mutual," Dana said, then hiccuped.

"Okay," Kathy said, shrugging. "What about Max? You two are attached at the hip?"

"Not his scene."

"But you invited your stepbrother. Why? Come on, Lauren."

"It's Laura."

"Terrence hates you," Dana said. "You're his stepsister, not his friend."

I walked away. I wasn't going to cry. I felt like crying. But I wasn't going to give her the satisfaction. Ugh. I hated Kathy Baker and Dana Cobb. Best to lose myself in the party. I roamed, looking for Max, but nobody could help me. It was hard for them to put two words together, let alone a sentence. I felt a hand clamp on my shoulder and whirled around.

It was Terrence. He wasn't alone.

"Laura, Laura, this is Freddy," Terrence said, and there was Freddy White. *The* Freddy White. AHHHHHH!!! He's so dreamy. He smiled all the way from his mouth to his eyes, which sparkled when he talked. He was a pretty boy just like all the other actors but he seemed genuinely nice and down to earth. I wanted to be his friend. I loved him in *Prime Crime*. He played the sidekick to Johnny Lee Grafton's character. Freddy White always played the sidekick. In *Eve of Destruction*, he'd be playing the sidekick too, no doubt. He'd probably be among the first to go.

"It's so nice to meet you. Big fan. Like, big fan," I said. My God, I sounded like an idiot. I shook his hand. Terrible idea, as mine was clammy.

"Nice to meet you too," he said. He looked puzzled. I couldn't blame him. My behavior wasn't that of a normal human being.

"She's my stepsister," Terrence said.

"Really?" he asked, eyeing me and then Terrence.

"It's true," I said.

"How's that working out?" he asked with just a brief hint of a smile.

"About as well as the plot of your movie," Terrence muttered. "Heading toward disaster but never quite getting there."

I laughed in spite of myself. Freddy smirked. "Oh, we'll get there in the movie," he said. "Haven't you heard? It's this year's *WarGames*—minus the creepy computer named Joshua. But even better! See, the bomb actually goes off in *Eve of Destruction*. Oops. I probably wasn't supposed to give away the ending." He sighed. "You know Hollywood—pick a subject and make the same movie over and over until they run out of ideas."

Now Terrence was looking at him with the same *I have a crush* fawn eyes. "Aren't you worried about getting fired for talking like that?" he asked.

"But this one is actually based on a book," I protested. "It's not . . ." My voice trailed off. Would Freddy White think I was a dork now? Had I just ruined this moment?

"That's why I took the part," Freddy said. He smiled at me. "I love that book. It's one of my favorites."

I smiled back, forgetting Terrence was even on the same planet. "Mine too," I said.

"Scaring humans on a regular basis is a healthy thing to do," Freddy added. "Especially in Hollywood."

I got the feeling he didn't like being an actor at all. Then again, if I had to deal with people like Astrid Ogilvie all day, I couldn't blame him.

"Why do you say that?" I asked.

He lifted his shoulders and raised his eyebrows. The gesture read loud and clear: *Who the hell knows?* "Scared people are more honest," he said. "Fear cuts to the chase. It saves time."

I nodded. "Just like Boudreaux Beauchamp wrote in *Eve*: 'Short time to live . . .'"

"'Long time to die,'" he quoted with me in unison.

My crush was growing by the minute.

In keeping with the End of Days, however, somebody chose that moment to put *1999*[1] on Max's boom box. Whoever it was cranked the volume to ten. People were drunk, so they started dancing. Funny how Max's parties felt like the same movie over and over. Except that now we had real live movie stars. I wanted to dance with Freddy.

---

1 Prince, *1999*, Warner Bros, 1982.

The feeling wasn't mutual. He took the opportunity to wave goodbye to Terrence and me. I couldn't ask him to stay. I was Laura Nobody from Griffin Flat, and he was *the* Freddy White. Also, conversation was no longer possible over distorted Prince and the excited shrieking of our town's brain-dead. I could only wave back as he turned and disappeared into the night.

After that, I relented and gave into Max's demand to dip into his private stash of moonshine. His family kept it in the basement. The music sounded muffled from down here. The air was still and dank. Max was all business, eyes roving over shelves of mason jars, squinting in the low light of a single bulb. Each one was dated.

"Circa 1962. Seems appropriate since we're on the edge of nuclear annihilation," I said.

"It's a movie. Not real life," he said.

"When did you get so smart?" I asked.

He plucked the 1963 jar from the shelf and unscrewed the cap. I caught a whiff of that horrible antiseptic smell, like a hospital. Fitting, as we could very easily end up there after drinking this stuff. "I've always been smart," he said, taking a sip and then wincing. "It burns—literally my esophagus."

I took the jar.

"How was Thanksgiving?" Max asked.

Bracing myself, I swallowed a gulp of the fiery clear liquid. It did burn. But then my belly felt warm. I shrugged. Ah, Turkey Day. Mom, Dennis, me, plus Granny and new Grandmother and Pops, made it quite the *Guess Who's Coming to Dinner*[1] sequel. Highlights included: a racial slur, a senile-old-woman

---

1 It's a 1967 major motion picture drama starring Katharine Houghton, Sidney Poitier, Katharine Hepburn, and Spencer Tracy. In the film, a daughter brings home her black fiancé to meet her parents, who are white.

reference, an abundance of profanity, a discussion over the FEMA pamphlet that was put on our doorstep (which turned into bickering over politics), running out of alcohol. "It could have been worse, I guess," I said.

"Really?"

I took another sip. It went down easier this tip. "Anything can be worse, Max.

"Forever Young"[1] woke me up the next morning. I hated that song. And true to my words last night, even a song like this one could get worse. It wasn't the original. It was Max's horrible a cappella rendition, right in my ear.

"Good morning, Laura."

My head throbbed. I couldn't open my eyes. "What's good about it?"

"Well, I stayed up all night trying to figure out what happened to the sun . . . and then it dawned on me." He imitated a cheesy comedy club cymbal crash, then burst out in fake laughter. "Thank you, ladies and germs. I'll be here all night."

I groaned and whacked him with a pillow. "How come you never get hungover?"

"It's my moonshine. Specially made for my exact body type and metabolism." He whacked me back. "Now, get up. We need to turn you into an actress."

---

1 Alphaville, *Forever Young*, WEA, 1984.

ECONOMY PICTURES

Congratulations, Contest Winner,

In association with DJ Crazy Bob's morning show on FM 95.6, we are pleased to welcome you and a guest to the set of *Eve of Destruction*. The prize is a walk-on role for you and your guest. Your part will take place on the mountain overlooking a smoldering pile of debris, where Pikesville once stood. Your character will die. It is imperative that you and your guest behave and act responsibly.

Enclosed are two copies of each form, a talent release form, and a liability release form. Please be advised that by signing these forms, Economy Pictures can use your likeness and name in marketing material for the film, and in the event of an accident, Economy Pictures is not liable for any injuries (bodily, mental, or emotional) and/ or death during the filming of *Eve of Destruction*. If you are under eighteen years of age, a parent or guardian must also sign. On the date of your arrival, you will be asked to turn in these forms to a production assistant.

Please be on time. And remember to have fun on the set of *Eve of Destruction*.

Sincerely,
Paul Greer
Senior Vice President of Production

Talent authorizes, as part of Production and for the compensation stated above, Producer to:

1. Photograph Talent and record his/her voice and likeness for the purpose of Production, whether by film, videotape, magnetic tape, or otherwise;

2. Make copies of the photographs and recordings so made;

3. Use Talent's name and likeness for the purposes of education, promotion, or advertising of the sale or trading in the photographs, recordings, and any copies so made.

Talent understands the master tape remains the property of the Producer and, unless otherwise stated, that there will be no restrictions on the number of times that Talent's name and likeness may be used. Also, unless otherwise stated, there will be no restrictions on the geographical distribution of Production.

Talent understands the terms described in this contract. He/she is over 18 years of age and has the authority to sign this contract and grant Producer the rights given under this contract.

If Talent is a minor under the laws of the state where his/her appearance is recorded, his/her guardian has the authority to sign this contract and grant Producer the rights given under this contract:

_____   _____

Parent/Legal Guardian Signature   Date

_____   _____

Talent Signature   Date

ACCIDENT WAIVER AND
RELEASE OF LIABILITY FORM

I HEREBY ASSUME ALL OF THE RISKS OF PAR-
TICIPATING IN ANY/ALL ACTIVITIES ASSOCIATED
WITH THIS FILM, including by way of example and not
limited to, any risks that may arise from negligence or
carelessness on the part of the persons or entities being
released, from dangerous or defective equipment or property owned, maintained, or controlled by them, or because
of their possible liability without fault.

I certify that I am physically fit, have sufficiently prepared or trained for participation in this activity, and have
not been advised to not participate by a qualified medical
professional. I certify that there are no health-related reasons or problems which preclude my participation in this
activity.

I acknowledge that this Accident Waiver and Release
of Liability Form will be used by the event holders,
sponsors, and organizers of the activity in which I may
participate, and that it will govern my actions and respon-
sibilities at said activity.

In consideration of my application and permitting
me to participate in this activity, I hereby take action for
myself, my executors, administrators, heirs, next of kin,
successors, and assigns as follows:

(A) I WAIVE, RELEASE, AND DISCHARGE from any
and all liability, including but not limited to liability
arising from the negligence or fault of the entities or persons released, for my death, disability, personal injury,
property damage, property theft, or actions of any kind
which may hereafter occur to me including my traveling
to and from this activity, THE FOLLOWING ENTITIES

OR PERSONS: Economy Pictures, BC-AD Productions, Albert Burg Films and/or their directors, officers, employees, volunteers, representatives, and agents, and the activity holders, sponsors, and volunteers;

(B) INDEMNIFY, HOLD HARMLESS, AND PROMISE NOT TO SUE the entities or persons mentioned in this paragraph from any and all liabilities or claims made as a result of participation in this activity, whether caused by the negligence of release or otherwise.

I acknowledge that Economy Pictures, BC-AD Productions, Albert Burg Films, and their directors, officers, volunteers, representatives, and agents are NOT responsible for the errors, omissions, acts, or failures to act of any party or entity conducting a specific activity on their behalf.

I acknowledge that this activity may involve a test of a person's physical and mental limits and carries with it the potential for death, serious injury, and property loss. The risks include, but are not limited to, those caused by terrain, facilities, temperature, weather, condition of participants, equipment, vehicular traffic, lack of hydration, and actions of other people including, but not limited to, participants, volunteers, monitors, and/or producers of the activity. These risks are not only inherent to participants, but are also present for volunteers.

I hereby consent to receive medical treatment which may be deemed advisable in the event of injury, accident, and/or illness during this activity.

I understand while participating in this activity, I may be photographed. I agree to allow my photo, video, or film likeness to be used for any legitimate purpose by the activity holders, producers, sponsors, organizers, and assigns.

The Accident Waiver and Release of Liability Form shall be construed broadly to provide a release and waiver to the maximum extent permissible under applicable law.

I CERTIFY THAT I HAVE READ THIS DOCUMENT AND I FULLY UNDERSTAND ITS CONTENT. I AM AWARE THAT THIS IS A RELEASE OF LIABILITY AND A CONTRACT AND I SIGN IT OF MY OWN FREE WILL.

_____   _____
Participant's Signature   Date

_____   _____
Participant's Name   Age

_____   _____
Parent/Guardian Signature   Date
(If under 18 years old, Parent or Guardian must also sign.)

Chapter Twelve

Dad forgot to call on Thanksgiving, even though he'd said he would. I didn't hear from him until late Saturday night. The phone woke up Dennis, who ran to the kitchen. I knew this because I heard him curse when he stubbed his toe on the sofa table, the one Mom bought on sale on Black Friday.[1]

"Oh, thank God. Danny, I thought something had happened to Terrence," he said.

I hesitated upstairs, standing outside my bedroom, listening.

"I'll get her," Dennis said, He jumped, seeing me hurrying down the stairs. "It's your dad." As we passed each other, he put his index finger over his mouth and went back to bed.

Thank goodness it wasn't Mom who answered the phone. The yelling would have woken up the entire neighborhood.

Dennis told me right after the wedding ceremony, during the reception in fact, that stepdads were better than real dads

---

1 Since 1952, it is regarded as the beginning of the Christmas shopping season. It helps stores get back in the black after being in the red all year.

because they stepped up when real dads stepped down. I smiled and didn't believe him. But lately—

"Ladybug," Dad said. *The worst nickname ever.* "I'm sorry"—the two words he always started off with in a conversation with me—"I know I was supposed to call"—*but*—"but things have been"—*chaotic . . . insane . . . busy . . . choose your own word in place*—"it's been—"

Dad was slipping in his excuses. I could have sworn I heard someone yell his name. Maybe his train of thought was off, or maybe the explanations were running thin, but it was like his mind was elsewhere.

"Dad, is everything okay?" I asked.

"Of course, Ladybug," he said, though his voice was shaky.

"You can tell me anything."

"Ladybug, you're better off not knowing some things."

"Sergeant!" I could hear the man clearly that time.

Dad sighed. "Ladybug, I'm sorry but I've got to go—"

"Dad, you seem worried."

"I am."

The dial tone clicked, and I stood there in the kitchen, staring at my mom, who was staring at me with her arms crossed and her foot tapping.

"Your dad," she said, but it was more of a statement than a question.

"Yes."

"I should have known. He has no concept of time."

Chapter Thirteen

The lingering smell of the rotting pumpkins set the mood—at least for me. The Harvest Party/Welcome Party had waited until after Thanksgiving to address the task of Halloween cleanup. Typical. Every other local was gushing over the invited guests. The ones who'd shown, anyway. Director Norman Edman looked intimidating, though his wire-rim glasses were smudged and his scraggly beard—I think you'd call that a beard—matched his hair, which looked like he hadn't combed it in a week and was incredibly shaggy and wouldn't fit in his baseball cap with the word *Eve* embroidered on. Granny would have made him get a haircut. His voice was groggy like he had been nonstop yelling. I was still intimidated by his presence. He had just sent the screenwriter—Eddie Payne, a "wildly charismatic genius"— back to the typewriter for a "rewrite" to fix the "issues" that he deemed "issues."

Meaning: the girl who'd won the radio contest had picked a black kid as her plus-one.

That's what I guessed, anyway. I was eavesdropping on Mr.

Edman's hushed conversation with a man in a suit, a man whose suit was pricey, a man who seemed more important than anyone else present. If I'd learned anything by living in Griffin Flat, it was the art of gossiping. You took snippets of what you overheard and spun them into outrageous truth.

In my defense, Mom said that if I happened to come across any Hollywood type, she wanted me to introduce myself. Apparently so they'd remember me. Or maybe just to be polite? Sadly for her, I was too chicken to get too close. On the plus side, they weren't talking about Terrence anymore—or the problem of actually having (God forbid) two black teenagers in the same movie who *weren't* criminals.

"I know a guy who knows a guy who knows a guy with clearance that can get us through the gate," Mr. Edman was whispering. "I mean, I know you have to worry about liability. You're the exec producer. But it's safe. As long as we don't touch anything, we'll be fine. Trust me."

The man nodded. "Fine. We'll amend the contract so that *you're* liable."

"No . . . I mean, *yes*, but the point is—" Mr. Edman broke off and glared at me. "Are you lost, young lady?"

I shook my head and darted away, searching for Max. Lucky for me, Mayor Hershott chose that moment to take the stage and address the crowd. He tapped the mic at the front of the stage, and the screech of feedback prompted everyone to turn.

"Welcome to Griffin Flat," Mayor Hershott proclaimed. He paused dramatically, telegraphing a joke. "It's an honor that our little town will be *off* the map real soon."

The crowd cheered.

The Griffin Flat High School Band was setting up behind him. In their red-and-gold uniforms and their instruments polished to shine, they played the school song, which really was "The Victors"—the University of Michigan fight song, with different lyrics, of course.

The crowd cheered, and the band jumped around as if the

football team had scored the winning touchdown in state (which would never happen). Astrid Ogilvie walked past. I tried to say hi but I chickened out. She'd been kind of rude the other night, and I didn't really want to feel small again.

"Hey. Laura, right?" Freddy said, poking me on the arm.

"Yeah, it's Laura, hey," I said, trying not to get overexcited.

I smiled. He smiled. Then he asked where Terrence was, and I pointed him out in the crowd. He was with Rodney next to the dessert table.

"And our stars—Astrid Ogilvie, Freddy White, and Owen Douglas," Mayor Hershott said as the crowd erupted in cheers and the band blew its horns and pounded its drums.

The stars waved to the crowd.

It was surreal. We hadn't had movie stars in our small town. This was new, and though it was exciting it was kind of nerve-racking. We were afraid to do the wrong thing, say the wrong thing; we were on edge. No one wanted the people from California to think we were dumb southern rednecks.

"Thanks for the hospitality," Owen said.

"Yes, thank *y'all* so much," Astrid said, taking the microphone from Owen. "It's an honor to be here, *y'all*." The fake southern accent that she was using was downright demeaning. The way she said *y'all* made my skin crawl.

"I love you, Astrid," said a boy in the crowd. I knew that boy—Max.

"I love you too," she said, blowing a kiss.

I was going to have to schedule a doctor's appointment because I sprained my eyeballs from rolling them too hard.

Max pointed at me and laughed. He was bent over, grabbing his stomach, and people were staring, but he thought he pulled a fast one. His comedy was questionable.

Freddy said that he was happy to be here and thanked everyone for being so welcoming to a boy from California. Freddy was the only one who mingled with the crowd, unlike Owen, who stayed off to the side of the stage, and Astrid, who spoke in a condescending manner. But most of the townspeople were oblivious; they saw how pretty she was and how big her boobs were. Peony Roth wasn't here. And according to the gossip on the street, she liked the stuff that started with a lowercase C. People were fed up with her shenanigans. People at Economy Pictures were fed up with her shenanigans. Her contract was null and void. She was sent off to do some "charity work," according to the press. In reality, she was at her fifth stint at the Betty. Who was going to take over the part of Helen Allen?

Bruce Coleman, producing partner with Anthony Dillard (BC-AD Productions), came to the microphone and hit it a couple of times before speaking. "Thank you," he said slowly. "Thank you for having this party to welcome us to Griffin Flat, or should I say, Pikesville?" He laughed at his own joke, which wasn't even funny. "Ha. Well, I am glad that your town won. It is a nice town. I've met so many friendly people. I hope that we make you proud. We're going to make history here. Just you wait. Just you wait."

Mayor Hershott was handed the microphone, and we got back to the night's festivities. I wanted dinner.

by ADA BRYANT
Entertainment Editor

Little Rock—Laura Ratliff, of Griffin Flat, Arkansas, has won a walk-on role in *Eve of Destruction*, directed by Norman Edman. The film is based on the novella by Boudreaux Beauchamp. It is the story of a small town on the brink of annihilation. Beauchamp took inspiration from the nationwide Civil Defense drill that took place on June 14, 1954, at exactly 10 A.M.

DJ Crazy Bob on Station 95.6 held the contest in association with Economy Pictures and BC-AD Productions.

"The idea of giving a local a chance of celebrity was enticing to everyone involved with the project," said George Louis Gould, head of Economy Pictures. "We are excited to welcome Laura Ratliff into the Economy family."

On Thursday, November 15, Laura Ratliff was caller number nine and answered three questions correctly to win the grand prize.

"That little girl is crazy smart—like crazy smart. Hell, the only reason I knew those answers is because they were written down for me before the show," DJ Crazy Bob said about Ratliff.

Ms. Ratliff, a junior at Griffin Flat High School, is a regular student who studies hard and is involved in extracurricular activities, such as science club, and is creating her own comic book with a friend, but on Monday morning she'll transform into a nuke victim.

"I'm a huge fan of the book. I can't believe that I get to be in the movie," Ratliff said, adding, "I don't want to screw up."

Per contest guidelines, Ratliff gets to bring one guest, and she chose her stepbrother, Terrence Jennings, to be that person.

"I was shocked that she picked me. Don't get me wrong, I'm glad," Jennings said, excited to lend his acting skills to his role. "I've done one school production, and that was *Romeo and Juliet*. I played Friar Laurence."

Even though this is not the first time memorizing lines for Jennings, it will be for Ratliff.

"I've never tried out for the school play. In fact, Mrs. Frazier once told me that my acting is scary, and that I kill the spirit of the stage. So, yeah, I probably shouldn't have said that out loud," said Ratliff, on her lack of acting lessons.

"No worries," said Edman. "We have a rough treatment of the script. We all saw *WarGames* last year, which was a master class on poor acting. Maybe I shouldn't have said that out loud. Oh well, we all witnessed it, didn't we?"

Edman is known to be a director that is very hands-on, to put it bluntly with his actors. It was no surprise that all of Hollywood wants to work with him.

"I'm nervous," Ratliff said. "But who wouldn't be?"

For a project that some thought would not see the light of day, they are now days away from shooting in small town Griffin Flat, Arkansas, population a little over 8,000. Located in the hills of the Ozark Mountains, Griffin Flat is in proximity to two ticking time bombs; there is the Titan II Missile complex and Nuclear One, a power plant in nearby Russellville. Surrounded by possible annihilation, this is the perfect backdrop of a movie that shows humanity at the brink of destruction, though the movie, like the book, promises redemption in the face of morality.

Griffin Flat, which is the location for the fictional Pikesville, a setting in literature that one has compared to William Faulkner's Yoknapatawpha County. Though to be fair, Beauchamp's writing has a tinge of the Faulkneresque, with his eccentric characters and lively, somewhat off-putting dialogue. He is a true southern writer in the sense of where he was born but not where he grew up.

"I don't know if it's every writer's dream to see their work on the silver screen, but it certainly will be an experience. And life is full of experiences. I am invited to the set and I plan to witness as much as I can," Beauchamp said. "I truly hope that they bring my novella to life."

But for Laura Ratliff, being on the screen means as much to her as it does her friends and family. We reached for comment from those closest to her, and these were the responses:

Mom Edna Jennings said, "I'm so proud of my little girl."

"It's been a tough year, and I'm glad that she has this in her life right now. She needs to have something good happen to her. I've been praying that the Lord moves in her life and this is just the ticket for her to minister," Virginia Park, Ratliff's grandmother, said.

Reggie Jennings, or Pops, Ratliff's stepgrandfather, said, "She's going to shine on that set. I'm glad that my new granddaughter is able to experience this with her stepbrother, Terrence."

"Laura Ratliff is going to make our town proud. As will I," said Griffin Flat Mayor Curtis Hershott, who also has a small walk-on role.

Sergeant Danny Ratliff, Laura's father, was asked to comment for this article, but he was unavailable. However, the United States Air Force sends its congratulations to Laura and looks forward to seeing the finished product in a theater.

Filming in Griffin Flat is expected to last two weeks.

Chapter Fourteen

I thought something had happened when Mom called in a panic. Like Granny had died or worse. "Get down here now," Mom said. That's all she said. No explanation. No why. Just "get down here."

So I did.

I rode my bike, sat it up against the brick building, and walked inside. Mom was dealing with a guest who was adamant about something, so I didn't get why I had to come down here right then. When Mom had a moment free, she told me—scratch that—she asked me, "Guess who's staying here?" I hated guessing. But I played along. The governor? An actor? The president? *No* was the answer to all of those.

"Who, then?" I asked.

"The author."

Now, you're probably thinking, *Why get so excited about the author?*

That guy, Boudreaux Beauchamp, was sort of, could be

described as, a recluse. Howard Hughesing[1] it. But he was here, staying in our little town, in Mom's hotel.

"He wants to meet you," a tiny man carrying a clipboard and a red pen said behind me. "I'm Mr. Beauchamp's assistant."

"Get out of town," I said.

"I wish."

"Wait—why does he want to meet me?" I asked.

"Your mother has been pestering Mr. Beauchamp all day."

How embarrassing.

"He'd like to do so now," the assistant said.

I looked bad. I had ridden the hayride a couple of times with Max and fallen off once getting off. (It took real skill to fall going upstairs, and trip over completely nothing—I had that skill.) I smelled. I'd gone home and was just about to hop in the shower when Mom called and told me to get my butt down here. So I did. Smelly. Hair a rat's nest. And dirt under my fingernails. I was pretty.

Boudreaux Beauchamp sat in the corner, away from the commotion. The crew had just arrived back from setting up the lighting on the downtown square. Tomorrow was going to be a night shoot. Who knew what they were filming. You know how Hollywood liked to rewrite literature.

"Mr. Beauchamp," the assistant said, then yelled since Mr. Beauchamp was an eighty-year-old man who was hard of hearing.

"I heard you the first time," he said (so apparently, he wasn't hard of hearing), closing his notebook and laying his fancy fountain pen beside it.

"Sit," the assistant whispered, and I did. Afraid of him and Mr. Beauchamp.

---

1 Howard Hughes was an eccentric man, a recluse who wanted to be alone. He locked himself in a room for four months eating nothing but chocolate bars, drinking milk, and peeing in empty bottles. Oh, and he was obsessed with green peas.

Mr. Beauchamp sat in front of me, his legs crossed, one hand on his knee, the other laid flat on the tabletop. Every so often, he lifted his hand and clicked the tabletop with his long fingernails as if he were playing the piano, and I watched as he tapped his index finger three times before he picked up his complimentary cup of coffee—black—and took a long sip.

"I'm trying to read you, Laura Ratliff," he said, watching me.

I pulled my sleeves down over my wrists. "What do I say?" I asked.

"You're hard to read."

"Do you think that's a good thing?"

"What do you think?" he asked.

Honestly, I didn't like how he answered my question with a question.

"I don't know," I said slowly.

He picked up his pen and tapped it on his notebook. "So, Laura, what's your story?"

"Are you writing a new book?" I asked, smiling.

"Maybe."

Beauchamp hadn't published a new book in years. He was becoming like J. D. Salinger[1] or Harper Lee.[2] Withdrawn from public life—a recluse—cutting off all contact with people. Until one day he appeared in the pages of *Vanity Fair*.[3] He was sitting under a lamp. A shadow from his hat sort of made a mushroom-like cloud shadow on the wall. He was the nukeman, or so many had dubbed him. He was the author that killed millions and left millions wanting more. He left the end of *Eve of Destruction* pretty vague. It was one of those endings that you throw the book across the room and curse the author

---

1 American author who is famous for writing *The Catcher in the Rye*, published in 1951.

2 American author who is famous for writing *To Kill a Mockingbird*, published in 1960.

3 A magazine that was resurrected in February 1983.

for leaving such an unsatisfying conclusion. In the *Vanity Fair* article, Beauchamp admitted to the world he had been writing, and Hollywood would be filming, one of the most beloved novellas. Finally.

It is time in this nuclear climate to finish this story for a new generation to become disillusioned with the world.[1]

I scooted closer to the table and asked, "Are we finally going to find out what happened to—"

He raised his hand for me to stop.

"I'm not going to answer your questions about what I'm writing," he said.

I guess I pouted because he grabbed my hand and squeezed.

"There, there," he said, patronizing me. "But I will tell you the title, and you can form your own conclusions. *Forecast for Extinction*," he said, leaning back on his chair. "Pretty good, don't you think?"

There were so many ways the story could go, but he wouldn't tell me. In fact, he went back to taking notes.

"Brunette, sixteen, pretty blue eyes—pretty green eyes," he said, peering over his reading glasses and staring at me. "You'd be a perfect character."

"A mutant, you mean, because the bomb went off and everyone died when the bomb went off. Remember? You wrote it," I said.

"I do. I remember every godawful word."

"Don't say that. It's one of my favorites."

"I'm sorry."

"Why did you stay out of the public eye for so long?"

"Nothing else to say."

"Nothing else to say? Says the guy who's writing a sequel to *Eve of Destruction*."

He smiled, taking another drink of his complimentary coffee,

---

1 Excerpt from Hamilton Stewart's article, "Boudreaux Beauchamp, Obscure Author," *Vanity Fair*, January 1984.

and snapped his fingers for his assistant to come. "You know, Laura, your mom mentioned that you want to be a writer."

"She did?" That was news to me.

He nodded.

"Well, to be honest, I like to write comics as a hobby. My friend Max and I are creating one."

"Is it about nuclear war? Because there's a market," he says, smirking.

"It's about superheroes."

"You have your niche. Do you want my advice?"

"Sure," I said, leaning forward.

"Don't—chuck it."

That was helpful.

"Honestly, what's the point?" He snapped his fingers again for his assistant, who dug in his pocket for a flask and poured.

"If you want some good stuff, I can hook you up," I said, leaning back on my chair.

"You're a child," he said.

I took offense to the word *child*.

"Okay, I'll take the good stuff. And I assume in return you want details," he said.

"I was just being nice, but—"

"Everybody wants something from someone," he said. "I'll answer your question."

"I would like to know what happens after—"

"After?" he asked.

"After."

"I don't know, but don't worry," he said.

"Don't worry about what?" I asked.

"Don't worry, we won't survive," he said.

"*We?*" I asked.

"I mean *they*. I mean *they*. Hell, I mean *we* too. It's only a matter of time before we do this. It is in our nature to destroy ourselves."

"What are you even talking about?" I asked.

"Unfortunately, humanity will one day enter a nuclear war. I *hope* humanity survives."

He was on a tirade now.

"But there's no way the human race will survive. Too many believe in the magic man in the sky while having power over nuclear weapons. We're *Homo sapiens*—the only species smart enough to create its own extinction and the only species stupid enough to do it. One big bang and we all fall down. We're going to have a ringside seat to Armageddon. Victory to the country that recovers first after a nuclear war."

I felt sick to my stomach.

"Oh—about the book," he said, smiling. "It seems fitting to begin with 'The End.'"

I grabbed his cup of complimentary "coffee" and chugged.

Chapter Fifteen

I came running down the hall and nearly tripped over Max at my locker. He was sitting on the floor with books strewn all around him in front of lockers that had been spray-painted white.

"Who did this?" I asked, standing in front of him.

"Seniors, I think," he said.

The FEMA pamphlet did say all interior walls should be painted antiflash white, and the walls in this hall are basically lockers. So I guessed they were doing us a favor. You know, saving lives and all.

"They're in the principal's office," he added.

"Getting a lecture or an award for a job well done?"

"Your guess is as good as mine."

I touched one of the lockers with my pinkie to make sure it was dry before sitting down on the floor beside him. I didn't want a bunch of wet white paint on my purple shirt.

"So why are you not in homeroom?" I asked.

"I could ask you the same thing," he said.

"I overslept."

"Likely story," he said, picking at his braces.

Max's nerd transformation was now complete. Full-on metal mouth.

"Don't even ask." Max spoke while drooling. "I've got the headgear too."

"Oh, my gosh, I'm so sorry," I said, thankful that my parents weren't too concerned about the well-being of my teeth. Max, on the other hand, had parentitis. "Do they hurt?" I asked.

He nodded and tossed one notebook aside and then started on another.

"Homework?" I asked.

"Yup," he said, flipping the pages of his western civ book.

He always waited until the last minute to do his homework. He was, like, crazy smart but kind of had a hard time focusing.

"I miss the days when homework was just coloring," he said, scratching out a sentence.

"Me too."

"And I wish that Mr. Meyer didn't require us to write out the questions too. I mean, come on. I hate that man."

"I had him last year. I got Mom to make sure that I didn't have him this year."

"I should have done that. We have new partners in science today," he said.

"For you," I said with a laugh.

"I've been thinking about pulling the shower string," he said, nodding.

"Do it. It's liberating."

"Mr. Truitt would smell a conspiracy. Two of his smartest students breaking the rules."

"Oh, I love a good conspiracy," I said.

"Me too," he said, leaning in close. I could smell his foul Cheetos breath. "Did you know there have been twenty-six nuclear tests this year?"

"Is that a lot?" I asked.

"There've been two this month alone. France and the USSR

did tests. This year the USSR have done sixteen; we, the United State, have done six, France has done three; and Great Britain has done one. At least, that's all that I could find. We've probably done more than six. But sixteen for the USSR, shit—this is scary as hell. If it does happen, I would want to be vaporized right away. Fuck getting cooked and being in agonizing pain."

"How do you know this?" I asked.

"Classified."

I side-eyed him. And then he spilled. "Hacking," he said.

WarGames certainly did a number on him.

"I think all these sirens are getting us ready for the big one," he said.

"I hope not," I said.

"Come on. The big bang to end all big bangs. Isn't your dad preparing for World War Three?"

He had me there. And he had me somewhere else: my dad lived in a world of classified information. Just like *1984*. What a book to have an anniversary. I hoped I was as smart as George Orwell when I grew up. It would be nice to know the nightmares that occurred to me now would manifest themselves thirty-six years later.

They probably would. The whole state of Arkansas was almost a cover-up. Four years ago, it was almost erased from existence after a nuclear missile silo accident. *It* meaning Arkansas. Thankfully, nothing happened, and we Arkansans were saved, meant to live another day to tell the ordeal, which hardly anyone would believe. Arkansas almost nuked themselves. Max would like to say how could we tell the difference? Ha. Ha. Very funny. But seriously. American flags would have to be replaced; instead of fifty stars, there would only be a need for forty-nine.

We, as make-believe historians, like to rewrite history.

Maybe we are Oceania and Mr. Meyer is Big Brother himself.

We were averaging three sirens a week, which wasn't normal at all. Since the start of the school year (school started two months ago), we'd had thirty-four of what our parents would call duck-and-cover drills. It was easy to say that the administration was overreacting, but was it? The editor of the *Shiner News* assigned me an article for the school paper on why there were so many sirens in early October. I dug and dug. I had some findings but nothing concrete. No one gave their name. I even went to my dad and asked, but he couldn't tell me anything, and most definitely wouldn't go on record, and wouldn't be anonymous either. No one would be my Deep Throat.[1] When I turned my story in to the editor, who turned it into our advisor (we don't have a free press at GFHS), it was redacted so much that the only thing left was my name, and that was misspelled. The editor still hadn't fixed my byline, even though I told her half a dozen times that my name is *Laura*, not *Lauren*.

"I'm telling you, Laura, the BOOM is coming," Max said, using his hands to show an explosion.

People were wrong; just because you have lemons does not mean you have to make lemonade—the same argument goes for a nuclear bomb.

"I'm afraid we won't live past tomorrow," I said.

We were in agreement.

He'd been hard hit in his family too. The sickness of a questionable tomorrow. You know—my granny believed in the Rapture. Like Jesus descending from heaven to take all the believers back with him. Saving them from all the trials, tribulation, and damnation. Don't get the mark. And pray like it's your last prayer ever. She lives for today by making sure she has a tomorrow in heaven. She does that by, of course, sending hundreds of dollars, money she doesn't have, to Reverend Lowry. But Max's family's version of a questionable tomorrow was different. His mom was racking up the credit card debt. Max told me they were in dire financial troubles, but it wouldn't matter.

---

1 The name of the secret informant who gave information to *Washington Post* reporters Bob Woodward and Carl Bernstein that led to Watergate and the eventual resignation of President Richard Nixon.

There was not going to be a tomorrow. A nuke was going to take care of that.

"Well, I've got western civ, English, lunch, and then chemistry. On the upside, I'm one chemical spill away from superpowers," he said, grabbing his lab sheet to finish before the bell rang. "What do we call the science of classifying living things?" he asked.

"Racism?"

"Good one. I'm going to write that down. Maybe Mr. Truitt has a sense of humor today."

"Do you ever wonder if we're living in a world where the tinfoil hats are right?" I asked.

"Every single day of my life."

NOTICE

Instruction to Patrons on Premises in
Case of Nuclear Bomb Attack . . .

WARNING: THE END IS NEAR . . .

Windows are not safe zones, so stay clear.

Electronic devices will not work, so no need to carry your Walkman around.

Air quality may be low, so refrain from taking as many large breaths as possible.

Radiation is everywhere, so find radiation-free zones like your local library or fire station.

Environments may change because of events, so summer may come early this year.

Food will be affected by radiation, so find alternatives to food.

Umbrellas, though unproven, may be used as fallout protection.

Clothing should be removed because of radiation absorption. No need to feel embarrassed if your skin is falling off.

Kitchen appliances lined with lead may be effective in shielding from the blast. However, it is unproven and untested.

Energy should not be wasted on activities not pertinent to survival. Please refrain from coitus so to avoid mutated offspring.

Do not stand during the blast. Items of taller height are most effected by the explosion. Bending over and placing your head firmly between your legs is a good strategy due to stability and overall awareness.

Thank You. And Please Enjoy Your Stay At The Flat Inn.

Chapter Sixteen

I was reading *1984* comfortably on the couch when the phone rang. It was Mom.

"We'll get back to our normal life soon, but for now I need you both to step up," Mom said, as if we were new to this family. Also, she'd neglected to say "hello." But I got it. Both Mom and Dennis worked. I had done my own laundry for years now. When Terrence was at his mom's, I was usually at home alone or until Dennis got off work.

"Get dinner at the diner. Don't wait for us. It's going to be another late one."

I hung up the phone right when Terrence came in through the garage.

"We're supposed to get dinner at the diner," I said.

"Let me change and we'll go."

I turned on the TV and slumped in the wingback pink chair. The same chair Mom would make me sit in during time-outs. I grabbed the remote and turned on the TV. *Kids*

Incorporated[1] was on. The *TV Guide* said, *Episode 26 Civic Day Parade: Kids Inc. want to make a float for the Civic Day Parade, but everyone wanted to do a tribute to something different. Renee proves that they have to work together in order to make the float spectacular.* Cheesy. Stacy's my favorite. I was probably not the target audience for *Kids Incorporated*, but it was fun and I liked it. Just like how I liked MTV. Mom and Dennis didn't care if Terrence and I watched MTV. Max couldn't. He lived in a pretty strict home. So whenever I was over at his house and we had MTV on, we'd have to have one ear listening for his parents' vehicle pulling into the driveway. Once we were caught, and he was grounded for a month, and I was labeled as a "bad influence." I wasn't allowed over there for two months. Not until the affair was found out by the entire town and my parents' divorce came through did Max's mom relent and say I needed a positive influence in my life— whatever that meant.

Terrence was still in the shower. He took longer than I did. He used all the hot water, so when he was at his mom's house, it felt like a vacation. I didn't do sports. In the ninth grade, I went out for the girls' basketball team. I didn't make it. In fact, Coach Thomas told me it would be in my best interest to never try out for a sport ever again.

"Ready?" Terrence asked, rounding the corner from his room.

"Yeah, for almost an hour."

"Hey, it takes time to get this good-looking," he said, picking his hair.

The diner was busy for a Monday night. Most people were talking about the shooting of scenes that had gone on in town. How exciting it was. How crazy it was. How they couldn't wait for it to be over. How everything would be back to normal.

---

1 A TV program that premiered in 1983 and was set around a musical group.

Those were the ones sitting at the counter because their usual corner booth was taken.

"I can't wait for this movie nonsense to be done with," Brenda Leigh said. I thought she was just angry that they didn't ask her for her help with hair and makeup.

We didn't usually get tourists, so the displeasure of many was felt. Griffin Flat was small and it would remain small—no matter how many people wanted to see it grow.

"Mom," Terrence said, waiting for me to decide between the cheeseburger and fries or French dip and fries.

Ms. Wilcox was wearing her yellow blazer. She was a realtor. She was good at her job. Ironically, she helped Mom and Dad buy the house we had been living in before. The one Granny lived in now. She was nice. She never said anything mean about me—at least, not to my face. But she was still angry. Terrence said he couldn't talk about his dad ever at his mom's house. It made her mad. Not sad mad. Just mad. Mad that he put her through that. She was the woman scorned. The bitter woman. She owned it, though. I think she was just upset that it made her upset. And embarrassed. And I got that. Because I had been embarrassed when it'd happened. You think your parents are happy and in love, and then they turn out to not be. It kind of crushes your psyche.

"You two looking forward to tomorrow?" she asked us.

"Mmm-hmmm."

"It's really nice of you to take your . . . stepbrother with you. You're just one happy family, aren't you? The perfect little stepsister," she said.

"Mom," Terrence said.

She smiled at her son. "I suppose I should ask how your dad is?"

"He's good. Busy. With the FEMA pamphlet and all," he said.

"Yeah, I bet he is. I hear Jay Nelson is making a killing selling insurance to everyone, even the old. Scum of the earth, he is. Selling insurance for the apocalypse." She looked around the diner. "We can't really gossip in here; we're within the city limits."

I laughed. So did Terrence. She did not.

"How's your mom, Laura?" she asked.

"My mom?" I asked. She had never asked about her before.

"The woman that stole my husband," she clarified.

"Mom—" Terrence said.

"Hester Prynne," she said.

"Mom—"

"Good for him for finding an older woman that can keep up with him. I'm too young and too in shape for him anyway," she said.

"Mom—"

"So have you seen your dad lately, Laura?" she asked.

"No, I haven't," I said.

"That's a shame. It really is. Your mom and your dad didn't really think—"

"Mom—" Terrence said.

She sighed. "Your mom and my ex-husband are coming up on their one-year anniversary soon, aren't they?"

I nodded.

"I can't believe they made it almost a year. Breaking up a marriage and then expecting it to be real love. Cheating is cheating, and there is no happiness in that. There hasn't been a marriage that worked when it's based on adultery," she said.

"Johnny Cash and June Carter," I said.

She chuckled but then gave me the death glare.

"Well, wasn't your parents' wedding, wasn't that a spectacle?" she said.

The spectacle, or wedding, as most refer to it as. What the local newspaper called a beautiful affair, what the gossip nellies called a white homewrecker (from a respectable family) marrying a colored man (It's 1984, for goodness' sake! You'd think we'd be past this), was a crime against nature (and good Lord, but many spoke that in whispered tones). It was a spectacle, that's what it was. Everyone was there—well, not Granny— but everyone in town was. My mom wore white (Who was she fooling?), and I wore a pink dress since I was the maid of honor. Terrence was his dad's best man. We were the Brady Bunch (we were both Jan). Our integration into our new normal went as well as could be expected, though at times it felt like segregation, but my mom tried her best to make everything separate but equal.

"Have fun tomorrow, my children, and I do mean that," Terrence's mom said, squeezing both our hands.

We ordered the food, ate the food, and headed home.

Terrence apologized for his mom, but I said it didn't really matter. I understood why she was upset. I was too.

nu·cle·ar war (\ˈnü-klē-ər , ˈnyü- , nonstandard -kyə-lər) (\ˈwȯr \)
noun
    a war in which nuclear weapons are used.

nu·cle·ar fam·i·ly (\ˈnü-klē-ər , ˈnyü- , nonstandard -kyə-lər)
(\ˈfam-lē , ˈfa-mə- \)
noun
    a couple and their dependent children, regarded as a basic
social unit.

Chapter Seventeen

Terrence was still getting ready. He had changed his clothes at least twice. I won't say how many times I'd changed mine. But now I sat eating my scrambled eggs, crispy bacon, and whole wheat toast, though my stomach was aching from fear. It felt like the first day of school. New outfit? Check. Big breakfast? Check. Standing in front of the grandfather clock for a Polaroid? Check. (Terrence still had to take his.)

We both had excused absences today.

The phone rang. I assumed it was a Hollywood person. (I actually assumed it was a Hollywood person who'd decided, on second thought, that *Eve of Destruction* didn't need any Griffin Flat locals for their movie—the town was enough.) Dennis answered.

"Yes, I'll accept the charges . . ." He frowned, staring at my mom, then thrust the phone toward her. "Danny."

I stiffened. *Dad?* Why was he calling collect?

Mom wiped her mouth on her napkin and placed it on her chair. She took off her earring to position the transmitting and receiving ends correctly against her cheek and mouth, because apparently there was a proper way to speak on the telephone—as if God were watching. "Hello?" She sighed heavily. "No, this is a fine time . . . I can't hear you—speak up." She threw a hand up and turned to Dennis and shook her head. "There's too much static on the line. Call back!" She marched back to Dennis and slammed the phone down on the hook.

Dennis and I stared at her.

"I couldn't hear a thing he was saying," Mom said.

Terrence bounded down the stairs and into the kitchen. He took a look around. "What's going on?"

Dennis shrugged and turned up the TV. Robert De Niro was being interviewed on *The Today Show* by Jane Pauley and Bryant Gumbel. I tried to focus on the screen, but it went blank, exploding with a *BEEEEEEEEEEEEEEEEEEP.*

I winced at the sudden spike in volume.

Dennis leapt forward to turn it down.

BEEEEEEEEEEEEEEEEEEEEEEEEEEEEEEEEEEEEP

Words appeared on the screen, printed in the sort of grim font reserved for statewide standardized testing.

EMERGENCY BROADCAST SYSTEM.

"This is a test of the Emergency Broadcast System," a man's voice announced. I knew his voice; everyone did. But for the first time I noticed that he sounded strangely cheerful, as if he'd been brainwashed by a cult. "The broadcasters in your area, in voluntary cooperation with federal, state, and local authorities, have developed this system to keep you informed in the event of an emergency. If this had been an actual emergency, the attention signal you just heard would have been followed by official information, news, or instructions. This station serves the Central Arkansas area. This concludes the test of the Emergency Broadcast System."

BEEEEEEEEEEEEEEEEEEEEEEEEEEEEEEEEEEP. Robert De Niro reappeared. Everyone relaxed.

"Do you think the two are related?" I asked, using my fork to point to the TV and the phone in the kitchen.

"*What* two?" Mom asked irritably.

I shrugged, my eyes on Terrence. "The reason Dad called and the reason there was a warning about an 'actual emergency.' Seems to be happening a lot. Weird, right?"

Nobody answered. Probably all for the best. After all, as Max put it, I needed to become an actress.

Chapter Eighteen

Terrence drove us to the set at the fairgrounds. There were so many NO PARKING signs that we finally had to ask a police officer where to go. "This general area," he said, pointing in a circle. We parked and walked the long way to a double-wide that had been converted into a front office. We checked in, had to show ID, and turned in our signed forms.

"Congratulations," said the lady at the desk. "You will have a lot of fun."

I recognized her; she was a volunteer from the local law office my parents used in their divorce. I forgot her name. Apparently she didn't have to wear a name tag. Which made sense: she was in charge of the "confidentiality agreements." The people in charge of the movie really wanted to make sure that we didn't *talk* about the movie *outside* the movie. We had to agree to this in about six hundred different ways.

She handed us two stickers to put on our shirts.

A tiny redheaded man stood at the door, wearing a sweater-vest and skinny jeans. He carried a clipboard and looked at his watch a lot. "That's Tyson," said the lady at the desk. "He'll be your eyes and ears. He's a head production assistant."

He looked at us and nodded.

"Okay, you'll meet with the script supervisor and then costume. And then meet with the director." She was so excited about her part-time job.

"Laura and Terrence," Tyson said, looking at his clipboard and flipping over a to-do list. We said yes, and he crossed off our names. "Follow me."

We exited through the back door and down a flight of wooden steps to the county fairgrounds. What usually held fair equipment, rides, and games now held trailers and golf carts and mopeds. And lots of people with walkie-talkies and clipboards and carts being wheeled and boxes being moved. Clothes being carried and people walking around in robes and smoking cigarettes. We were no longer in Griffin Flat.

Terrence and I followed Tyson to a golf cart. He got in the driver's seat, and I sat beside him. Terrence sat in the back. Tyson took his sunglasses from his shirt and put them on. It was overcast, but I guess he wanted to look the part of a Hollywood player.

We, as in Terrence and I, held on for dear life as the gas pedal was firmly pushed to the floor and we took off down the dirt road. Past where the ring toss and guess-your-weight games would be, also where the guess-your-weight game operator was punched in the face after a woman was offended by his guess.

"So you're in high school?" Tyson asked, trying to make small talk.

"Yes, we're juniors," I said.

"And how do you know each other? Friends?"

Terrence tapped me on the shoulder. "We're brother and sister," he said, conveniently leaving out the "step."

Tyson looked at me and then turned to look Terrence. "Don't you see the family resemblance?" I asked, trying not to laugh.

The look on his face confirmed that he thought we were serious until he shook his head, gave a short laugh, and said, "Funny."

"We think so," Terrence said.

Tyson looked back at him and swerved. I screamed, and he course-corrected.

"Oops," Tyson said.

"Your last word on this earth was going to be 'oops,'" I said.

He smiled, pushing up his sunglasses with his middle finger. Then he took a deep breath and continued driving down the bumpy road, stopping in front of a trailer. "This is your stop," he said. He kicked his feet up over the steering wheel.

"Not going inside?" I asked.

He shook his head. "I'll wait out here."

We walked up the stairs and knocked on the door. It flew open. "Nuke me!" a man greeted us. He smiled widely. He was balding and pale, with a pencil-thin black mustache. He wore a purple-and-green scarf around his neck and a pincushion on his wrist. "Welcome. I'll be with you shortly."

His name was Raymond—pronounced "Ray-MOND"—Sinclair. He encouraged us to repeat his name back to him with "a tinge of hoity-toity." He said he had worked on *Dynasty*.[1] I loved that show. The shoulder pads were bigger than the egos. Alexis was my favorite.

Terrence and I sat on a couch near the huge window. I caught a glimpse of Astrid, who was getting sized for the "Civic Pride Scene." I tried not to make eye contact with her, but failed.

"*L* name, right?" she said, glancing up while picking at her cuticles.

"It's Laura," I said.

---

1 ABC soap opera set in Denver, Colorado. It premiered in 1981. It's produced by Aaron Spelling and stars John Forsythe as oil magnate Blake Carrington; Linda Evans as his secretary/wife, Krystle; and Joan Collins as Blake's ex-wife, Alexis.

"Got it—*L* name. Terrence, right?"

"*T* name," he said without smiling.

"He-e-ey," she said, suddenly sounding very creepy. "Funny man." She probably meant for it to be very sexy. But everyone with a British accent sounded sexy.

I tried not to think about Astrid, but to concentrate on my role. I could see my pale pink dress with capped sleeves hanging on a rack full of clothes. It was so pretty. I couldn't wait to try it on. Terrence's black pants, white button-down shirt, and black leather jacket were hanging right beside it.

Astrid stepped off the stool and walked toward me. "Amateurs are fun, but let's try not to mess up, 'kay?" she said, unzipping her dress to show her bare back.

Was she trying to be intimidating? Terrence stared, though. Astrid was pretty, I'd give her that, but she most definitely forgot to turn off the bitch switch before coming to our town.

"Laura, we're ready for you," said Raymond, placing the tape measure around his neck.

I got on the stool where Astrid once stood, and tried to hold still with my arms stretched out like I was getting ready to take off. They were going to have to take in the boob area on the dress. Apparently Peony Roth was much more blessed in that department than I was. I was taking Peony's part today, though technically not Peony's role. Still an extra, but I was going to be on camera.

Astrid laughed. I wanted to cry as each pin pierced my skin.

"Pain is beauty," Raymond said. "But try not to bleed on the dress."

I hobbled off the stool and waddled my way behind a partition and somehow got out of the dress without doing any harm to it.

I sat in the beauty parlor chair. It was Kitty's turn to turn me into a swan.

Kitty Van Pelt, the hair and makeup extraordinaire, wore her hair crimped with pink stripes. Actually, she wore a lot of pink. Tights, skirt, long-sleeve shirt, vest—all pink. Including her makeup. Pink was her signature color. (She was a character. But really sweet.) She spoke at a high pitch, and squealed and smiled as she did her job.

Astrid sat in the beauty parlor chair beside me, filing her nails with an emery board that she had pulled out of her *Nuke Me* tote bag. I saw that she had two books in there, *Eve of Destruction* and *1984*.

"Oh, I'm reading that for class at my school," I said. I pointed at the special-edition *1984* anniversary cover. "How do you like it?"

"Oh," she said, tracing my eye line to her tote bag. She shook her head. "My tutor gave me the CliffsNotes. I haven't read it yet."

I continued to stare at her as she went back to focusing on her hangnail. I wondered if she'd even read *Eve*. Probably not.

Astrid sighed and pushed herself up from her chair. "I'll be back. You Americans bore me," she said, leaving the trailer with the door slamming shut behind her.

"Brilliant," Kitty said, mocking Astrid's posh accent. "Now, Laura, we're going for a natural look. You did win the pageant, after all."

"What pageant?" Terrence asked.

"What pageant?" Kitty asked, dropping her eyelash curler and placing her hands on her hips.

"I honestly can't believe you asked that," Raymond chimed in.

"I don't know. That's why I asked," Terrence said.

"Have you read the book?" she asked.

Terrence shook his head.

"Read the book." She picked up the eyelash curler and went for my right eye.

"We're going to go for a special-occasion look. Something strong to hold up the mushroom-shaped crown," Kitty said.

"The what now?" Terrence asked.

"Read the book." Kitty brushed my hair and smiled at herself in the mirror. "Well, our little Miss Laura was crowned Ms. Atomic Bomb."

"Miss What?" Terrence asked.

Raymond rolled his eyes, marched over to Astrid's tote, and picked out the paperback copy of *Eve of Destruction*. "Read the book!" he cried, literally throwing it at Terrence's head.

I tried not to laugh. Terrence gave me a look that said, "Everyone involved in this movie is totally insane."

"Now, what are we going to do for the radiation scars?" Kitty said, talking to herself as she mixed a couple of eye shadows together.

Poor Terrence. He wouldn't have felt so lost if he'd only read the book.

Chapter Nineteen

Now, to be completely honest, I didn't have high hopes for this film. Yes, the fairgrounds felt extra creepy. But this was the director of *Kinship*. Ergo: he'd cast an Asian actress, Kai Yu, in the starring role, and she'd died while filming, so instead of suspending the project, he hired a *white* actress to take her place, Maxie Frey. Maxie the actress always reminded me of Maxie the Pads, which in turn reminded me of horrendous, debilitating cramps. Maybe that's why I hated her.

Mr. Edman stood in the middle of the barren set—talking animatedly to a man in a backward baseball cap, who was smoking a cigarette and looked like he hadn't showered in days. Both had wires and Walkman headphones dangling from their necks.

I strained my ears to listen.

"I heard what Bruce and Anthony did," Director Edman whispered loudly. "A bunch of cheapskates."

Tyson cleared his throat. That got their attention.

"This is Laura," he announced. "And this is Terrence," he added, trying to defuse the tension. "She won the radio contest, and he's her guest, *as guaranteed by the rules of the prize give-away*."

I frowned.

Mr. Edman shook his head. "Terrence, buddy, happy to meet you, but you really put us in a pickle." With that, he turned back to the baseball cap–wearing smoker.

Interesting: The director of *Eve of Destruction* wasn't happy to meet *me*. He didn't even consider me worthy of being acknowledged. Yet I was the one who'd won the contest "as guaranteed by the rules" . . . blah, blah, blah. Terrence tucked his hands in his pockets, something he did whenever he got nervous or embarrassed. I felt for him. In similar situations I fiddled with one of the two extra scrunchies I always kept on my wrist.

"Listen, Eddie, it *has* to work," Norman Edman continued, as if we weren't there.

Aha! This was Eddie Payne, the so-called wildly charismatic genius. Funny: he looked like a grown-up version of Max, minus the baseball cap and cloud of smoke.

Eddie's eyes flashed to Terrence. He dropped his cigarette and stomped it out under his Converse high-tops. "Shit. It is what it is," he said. (More croaked than said. Eddie sounded like Mr. Welsh, our math teacher, who had a carton-a-week habit, or like an evil frog villain from a fairy tale who also smoked a carton of cigarettes a week.) He vanished into one of the trailers.

Mr. Edman sighed and approached us. "I'm Norman Edman," he said.

It occurred to me that he hadn't introduced himself to me at the welcome party. Not that he had any reason to; it was just interesting that I hadn't officially met him.

He extended a hand to Terrence.

"You want to shake?" Terrence asked, folding his arms across his chest.

"Pardon?" Mr. Edman said, his Hollywood smile intact.

"You know, with me being not white and all."

I cringed but bit my lip to keep from laughing.

Mr. Edman's Hollywood smile faltered. "Excuse me?"

After that I closed my eyes. I could envision how this would play out. Terrence would get us kicked off the movie set. Which was probably all for the best in the long run, except that I wanted to see Freddy White again. (I'll admit that here. Best just to get it out of the way.) But when I opened my eyes again, I saw that Terrence had accepted the handshake.

"It is what it is," Terrence said in a dead-on impersonation of Eddie Payne.

Now Mr. Edman looked as if he were about to vomit. He still tried to be sunny. "I'm not racist," he said, pulling away. "I have plenty of black friends."

"Good for you," Terrence replied. "I have hardly any."

Then I actually did laugh. I couldn't help it. My stepbrother laughed too. That made things better. It got rid of Mr. Edman, at least.

At 11 A.M. I commented—very quietly, to nobody in particular—that we'd arrived at 8 A.M.

Terrence's stomach growled. He'd been too busy earlier this morning trying on different clothes to eat breakfast. I, on the other hand, had eaten breakfast and was hungry just the same. Another vice of mine—when I was nervous I liked to eat.

A very ominous "it's time" was yelled over a bullhorn. That was meant for me. I got up, everyone staring, and walked over to the set like I was walking down the green mile.

Astrid climbed into the 1954 cherry-red Chevrolet convertible beside me and snickered. "Thank God you won Miss A-Bomb. I don't have the upper-body strength to hold that thing up."

I could be wrong, but it sounded like a clever way of calling me fat. I smiled. I was going to take the high road all the way to hell if I had to.

"Now, just wave," Norman said to us. "Just wave to the

crowd when they're here. Just wave, smile, and wave, like you have no care in the world. You just won, Laura. Astrid, you came in second."

I gave a short laugh. *No laughing, Laura*, I said to myself, because when I did, the pins holding this monstrosity dug into my skull. I was going to have to wear this all through breaks. Kitty would come and do a touch-up, but I was instructed not to move. If I did, there would be bloodshed—as in my own.

"Don't be all high and mighty. I asked Norman to give someone else this part. An extra. I did not want to wear that godawful thing," Astrid said, poking at the mushroom cloud that was possibly digging into my brain. "Think of my poor head. My hair. I'm good with coming in second."

"Lunch!" someone screamed, and everyone stopped what they were doing and, like a hog heading for a trough, they ran.

Just like in the school cafeteria, everyone sat in their respective cliques. Crew on one side. Production on the other. Talent ate in their trailers. Terrence and I? Well, we found a picnic table next to the Porta Potties. We liked to keep it classy. Individual boxes filled with sandwiches and a little package of potato chips, a pickle, and a cookie. Terrence and I each grabbed a lemon-lime soda from a cooler.

"You'll enjoy tomorrow. Sloppy joes," said a scruffy-looking man. His gray hair went every which way, his beard was unkempt and looked like a Dalmatian's, and the dark circles under his eyes were large but were slightly covered by huge black-rimmed glasses. "I'm Dylan Paige," he said. "Cinematographer. You'll see me around. Usually with a handheld."

"Nice to meet you," I said.

"You too," he said. "You two seem to have manners, unlike some people." He looked over his shoulder down the lane toward the trailers. "But I've been around worse."

"How many movies have you worked on?" Terrence asked.

"Thirty or so," he said. "But I've only been on this job for the last five or so in my career."

"That's impressive, man."

"Well, I did take a pay cut to work on *WarGames*."

"So you've met Matthew Broderick and Ally Sheedy?"

He nodded. "I was hoping that they'd be in this too instead of the talent we have," he muttered quietly. "They've got attitude problems."

"Yeah, they're not that friendly," I said.

"Except Freddy," Terrence said.

"Oh, yeah, Freddy's nice," Dylan said. "And Owen at least keeps to himself . . . But the girl." He shook his head. "Sometimes stereotypes are true. We're already taking bets on how many takes it will take for Astrid to die. I've got my money on six. You want in?"

Terrence and I looked at each other and nodded. We decided to go in on eight.

By the time we got back from lunch, we were already behind schedule according to Tyson, who kept on relaying that message from Norman, the director. Well, I guessed he could be annoyed. It was his picture, after all. But Astrid was in a mood and took it out on anyone she came in contact with. (Kitty, Raymond, Eddie—even Norman. They could do no wrong, but she was right. All the time, or so she claimed. A lot.) Like the guides say to tourists on African safaris, don't make eye contact. She was a predator and we were her prey.

But like the tabloids screamed with their headlines, Astrid Ogilvie was an entitled whiner with unreasonable expectations for life. I rolled my eyes but didn't move anything else for fear of decapitation. I looked like a fool sitting here in my pink dress and Miss Atomic Bomb crown. Astrid didn't. She wore white— or, as she called it, virginal white.

"It pays to come in second place," she said, snickering.

I wanted to lean over and send the full force of my mushroom cloud over her head. But I didn't. I had self-control, and my body physically wouldn't allow it without doing bodily harm to myself.

We sat in a bus at the end of "Main Street," which in real life was Sixth Street. Terrence sat beside Freddy. Astrid didn't want to sit by me, but it being the only seat, she had to. Sometimes we had to do things we didn't want to do to get from point A to point B.

Astrid and I didn't talk. I tried talking to her, but she didn't find the need or the desire to. When Astrid got on the bus she made it all about her. She rolled her eyes and scoffed. "Owen has jumped the shark[1] as a human being."

I laughed, and she did too. That would be our only interaction.

Owen wasn't in this scene technically. He had one shot where he was seen from the crowd. The crowd. Extras were lined up and down the blocks. They were dressed in attire from the 1950s. Stereotypical clothing: white blouses, poodle skirts, house dresses, ladies' suits, low heels, black-and-white saddle shoes, and the bad-boy leather jackets, jeans rolled up, short-sleeved shirts—it was June, of course.

Terrence was in the scene as well, in the crowd on the opposite side as Freddy to give the illusion of a diverse town. It was Pikesville, after all, but Pikesville did look a lot like Griffin Flat.

Half the school was here. But Max wasn't. He thought this movie-making business in our town was stupid and wouldn't end well.

---

1 Meaning to show how brave he was or how hard he was trying. Like how the Fonz wore swim trunks and his trademark leather jacket and literally jumped over a shark while on water skis. Two thumbs up. Ayyy. It was absurd because Fonzie already proved how brave he was by jumping over tons of barrels with his motorcycle in a previous episode. Honestly, I was only watching *Happy Days* because of how cute Ron Howard is. He has great thick red hair. Though I stopped watching when Ron left the show in 1980. The show was never the same again. It was canceled back in September.

Kitty came up behind me and literally used a whole aerosol can of Aqua Net before she pulled another can of Aqua Net out of her utility belt, shook it, and sprayed my beehive into place.

Then she touched up my makeup. And Raymond straightened my pink dress and buffed my white leather Mary Jane shoes. I looked like an overgrown toddler.

"Laura," Astrid said.

"Hey, you got my name right."

She looked at me like I was stupid. "Oh, don't be so dramatic," she said, smiling and waving occasionally to the crowd.

"Quiet on the set. Quiet on the set."

"And action!"

NOTICE OF FILMING

This area is being used to photograph and record video and film footage in connection with the promotional and publicity campaign of the movie *Eve of Destruction*. By your presence in this area, you acknowledge that you have been informed that you may be photographed and recorded as part of the release in home video and/or any media now known or hereafter devised, in perpetuity throughout the universe and the advertising and publicity thereof. Further, by your presence here, you grant your permission for your likeness and voice to be included therein without compensation, credit, or other consideration. If you do not wish to be photographed or recorded, or appear under these conditions, you should leave this area immediately. You will be reminded of this on each day of shooting. Thank you for your cooperation.

EXT.CITY—AFTERNOON

It is a bright, crisp southern day in June 1954, and the small-town Miss Atomic Bomb parade could be something out of a Norman Rockwell painting. Main Street is lined with townspeople applauding as the Miss Atomic Bomb, HELEN ALLEN, and runner-up, MARTHA WELLS, are driven in a bright cherry-red 1954 Chevrolet convertible. They wave to the crowd, smiling, laughing, and having a great time.

HELEN sees HANK. HELEN smiles.

                 HELEN
               (mouths)
                  Hi.

                              FADE OUT.

No one knew her. Helen Allen wasn't popular and certainly did not have the eye of the boys at Jefferson High. But she saw one boy with a twinkle in his eye. The way he smiled. The way he said her name when she would accidentally on purpose rush pass him in the hall. "Excuse me. I apologize," she would say.

He would counter with, "No problem, Helen."

Helen's heart skipped a beat. She would do anything for him.

That night as she sat with a mushroom cloud on her head, as she was crowned Miss Atomic Bomb in the back of a convertible, waving to an adoring crowd that barely knew her name, she saw him. Hank. She was in love. And it took an atom bomb for him to realize the lengths she would go to for him.

Eve of Destruction, *Book, page 5.*

Chapter Twenty

It was a lot different from what I thought it would be. Confined to one central location, doing the same part over and over again, repeating the one line over and over again. "Let's do it one more time . . . One final take . . . Just like that . . . Okay one last time . . . That will do . . . Cut."

Exhausting. Boring. It was drudgery, not glamour.

We started filming that one scene at 3 p.m., and by 6:30, I couldn't stop yawning. They got enough crowd shots, so Terrence was allowed to leave. He fell asleep in Freddy's trailer. Raymond took back the dress, and Kitty helped take down my mushroom-cloud crown hair but not before taking a Polaroid and giving it to me as a memento.

I said good-bye to Kitty, then went looking for Terrence so we could go home. I was so tired. But when I turned a corner around a trailer, I saw Mr. Edman talking with Mr. Paige, the cinematographer. They were deep in conversation, but not too quiet. I heard every single word. They were standing below a light post, as if they were playing a scene in some film noir involving an illicit conversation.

"My guy didn't come through, so we're going to get creative. Trust me, it will work out. The footage will be absolutely fantastic," Mr. Edman said.

Mr. Paige didn't agree. He used his index finger as a weapon, stabbing Mr. Edman in the chest. "If we get caught, my ass is on the line, and I'm sure as hell not going to prison over this movie," he said.

"We won't," Mr. Edman said. "Trust me."

A coyote howled in the distance. The two of them scurried away. I did, too—not because of the coyote but because I didn't want Mr. Edman or Mr. Paige to catch me eavesdropping. Coyotes didn't scare me at all. The only people who were scared of them were outsiders.

I found Terrence in Freddy's trailer sitting on a couch playing *Mario Bros.* on Atari. I climbed over Terrence's feet and sat between them.

"Score!" Terrence said, leaning over me to high-five Freddy.

"I've got winner," I said.

"Okay," Terrence said.

"Fine by me," Freddy said, giving me a nudge with his shoulder.

We played for another hour and a half. Freddy went to dinner. I had homework to finish, so.

Terrence drove us home. We were both so exhausted. Mom and Dennis were just setting the table, so perfect timing. Mom asked about our day while scooping mashed potatoes out of a bowl. But neither Terrence nor I took any. We both fell asleep at the dinner table. I woke up for a moment when Dennis tried to remove the fork I held in my hand.

"Eve of Destruction" Films in Griffin Flat

by TROY MARTIN
Staff writer

Little Rock—The production of *Eve of Destruction* continued in the small town this week.

More than 500 extras lined the sidewalks of the small town in the hopes of being one of the chosen few selected for pivotal scenes.

"I want them to look like people from the South," said Anthony Dillard, one half of the famous duo BC-AD Productions.

"I think the word he's looking for is *fat*," Bruce Coleman said. "But *real* is probably better."

"I guess the Jane Fonda videos are working," Anthony said with a laugh.

Extras have been lining the streets each and every day to have their one shot at fame.

"This is the closest I want to get to a bomb," said Otis Wilson, a resident of West Memphis, Arkansas.

People from as far away as Oklahoma have come to get their one shot at stardom. Some are camping out at the fairgrounds in Russellville in order to be here for the biggest shot of all, on December 6. The day when the bomb is set to drop.

The crew, with the help of some locals, have been rigging up some explosives.

"The bomb will drop. We're preparing everyone to not freak out," said Margaret Meadows, local deputy.

Filming began on November 26, and plans are to conclude on December 6.

"Everyone has been so nice," said Astrid Ogilvie, British actress. "I'll be sad to miss them when I get to go home."

A local girl, Laura Ratliff, 16, has already made her film debut thanks to being lucky caller number nine in DJ Crazy Bob's 95.6 radio contest. "It has been so surreal to be here. It's been fun but a lot of work," she said.

As far as the plot of the movie, it stays close to the source material of the novella by Boudreaux Beauchamp. In the film as well as the novella, it is June 14, 1954, and a Civil Defense drill will take place on the same day at the same time as major cities across the nation. However, instead of a drill with the sirens blaring and people seeking shelter, and instead of leaflets printed with, *This Might Have Been A Bomb!* being dropped from planes, a 15-megaton hydrogen bomb drops on the citizens of Pikesville.

Much of the movie is filmed in Griffin Flat, with one scene filmed at the state capitol.

"Arkansas has a lot to offer the film industry," said Mr. Edman. "I will be back to film again."

Eve of Destruction is set to hit theaters in the summer of 1985, putting Griffin Flat on the map and giving many locals a debut in a major motion picture.

Chapter Twenty-One

I'd be lying if I didn't say I missed doing experiments with the athlete flavor of the week. But that didn't make me want Mr. Truitt to reconsider my punishment.

"Nonononono—I'll do it," Max said, grabbing the beaker out of Rodney's hand.

Max sighed and looked longingly at the safety shower. He desperately wanted to pull that string. But he didn't. Unlike me, he had self-control as well as unrelenting fear of his mother.

I was on question number four and just about to pull out my calculator from my bag when I saw Mr. Truitt slam his grade book down on the table, and throw his glasses down too, and stomp his feet like the child I babysat once. (I retired right after.) A grown man throwing a temper tantrum was a sight to see.

"Laura, I need to see you at my desk," Mr. Truitt said.

The class oohed.

"Mr. Truitt, did I do something?" I asked.

"Why is it that everyone thinks they are in trouble when I call them to my desk?"

"Well—"

"No."

He sat down and nodded for me to take a seat. He scooted his chair closer to his desk and I did the same with the chair.

"I'm going to have to lift your punishment," he said.

"You're what now?"

"Grades haven't been good, and Coach Brooks is on the verge of having to play with five players, with no one on the bench academically eligible."

"I don't see how that's my fault."

"Laura—"

"I pulled the safety shower. I have to be punished."

"And you have."

"But—"

"Laura, please, take one for the team," he said.

"I don't like this one bit." I slid down in my chair. "What dumbass needs my help this week?" I asked.

He motioned toward Kevin Barnes. I groaned silently. I'd forgotten he even attended classes. I just thought he played games and went to parties. Maybe that wasn't fair. Actually, it was. Not all athletes were stupid, but the ones in Mr. Truitt's fourth-period chemistry class were. I found my apelike new lab partner (who reeked of cigarettes) sitting across from Max and Rodney. Max started snickering.

"Hush," I said. "It was worth it even though it didn't last long."

"Sure."

Kevin slid the lab manual over and smiled. I hated him at that moment. Why did Kevin have to be stupid? He was a senior and still in chemistry. But he was a star Shiner athlete who needed a grade boost. And needed me to get him there.

"We're helping the dummies one A at a time," Max said.

"Who you calling a dummy?" Rodney said.

"Um. You?"

"At least I'm street smart," Rodney said.

"I'm street smart," Max said.

"*Sesame Street* smart," said Rodney as he tried to light a Bunsen burner.

"Oh no, you just got owned," Kevin said, perking up.

"I did, didn't I?" Max said. He reached out for Rodney to shake his hand, which he did. (Max is a worthy opponent.) Max used his other hand to turn off the Bunsen burner before the entire school went kaboom. "Maybe I'll join the basketball team and then Laura can do my work too."

"Ha-ha. Not a chance," I said.

"Don't worry," Rodney said. "The only way you'll play basketball is if Governor Clinton enacted segregation again."

"Wow. That was a pretty good comeback. Well done," Max said. He clapped.

"Nothing to it." Rodney smiled.

"I'd say *burn*, but with you and all these chemicals together, that joke could go very wrong."

Chapter Twenty-Two

In Griffin Flat, the art supply shop, bookstore, and comic book emporium are one and the same. Dewayne Smith's, named after the owner, Dewayne Smith. As mentioned, he fed my X-Men and Flash habits, among others. But he also fed my Judy Blume habit. Max and I hit up the store as often as we could if time allowed and we had the money. In today's case it was an emergency; Max needed a new ruler. He'd broken the other one lunging for the TV set. I still wasn't sure on the details, even after Max's long and convoluted story.

Apparently, he'd heard the garage door open because his mom got home early from Bible study, and he couldn't use the TV remote control—because his dad had taken the batteries out and put them into the radio, just like it said to in the FEMA pamphlet—so Max had to turn the channel on the TV manually since he was watching *Top 20 Countdown* instead of PBS, and needed to switch to *Nova* before his mom caught him. How exactly that series of events resulted in the breaking of his ruler was unclear. But here we were.

Terrence tagged along. Before taking care of the ruler, Max darted behind the cash register to watch Dewayne Smith's TV. He had to work the set, slap it a couple of times and adjust the antennas, but here Max was allowed to watch as much TV as he wanted before he had to go home. I don't even really think he cared what was on, as long as it wasn't PBS. He was one of the few kids I knew who had cable TV, and his parents wouldn't let him watch any of it. (There were porn channels, or so I'd heard.)

"Our shipment will be late this week," said Dewayne Smith. He was talking about the comic books.

"Noooooooo," I said, a little too loudly.

A few people in the store turned and stared. But only for a second. They understood. Most of the people who came here weren't of the Kevin Barnes variety.

I went to the Judy Blume shelf. I needed my favorite author to tell me how to handle life right about now. She had gotten me through tough times before. Whenever I needed help, I'd go to my mom, and she'd gift me with enough to buy a Judy Blume paperback. Or she'd buy them herself. When she couldn't find the right words, which was often, she'd let Judy Blume do the talking. When I got my period, I was handed *Are You There God? It's Me, Margaret*. When Mom felt like I gawked at Christian Slater too long, she handed me *Forever*. I dog-eared the juicy parts for reference. When Mom and Dad were getting a divorce, she accidentally handed me *Tiger Eyes* instead of *It's Not the End of the World*. I had to wonder why she had *Tiger Eyes* at the ready. I called Dad every day for a month, making sure he was okay. Mom gave Terrence *Then Again, Maybe I Won't*, and gave me *Deenie* for another reason I'd rather not share.

"Any new Blume today?" Terrence asked, wandering back to the book area.

"No. It's sad, really," I said.

He laughed.

"No practice today?" I asked.

"Canceled due to the movie," he said. "So is this what you and Max like to do for fun?"

"Yeah, it's exciting," I said, trying to sound as deadpan as humanly possible.

"Dad and Edna are working late again," he said, picking up *Smart Women*.

"It's still really weird hearing my mom's first name," I said.

"The same goes for me when I hear you call my dad Dennis," he said, walking over to the comic books. "So what's good?"

"I can't believe you just asked what's good," Max called, still in a trance in front of the TV screen.

"Don't mind him," I said.

"I never do," Terrence said with a laugh.

"Ha-ha. Very funny," Max said, not losing eye contact with the inanimate object. I shuffled over to the comic book section. Terrence hung over my shoulder, eyeing the comics curiously. Unlike Max, I was happy to give him a tutorial and tell him what was good.

"This one is *Peter Parker and the Amazing Spider-Man*.[1] It's pretty good. I'm more of a Firestorm[2] girl, okay, but the X-Men? I freaking love the X-Men.[3] Are you into DC[4] or Marvel?[5] Because I like both. But DC has the best supervillains . . ." I broke off, looking at him looking at me as if I'd been speaking in Russian. "You have no idea what I'm talking about, do you?"

"No. But it's cool," he said.

---

1 Marvel. Vol.1 #259, December 1984. Contains the story of Mary Jane Watson.

2 DC. Ronnie Raymond is a high school student and Martin Stein is a Nobel Prize–winning physicist; an accident fused them together. Their first appearance was in *Firestorm: Nuclear Man* #1, March 1978.

3 Marvel. Stan Lee and Jack Kirby created mutants who were born that way.

4 DC Comics, founded in 1934 by Malcolm Wheeler-Nicholson.

5 Marvel Comics, founded in 1939 by Martin Goodman.

I smiled.

He turned and picked up a copy of *Batman,* near the bottom of the rack. "A lot of superheroes are orphans," he said.

"Batman, Superman, Spider-Man," Max said, listing off the super orphanage.

"Why?" Terrence asked.

"Character development," Max said. "It's great to give them a tragic backstory."

"I'm not an orphan, but I feel like one," I said, not thinking before speaking.

Luckily Terrence never asked what I meant. He just listened to me talk.

"I'm not an orphan in the traditional sense, like Annie, but my mom is newly married to your dad, and my dad is off—"

"Saving the world from annihilation," Terrence chimed in, finishing my thought.

"Funny that we are dealing with the fallout," I grumbled.

"Survivors of the aftermath," Terrence said in a dramatic doomsday voice. When I laughed, he added, "Sorry. It's the comic books. They're messing with me." He glanced at the snowy image on the TV screen at the front of the store. It looked like the local news . . . sort of.

"Now, what are your thoughts on *Star Wars*?" he asked.

"Oh, I've got thoughts," I said. "The first one was really, really good. *The Empire Strikes Back* was even better. But *Return of the Jedi* was . . . Honestly, I think they made it just to sell merchandise."

"Did you know that the movie was originally called *Revenge of the Jedi*?" Dewayne Smith asked from behind the register, eyes on the TV. "They made, like, only a hundred T-shirts. I got one. And when the time comes, I'm going to sell *that* merchandise and retire."

He might have been a grown-up, but Dewayne Smith was an even bigger nerd about movie and comic book trivia than we were.

Max hopped off his stool and walked over.

"Speaking of *Star Wars,* you two are like Luke and Leia," he said. "You know, *Return of the Jedi* Luke and Leia, when they find out they are brother and sister and Leia can officially be with Han."

"Are you Han in this situation?" Terrence asked with a smirk.

"Oh, goodness, no," Max said. "I'm more like Chewbacca."

I shook my head. "You're C3PO and you know it."

Max gave me a death glare.

Terrence shrugged. "At least nobody here said *I* was Lando Calrissian."[1]

---

1 The smooth-talking friend of Han Solo played by Billy Dee Williams, the one black character in all three films.

Chapter Twenty-Three

We shouldn't have been so excited to see Astrid Ogilvie die. But we were. Beyond excited, I'd say. It made the hassle of coming to the fairgrounds and sitting through take after take so much more bearable. It had only been a couple of days, and still I knew I never wanted to be an actress—even if it meant being a world-famous millionaire.

I found her sitting on a cloth chair with her name on it. It was facing away from the action. She was reading a copy of *Vogue*. It was as thick as a telephone book. I tapped her on the shoulder.

"Astrid, I hear you're dying today," I said.

"Why, yes, I am," she said, smacking her lips and not looking up.

"That's nice," I said.

"It is, isn't it?" she chirped.

"Have a nice death."

"Thanks, love. You too. Now, piss off."

• • •

The fire department was there in case it got out of hand.

It got so real so fast. Astrid's stunt double got injured in a trial run, which meant that the scene had to be cut, but that wouldn't do for Mr. Edman. He had his heart set on killing Astrid Ogilvie—I mean Martha Wells. He wanted everything as realistic as possible.

"I'm not afraid," Astrid said over and over to the director.

The producers were not going to be happy. All the ways it could go wrong. Her suit failing and her dying was another. But it was decided. Astrid Ogilvie would be set on fire.

"You're insane," Freddy said as we watched her get fitted into her fire-resistant suit.

"I know, but I'm kind of being bamboozled into it," she said.

"You can say no," I told her.

"Unlikely."

Dylan was going to do two shots. One with her in her regular clothes and then in the fire-resistant suit, which was, as the suit was ironically named, set on fire. In production they'd mesh them together—or so they said.

Astrid was going to die, all right.

She was looking at herself in one of those handheld mirrors, practicing her lines. She must have been a reincarnated silent movie actress because all her facial expressions and gestures with her hands were so overexaggerated.

"Stare much?" she asked, catching me looking at her.

I looked away.

"Ha. Ha. Ha. Ha. Ha. Ha. Ha. Ha," Astrid said, holding her abdomen.

"Are you okay?" I asked.

She buzzed her lips and then scrunched her face up tight.

"If you make a face like that, it'll stay that way," I said.

"Unlikely," she said.

"I warned you."

"As I was in Arkansas I saw a saw that could saw any saw I ever saw saw. If you happen to be in Arkansas and see a saw that can out-saw the saw I saw saw I'd like to see the saw you saw saw," she repeated, looking into her handheld mirror.

"We all do this," Owen said as he walked up to me. "It helps us say the words in the script better."

"It's a little disturbing," I told him.

He just smiled.

Astrid walked away, still looking in her handheld mirror. "You know New York, you need New York, you know you need unique New York."

It was downright cold. We were pretending that it was June even though in reality it was November turning into December. That was the thing with Arkansas weather; it had two settings: hellfire and hypothermia. The saying *"If you don't like the weather, wait five minutes"*—well, it was true. We had been known to go through all four seasons in one day.

"All right, Mr. DeMille, I'm ready for my close-up," Mayor Hershott said, walking up beside me. "Laura, how are you?"

"I'm good," I said.

He was dressed in a tweed jacket, tweed vest, tweed pants, tweed bow tie, and glasses, and his hair was combed to the side. I guessed tweed was popular in 1954.

"Betty bought a bit of butter, but she found the butter bitter, so Betty bought a bit of better butter to make the bitter butter better," said Mayor Hershott.

"Astrid was talking weird too—"

"Vocal exercises," he said. "Peter Piper picked a peck of pickled peppers. If Peter Piper picked a peck of pickled peppers, where's the peck of pickled peppers that Peter Piper picked?"

The director was standing next to the cinematographer, and they were arguing. The director would yell, and then the cinematographer would yell, and then the director would stomp his foot, and then the cinematographer would stomp his foot. The cinematographer walked away cursing and raising his arms in frustration, leaving the director biting his fingernails.

"Is everything okay?" I asked. "Everyone seems tense."

"Well, they are—the explosives aren't here yet, and the big blast is next Thursday," Tyson said, walking up beside me.

"There's actually going to be a bomb going off?" I asked.

"Of course," he said. "A big one."

"Is that smart?" I asked.

"What could go wrong?"

"Are you asking? Because a lot," I said.

He walked away, pulling his sunglasses down from the top of his head.

"The light is great. We need to get going," yelled the guy with a clipboard.

The director threw his arms in the air and decided it would do.

That was encouragement.

The set safety people were talking to Astrid. I was hoping they were talking some sense into her, but sadly no. She wanted to do this. Even though her stunt double was being treated with likely third-degree burns.

"Okay, quiet on the set. Quiet on the set," the director said.

"Action!" The guy who held the clapperboard closed it with a clap.

"NO! STOP," the director yelled. Everyone froze. "She's got red lipstick on her teeth. FIX!"

Kitty came running with a tissue, and rubbed and rubbed Astrid's two front teeth. Kitty reapplied the lipstick and made her smile.

"Okay, Quiet on the set. Quiet on the set," the director yelled again.

"This is going to be the best thing since sliced bread," Kitty whispered.

"Astrid's going to kick the bucket right before our eyes," Raymond said in a whisper.

I looked over to Freddy and Owen. They too were excited to watch fire engulf Astrid. It was Christmas morning for these people.

"And action!"

It's a calm and sunny Monday morning. The Wells family goes to the festivities for Operation Alert. Martha stands toward the back with her mother, father, and brother Willie. Mayor Forte informs the crowd of the public service announcement set forth by Civil Defense.

"The Reds will not let Pikesville live," says Mayor Forte. "You are instructed to go to your local shelters until the formidable threat has concluded."

Martha grabs Willie's hand as the sirens sound an air raid alert. The citizens of Pikesville talk and laugh as they slowly move to their designated fallout locations . . . paying no attention to the sleek missiles rising over the town of Pikesville.

At first, people think: airplanes dropping leaflets—This Is A Bomb!—a good old-fashioned propaganda technique to scare them.

Flash, Heat, and a Deafening Boom, and a Blast Wave that knocks people off their feet.

The sudden and overwhelming force sweeps down Main Street. People run. But there's no time to hide.

In the end, Willie is stronger. He dashes ahead. Martha loses his hand and becomes one of the many engulfed bodies turned to black char. But the mushroom cloud in the sky is an indication—fallout is coming.

Eve of Destruction, Book, page 9.

Chapter Twenty-Four

I awoke to light suffusing my room. As it faded, the ceiling fan slowly came to a stop. I squinted in the sudden darkness. It was quiet. My alarm clock was blank, not even blinking the dreaded 12:00. The dryer was off. Mom always did a load right before bed; I usually heard it rumbling if I woke up. The telltale sound of white noise or buzz of *some* sort of electronic appliance. Kind of comforting. Now nothing. The power did a fast *whoop* before shutting off.

My heart leapt. It had to be an EMP.[1] Right? Which only meant I was awake for the apocalypse.

They, as in the people who were in charge of doing the unthinkable, said once you see the flash, you have less than thirty seconds before the blast. *Flash. Blast. Boom.* I lay there

---

1 Electromagnetic pulse. Electronic devices will be shut down for a hundred miles in every direction due to the EMP generated by the blast. That includes cars, radios, televisions, clocks—anything, really, that runs on electricity. And they won't start up ever again.

in my bed with the covers up to my chin, waiting for the *blast*, *boom*, since apparently I had already had the *flash*.

But did I really want to be here in bed when the end of the world happened?

My first stop was the living room and then the kitchen. No lights on the VCR and no humming of the fridge. I tried a light switch in the dining room to be sure, but nothing. I even opened the fridge to see if the light was on—it wasn't. It was still cold, so I quickly shut it. We would need the food before the radiation came. Looking out the window, I saw nothing. The streetlamps that usually kept our cul-de-sac lit were out. It wasn't just our house.

They said that a bomb fifty miles away sounded like a giant door slamming the depths of hell.

I peeked in to Dennis and Mom's room, but they were asleep. Mom and Dennis asleep. Mom sprawled out all over the bed, leaving poor Dennis with a square inch of his own. Did they feel it?

We could have had the *flash*, but then it was too far away to see the *blast*. Even so, when was the fallout going to hit us?

Terrence's room was down the hall from mine. I could hear the snoring from outside the door. I cracked it open just to make sure. If he was awake, we could experience the *blast* and *boom* together. But he was asleep. I went to close the door, grabbing the knob, but ended up stubbing my toe on the doorframe (Stubbing your toe. It hurts like an atomic bomb went off in your foot and you have no one to blame but yourself) and yelped, waking up Terrence. "What are you doing?" he asked, half asleep.

"I saw a flash of light and all the power went off," I said.

"What?" he asked, rubbing his eyes.

"I'm waiting for the blast."

"What?" he asked again. "Did we just get hit?"

"I thought I'd be the only one awake for it."

"And?"

"And I didn't want to be alone," I said.

"Laura—" he started, but I closed the door before he could say anything.

I went back to my room but not before closing all the curtains in the house (*close the curtains, stay away from the windows, and do not look toward the light*) including in my room. My bed was by the window, so instead of getting back in bed, I made a makeshift one in my closet, and I might have hummed the entire Johnny Cash song "Ring of Fire"[1] to myself.

A little while later, there was a knock on my closet door.

"You want company?" Terrence asked.

He brought his pillow and comforter. He sat opposite me.

"I'm afraid of going to sleep and not waking up. I'm afraid that there won't be a tomorrow. That sounds really corny. Like something Scarlett O'Hara would say—I won't go hungry again, because I'll eat those radioactive radishes," I said to him.

He laughed. "Frankly, Laura, I don't give a damn."

"You had to," I said.

"Sorry, but yeah, I had to."

I kicked at his leg and he kicked at mine.

For the rest of the night, or morning, we contemplated whose fault it was—for the nuclear holocaust that would surely come, and for the one that never occurred.

The next morning, they said a transformer had blown, but seriously, I had my doubts.

Maybe that whole fictional life was creeping into my nonfictional life, but I thought we were all going to need psychological counseling after the movie wrapped.

---

1 "Ring of Fire" was written by June Carter Cash and Merle Kilgore. It was originally recorded by June's sister Anita Carter. However, it was most known as a Johnny Cash song that was released in April 1963. It's a mixture of country and rock and roll.

Chapter Twenty-Five

We stayed late after school so we could be extras in the Operation Tat-Type scene. I, with my fellow castmates, would be getting fake tattoos under my arms.

Makeup and hair were done on the stage, and wardrobe was in the gym locker rooms. The gym was where the scene was supposed to take place, but the acoustics were pretty bad (thank you, Kathy's dad, who donated the gym's sound system. His name, Peter Baker, was on a plaque that hung over the light switch next to the fire exit doors, but he forgot that insulation was important to soundproofing), so a location change was in order. We moved the whole operation to the cafeteria.

Half the crew came in and moved the tables, the food-serving counters, tray cart, fork-and-spoon dispenser, and milk cooler out into the hall, while the other half moved in the cots, hung the white cloth partitions, and moved in tiny chairs for everyone to wait on.

Kitty went "plain" with the makeup. A lot of beige. And Raymond dressed everyone, at least the girls, in white bras and skirts and Keds. All the male extras and talent would be shirtless with slacks. Boys were instructed by many a production assistant not to gawk, and girls were instructed not to giggle.

There was something to say about how a man could be seduced and manipulated by just a quick show of boobs, even if those were protected by a thin layer of fabric—in the case of my choice of brassiere, lace. Personally, I liked more of a rounded cup, but this bra was more pointy—take-out-an-eye pointy.

"Does there need to be a point with boobs like this?" Astrid asked.

"The nipple. They're the point on a bare breast," I said.

"Good one, Laura," she said.

She knew my name.

What were the '50s like? I only understood the '50s from the perspective of *Happy Days* and *Joanie Loves Chachi.*[1]

"I'm getting sick and tired of Hollywood portraying men as nothing but sexual objects. I know Hollywood does that with women, but that's different," said Owen.

"You can't be serious," Astrid said. "We're the eye candy."

"I wasn't being serious. I was being ironic."

"Oh, well, my point still remains," she said, pulling up her bra strap.

"Point," Freddy said, laughing.

Astrid mocked them by mimicking them.

There's something about this decade in movies that has a fascination with women's boobs. They're not that special. They hurt when you run. They hurt when you sleep.

In May, I went to the movies with Max. We saw *Sixteen*

---

1 *Joanie Loves Chachi* was a spin-off of *Happy Days*. It only aired for two seasons. It starred Erin Moran and Scott Baio as Joanie Cunningham and Chachi Arcola. They tried their hand at a traveling rock band. The show was canceled last year.

Candles.[1] When Samantha stared at Caroline while she took a shower, Max was doing the same thing. *Revenge of the Nerds*[2] was even worse.

Two years ago, Max and I went to Little Rock with my mom for a day of shopping at University Mall. We went over to the movie theater. Mom went to see *An Officer and a Gentleman*[3] with a friend, and Max and I were supposed to see *E.T. the Extra-Terrestrial* again, but we snuck in to see *Fast Times at Ridgemont High*,[4] starring Sean Penn, the greatest stoner of all time. When it got to the Phoebe Cates scene, Max had to leave the theater for a while.

They never showed a guy's you-know-what. All you ever saw from a guy was his ass. Thank you, *Footloose*.[5]

After the movie, Max was fascinated by Phoebe Cates. I think he was fascinated by Phoebe Cates's breasts.

"What a wonderfully structured, detailed, and fleshed-out character Linda Barrett is. She has such a huge screen presence. The actress really is a true find. God bless you, Cameron Crowe," he said, waiting for my mom in the theater lobby.

---

1 A major motion picture that premiered on May 4, 1984. It was directed by John Hughes. It starred Molly Ringwald, Michael Schoeffling, and Anthony Michael Hall.

2 A major motion picture that premiered on July 20, 1984. It was directed by Jeff Kanew. It starred Robert Carradine and Anthony Edwards.

3 A major motion picture that premiered on August 13, 1982. It was directed by Taylor Hackford. It starred Richard Gere, Debra Winger, and Louis Gossett Jr.

4 A major motion picture that premiered on August 13, 1982. It was directed by Amy Heckerling. It starred Jennifer Jason Leigh, Brian Backer, Phoebe Cates, Sean Penn, Judge Reinhold, Robert Romanus, and Ray Walston.

5 A major motion picture that premiered on February 17, 1984. It was directed by Herbert Ross. It starred Lori Singer, Dianne Wiest, Kevin Bacon, and John Lithgow.

"I think you mean the structure, details, and flesh of her boobs?" I said.

"Prude," he said.

"I'm not a prude," I said.

A lot of parents did not want their children to participate as extras in this scene. Sure, they had no problem with them participating in the death blast. Priorities. Permission slips were sent home, and only the ones who had it signed were allowed to be filmed. Max's mom did not agree, so he went home after school. Dana and Kathy were here but decided against it when they were ordered to remove their shirts. Terrence was here, and so were Kevin and Rodney. When a man walked in with a clipboard, checking off his to-do list, he took one look at Rodney and dropped his number two yellow pencil to the ground.

"Oh, nononononono," he said.

That made three.

Isaiah, Derek, Sam, Marcus, and Latitus walked in without their shirts on.

That made eight.

Deidra, Jessica, Andrea, Elise, and Rachel came in wearing nothing but their bras and skirts.

That made thirteen.

Suddenly I could only imagine Mr. Edman's head exploding. We were in the South, *not* an all-white region. What was he expecting?

Eve of Destruction became mainstream pretty fast, and I didn't really know how they, as in the bigwigs in the "industry," were going to take it.

"I don't think Hollywood has seen this many black people since *Roots*,"[1] joked Deidra to Jessica.

---

1 A 1977 miniseries based on Alex Haley's book *Roots: The Saga of an American Family*. It stared LeVar Burton in his acting debut as Kunta Kinte. Usually I watch him on *Reading Rainbow* on PBS.

The plan was to intermingle, white-black-white-black-white-black. I bet they wanted to do the entire movie in black and white. A strange problem to have, but it was 1984, and life still hadn't changed.

"We're good. We're good. We're good," the director repeated to himself. "This will be good. This will work. We will be fine."

I didn't see the problem, but if you'd been to the movie theater recently, you would understand. There hadn't been a lot of black actors in recent major motion pictures.

"Okay, okay, okay," the director said. "We need to rehearse."

Which we did. All of us with no speaking parts just stood in lines and whispered nonsense.

"Shut it, extras. The whispering is hurting my ears," Astrid screamed. "We've done enough practice."

I wanted to go behind the curtain, grab the needle that the prop department was setting up, and stab her in the eye.

Self-control. I needed self-control.

The director came in and ordered us to practice one last time before we got it on film. Astrid moaned and rolled her eyes. He was calmer than before, when he saw all the extras. He didn't say anything racist. He didn't really say anything at all. There were rumblings about the budget, which was already tight and was about to get even tighter. Over budget by a few hundred thousand. Probably over a million by the time the big scene rolled around. I couldn't comprehend that amount of money. I had five bucks to my name, and that was because Mom gave that to me just in case I needed some spending cash.

"I need more from you," the director said to Astrid, who was getting frustrated with the direction he was giving her.

She was about to walk off set when he called for a five-minute break.

The director left to take a phone call, probably from a finance man.

I went over to the food service table and grabbed a banana.

"He's in over his head," Astrid said, standing beside me and grabbing a grape off the vine in a bowl.

"What do you mean?" I asked.

"Oh, I'm not talking to you. I'm just thinking out loud," she said, smiling and taking another grape and popping it into her mouth.

"The light—we're going to lose the light," Mr. Edman yelled.

"Honestly, we're inside," Astrid said to herself, most definitely not to me.

I dropped the banana peel in the garbage.

The director was literally pulling his hair out. He was literally becoming bald before my eyes. "One take and we'll film," he said, yelling into his bullhorn, even though the cafeteria wasn't that big. "Quiet on the set. Quiet on the set. And action!"

The macabre scene comes after they prick their little fingers to actually test their blood.

They're given ID cards to carry in their wallets and clutches. Cards with their name, address, and blood type. The circle smeared with their blood. The students wait in line until their name is called.

"Next," says Nurse Murphy.

Helen moves forward, her arms at her sides. She's cold in nothing but her brassiere and skirt. She sits on a cot and waits for her turn, picking at the loose thread on her hem.

Nurse Murphy orders Helen to lift her arm. She wipes the X mark. Helen flinches at the coldness.

"Is it going to hurt?" Helen asks naively.

"Only for a bit, but don't worry—the pain will subside."

The tattoo gun buzzes as it comes toward her. She screams, but the nurse does not stop. The gun touches her skin. It tickles. She laughs, but the pain comes and she starts. Tears run down her cheeks, down her chin, onto her bosom.

"All done," Nurse Murphy says. "See, it didn't hurt one bit."

Helen's body, once pure, is now defiled with an O and a positive sign.

Eve of Destruction, *Book, page 14.*

Chapter Twenty-Six

The "congratulations; we made it one week" party was tonight. The temperature had dropped, but everyone was still determined to celebrate. So the school administration graciously opened the doors to the high school gym. The same gym where I got pelted during dodgeball last week.

I waited in line for food. BBQ and potato salad filled my plate, and a piece of Wonder Bread.

"It's, like, so totally going to look like a mushroom cloud. I worked it to a T. It's going to be so gnarly," Skeet said, scooping coleslaw onto his plate. Skeet's in charge of the explosives on set. He's the one who's going to be making the bomb look like the real thing.

"Gnarly," I said as he was trying to explain it to me.

"Righteous."

The last time I saw him—yesterday—he'd had a lit cigarette in his mouth. He was holding a stick of dynamite in his right hand and a brick of C-4 in his left. He could have taken out me and everyone around us that day. Unless he was holding props. It was hard to tell sometimes.

I found a table in the back for Max and me.

"They want to use my land," he said glumly as he sat. He placed a chocolate cupcake on my plate.

"Thanks and what?" I said, licking the frosting that I had swiped with my index finger.

"For your death scene."

"Cool."

"Not cool. That's my place, and my mom gave them permission to use it. Ugh. Annoying woman. She signed papers and everything."

"But it's going to be in a movie. That's pretty awesome."

"Ugh."

I shook my head. "You're being crazy."

"Am not. But I'll tell you what, I'm going to be there," he said.

"Why?" I asked.

"Because I'm going to be in this movie if my land is going to be in this movie."

"I thought you don't care about this movie."

"I don't."

"Well, I think you do."

He rolled his eyes and dug into his fried chicken leg like a dog gnawing on a bone.

"Can I have everyone's attention?" Mayor Hershott said to the crowd. His voice echoed throughout the gym.

A few people stopped eating and looked toward the stage, but most kept talking to who they were talking to and pretended that Mayor Hershott did not exist. I know I didn't go up to the stage.

"Thank you all for coming," said Mayor Hershott. "What an awesome turnout." Most people here had come for the food. "Everyone has been great this week. But we've got one week left with Hollywood, and let's make it the best week ever. Who's with me?"

Most kept on eating their lime-green salad and pickled eggs, but the kids cheered.

The director approached the microphone. Once again a piercing sound went through the speakers and made all of us, even the ones not paying attention, i.e., not me, place our hands over our ears and scream out in pain.

"Okay," he said, finally getting the attention back on him— even the ones who hadn't been paying attention to Mayor Hershott. "You all have been great with your turnout as extras this past week." People clapped for themselves. "I'm requesting an even bigger turnout for this upcoming Thursday's last but biggest shoot."

Next Thursday marked the end of the world for Pikesville. As the bomb went off, I would be watching from the top of Crow Mountain. *Blast. Heat. Radioactivity. End the Arms Race—Save the Human Race.* Really, one big bang and we all fall down. Winning the contest meant I got to survive. Sort of. (Sorry, spoiler alert for whoever hasn't read *Eve of Destruction* yet, but I died. The Red Warning from Mount De Soto and my death scene, the sacrificing my life for the boy I love. Like I said—spoiler alert.)

"I don't know why this morbid stuff is so fascinating to me," Freddy said.

"I think it's because no matter how bad our lives are, it could be a lot, lot worse."

"True. Where's Terrence?" he asked.

"Um," I said, looking around, "he's over there by the tree with Rodney."

He smiled, knocked his shoulder with mine, and walked away.

The director was still talking about what would happen after the bomb went off.

"I need smiles and happy faces. True, a lot of people are

going to die, but it's all worth it in the end. It's going to be visually appealing. You won't even know it's fake. There will be casualties, and if any of you all are interested in being a part of the blast sequence and also the aftermath scene, we would love to have you. We need bodies—dead ones. For the ones playing *live* victims, we are asking for you to come in ratty clothes from the early '50s—and surprise! If you choose to go the extra mile, a seventy-five-dollar bonus will be paid to those who shave their heads bald. Everyone will be covered in mud and other ways that our makeup department can come up with to mimic the effects of radiation. We will also be setting up the blast zone, and if you do live in the proximity of what we are calling ground zero, we need you to evacuate. For your inconvenience, every adult will be paid ten dollars and every child five. Starting at six A.M., we will be knocking on doors. The local police have agreed to help. Thank you for your understanding. And don't forget what Mr. Beauchamp said in his great novella: 'If you've seen one nuclear war, you've seen 'em all.'"

People clapped again, even more loudly. I didn't know if it was the promise of money or the excitement of seeing an explosion or coming face-to-face with the postapocalyptic boogeyman, the nuclear boogeyman on the brink of destruction, but everyone was interested in being a victim.

Chapter Twenty-Seven

Mr. Truitt was setting up the VCR. Movies were the greatest thing to happen to a class since the time we got to play Heads Up, Seven Up when we had a substitute teacher.

"Someone get the lights," Mr. Truitt said.

"What's going on, Teach?" Rodney asked, flipping the lights off.

Mr. Truitt didn't answer. Instead, Rodney pressed PLAY and went to his desk and sat down.

Dr. Doomsday or: How to Start World War III Without Even Trying—a play on the cinematic title *Dr. Strangelove or: How I Learned to Stop Worrying and Love the Bomb*[1]—subtitle: *History of Atomic Fusion.*

Our title: *What in the hell have we/they done?*

---

1 A political satire black comedy that premiered January 29, 1964, directed by Stanley Kubrick and starring Peter Sellers in three roles. Also starring Sterling Hayden, Keenan Wynn, Slim Pickens, and Darth Vader himself, James Earl Jones.

The man's voice was so robotic, rattling off so many statistics, one after another, and another, and another:

W-53 Titan II Thermonuclear Missile has a blast yield of nine megatons. Has been in service since 1962. It weighs over 8,000 pounds and is at least 600 times more powerful than atomic weapons dropped on Hiroshima and Nagasaki in 1945 at the end of World War II.

There are two types of assaults, that being Surface and Airburst. At the end of either, this is what you might expect in a generalized rural location.

Surface
3,100 dead; 9,460 injured.
Airburst
7,420 dead; 49,690 injured.

It is said that Airbursts don't produce any appreciable fallout, but ground bursts produce a great deal.

Distance from blast: 5 miles. Fallout will begin in 20 minutes.

Distance from blast: 25 miles. Fallout will begin in 1 hour.

Distance from blast: 100 miles. Fallout will begin in 3 to 5 hours.

Victory to the country that recovers first after a nuclear war. However, the only creatures guaranteed to survive a nuclear war, we are told, are cockroaches. For humankind the problems caused by radiation and the fallout seem insurmountable.

The screen went white, then got brighter, then there was a blast so loud that I thought it was going to knock out the television speakers.

I screamed. I couldn't help it. A shiver went down my spine, like someone was walking over my grave—as the saying went.

Everyone turned their head. I was having a panic attack. Mr. Truitt rushed toward me. He tried to calm me down. He grabbed my shoulders to keep me from shaking, but I kept struggling in his arms. I couldn't breathe. I could see my reflection in his silver tie-clip. The look on his face made me just as afraid as he was. My face was bright red and covered in tears. Rodney ran to get the nurse, and she came in just as fast as he'd left with a brown paper bag.

"Laura. Laura. Laura," the nurse said over and over again, "just breathe."

Mr. Truitt stopped the tape and turned off the TV. Kevin turned on the lights and we sat quietly. What was there to say? I had nucleomituphobia.[1] Like my teacher in ninth grade told us, "Don't worry about the possibility of war. If it happens, the school will be a target in the primary strike zone, and our obliteration will be swift, instantaneous, and painless." He was going through a divorce, and he was fired the next week after many of the parents complained.

Class was pretty much done after that until the bell rang. I kept breathing into my brown paper bag. I saw Mrs. Martin during gym class, where I talked about my feelings. I knew that I could never show my face again in chemistry. I was the girl who got freaked out over a fake nuke; what would I do if there was ever a real thing? A brown paper bag wasn't going to save me.

I didn't want to think about what happened in chemistry or Mrs. Martin's assertion that if I didn't come to terms with

---

1 Nucleomituphobia: the fear of nuclear weapons. Some people with this fear believe they will die because of a nuclear weapon. Also called nucleomitaphobia or nucleomitophobia. Associated words: fallout, radiation, thermonuclear warfare. Causes: external events and internal predispositions. Symptoms typically include extreme anxiety, dread, the fear of going outside and standing under the bomb, which would result in turning into a skeletonized version of a fleshless body, and of course anything associated with panic, such as shortness of breath, rapid breathing, irregular heartbeat, sweating, excessive sweating, nausea, dry mouth, inability to articulate words or sentences, and shaking. There is no cure.

my nucleomituphobia, I would most definitely have a nervous breakdown. So I focused on the comic and how our superheroine looked. Max kept on talking about her boobs. I wanted something different, and it always went back to her breasts. Ugh. Human nature, I guess. Everything about life is about the human body and sex. Bombs are very phallic. War is very homoerotic. I probably shouldn't be writing this. Future generations will read this and think humans were strange creatures obsessed with sex, but afraid of its destruction just the same. Oh, what complicated creatures we were/are.

Anyway, I couldn't describe her right, and Max and I were arguing over whether he was going to make her a brunette, a redhead, or a blonde. When Terrence came home and saw us basically at a standstill, he suggested we make her black. "I'm guessing there's not a lot of black superheroes," he said.

"Besides Vixen, Monica Rambeau aka Captain Marvel, Nubia—you know, Wonder Woman's twin—and Storm," Max said.

"You know your superheroes," Terrence said.

"I *know* my superheroes."

"Don't forget to add the boobs," Terrence said.

"See, no matter what she has up here, it's all about what's down here," I said pointing to my head and then to my boobs, for emphasis on my comic character.

"Gross! You're my stepsister."

Since Max wasn't showing me any of his drawings for *Big Sister*, I decided to take a crack at it.

"What's her name?" Terrence asked.

"I don't have one," I said. "Nothing seems right."

"Destiny," said Terrence. "That's her name."

I looked at her once again. She was Destiny. She had a destiny. It might have been too on the nose, but who cared. She was our Destiny. (Our goal was to finish our comic and show it to the producers, who had to know someone big in publishing.)

"So Rodney told me what happened in class today," Terrence said, sitting on the couch next to Max.

"I don't really want to talk about it," I said.

"But it happened again," he said.

Okay, yes, it had happened before. The first time was after gym class—a year ago. We played this game where we started in the middle of the football field and the teacher would blow his whistle and we all would run home, touch our front doors, and run back. If we could do it under fifteen minutes, the school would let us go home if the nukes were coming so we could die with our families. Kids ran around Griffin Flat, dodging traffic in the streets. If you couldn't, you'd stay put in the fallout shelter in the basement. The second time was in English when we were reading about Orson Welles's biggest practical joke ever, *The War of the Worlds*.[1] During Halloween week, we listened to the radio broadcast, and I started having a panic attack in class. Mrs. Barnes had to stop the tape. Can you imagine thinking it was real when it wasn't, and freaking out that of all the ways the world could end—this was it, aliens?

"Like I said, I don't want to talk about it."

"Why?"

"It was scary," I said.

"It *was* scary," Max said, chiming in.

"You look okay now," Terrence said.

"She had to talk to Mrs. Martin."

"The school counselor?" Terrence said, making a face. He had to see her too after the great affair became known to the whole school/town.

"Stop talking like I'm not here," I said.

"Well, are you cured?" he asked.

"What do you think?" I asked.

---

1 An adaptation of H. G. Wells's novel, *The War of the Worlds*, which was published in 1898, but the radio show occurred in 1938. People listening to the broadcast thought it was real, and it caused mass chaos.

"I'm going to take that as a no."

"Yeah, no. There is no cure for nucleomituphobia. You just have to deal with the symptoms and hope there are no consequences."

"There's not going to be a nuclear war," Terrence said.

"You don't know that. There could be . . ."

"There could be a nuclear accident," Max said, nodding. "There was one before. There could be another."

"Helpful, Max, helpful," Terrence said. "Laura, you need to get your mind on something else, that's all." He grabbed my notebook. "Now, don't forget to describe the boobs."

Chapter Twenty-Eight

Not everyone felt the same way I did about the thought of being blown off this planet. But a few did. And what do people say about grassroots? They grow with only one person—and that was me. I wanted to stay on planet Earth for as long as I could. I didn't want any outside forces deciding it for me. Besides, Mr. Truitt owed me. (For Kevin Barnes.) I stood at the front of the room and asked the class one simple question: "Do you want to die?" By the look on Mr. Truitt's face, he didn't like the direction my question was going.

"Yes, I had a panic attack. Yes, I am afraid of nuclear war. I have nucleomituphobia. It is a condition with no cure. And yes, I am embarrassed by it," I said.

Mr. Truitt's brow literally had sweat dripping from it. My little desire to talk to the class about my little episode yesterday made him nervous.

But I continued. "The whole idea of mutually assured destruction is a useless figure of speech that politicians use to scare the bejeebers out of everyone on this planet who has access to modern technologies. If you think about it, if a thermonuclear bomb destroys half the world, sending it back to the Dark Ages, we as a planet would be on even footing. No one would be better than the other. I'll ask y'all three questions. One: What would happen if a bomb exploded over Griffin Flat? Two: What would we do? And three: How would we survive? Don't kid yourself; no one wants to live through a nuclear war. Who would want to be around after? It would be easier to sit down on the couch and patiently wait to be vaporized than live during the unknown."

"Laura," Mr. Truitt said, standing up from his chair.

"Mr. Truitt, I'm almost done," I said.

He nodded, sitting back down.

"Just some thoughts. Imagine this scenario: a blinding flash outside your home is followed by a blast that shatters every window and wall. You are probably hurt pretty badly. Cut, broken, and bruised. A first aid kit will help, but only so far. You try to turn on a TV or radio, but who knows if there is a signal. But that will only help if there's not an EMP. If there is an EMP, then you're SOL. And I wouldn't try the phone—it's probably dead too. If you're getting an Emergency Broadcast System message, you'll be one of the lucky ones, so congratulations. You just lived through the first wave of a nuclear attack. But there's one problem . . . you're dead. By the time help gets to you, radioactive fallout will already be in your system. Not to mention the burns that cover your body, with the flash of light that you probably immediately looked at—remember to keep your eyes closed and covered—you'll be blind possibly have first-, second-, or third-degree burns. Wear white—it saves lives. And even if you lived through that—blind and patchy—then you'll have to deal with winds up to one hundred plus miles per hour and a firestorm that burns for hours on end. And sad to disappoint you, we're not turning into Firestorm. True, this is only speculation. No one knows what living hell is waiting for us if or when this actually happens. We're not prepared. The USSR has courses in their high schools. They know what to do to survive a nuclear war."

"So what's the point of doing homework? We're all going to die of radiation sickness," Rodney said.

"That's a pretty great outlook on something that's never, ever going to happen," Mr. Truitt said.

"You optimist, you," I said. "Not many people worry about a world war that goes nuclear, but what about one that gets started by mistake?"

"And on that note," Mr. Truitt said, interrupting me and my train of thought, "thanks, Laura, for your informative and yet dismal look on the outlook of—"

Mr. Truitt was interrupted by the sound of a boom. We as a group jumped. Someone ominously said, "It's the bomb," and then the sirens blared. It wasn't a Thursday.

We moved out into the hall and sat by the white lockers and waited. It was stupid. It was idiotic.

"What's the point?" I heard Kevin say across the hall. "Laura's right. We're all going to die."

He reached into his pocket and retrieved one of his clove cigarettes. And right there in front of teachers and his fellow classmates, he lit a match and blew smoke in his neighbor's face.

Coach Brooks pulled the cigarette from Kevin's mouth and stomped it out on the floor. But that made him grab another.

"No, Kevin's right," I said, not realizing I was speaking. The brain worked that way sometimes. "Come on, they're lying to us. Sitting here with our arms over our heads is not going to save us. This so-called drill won't save us. If this was real—if there were bombs coming right at us, it wouldn't matter anyway—what would we do? Hide under a desk like our parents did? Fallout shelters?" I stood up. The teachers stared at me. "Don't just sit on the floor with our arms over our heads as they tell us to do. What they don't tell you is that in the case of extreme apocalyptic disaster, there is nothing they or we can do.

If you manage to survive, your very own neighbors will shoot you and steal your food—but that's if the radiation doesn't get you first. First comes headaches and the continuous vomiting and hair falling out, skin falling off—"

"Laura, you're not serious," Kathy said.

"I am serious," I said.

"You're scaring us," Dana said.

"You should be scared," I said. "We will be praying for death."

Coach Brooks was walking toward me now. He grabbed my arm and dragged me down the hall.

"The Soviets are coming! The Soviets are coming! America is under attack—America is under attack from within."

I was in a lot of trouble. I was suspended from school again, this time for inciting a "riot." Suspended for telling the truth. I guessed truth equaled fear. And that made Principal Parker and Mrs. Martin nervous. Whatever. They'd probably die in the first wave anyway. Heartless? Maybe. Honest truth? Absolutely.

Chapter Twenty-Nine

Pops sat at the dining room table drinking his black coffee and eating leftover brownies from last night's dessert while reading the morning newspaper.

"You're here as my babysitter?" I asked, sitting on the bench beside him.

"I'm here as your pops," he said.

Mom and Dennis were at work, and I was at home. Suspension did that to you. Sure, I caused a ruckus, but I didn't say anything that was untrue.

"Do you want a brownie?" he asked.

I shook my head. "I'm not hungry."

He nodded and went back to reading his newspaper.

I sat twisting my scrunchie on my wrist like I always did when I was anxious or excited.

"Aren't you going to ask me about why I'm suspended from school? But I bet Mom and Dennis already told you, didn't they?" I asked.

"They told me a version," he said. "When you're ready, you can tell me yours."

"I didn't say anything that wasn't the truth."

"Laura, are you truly afraid that there is going to be a nuclear war?" he asked.

"Who told you that?" I asked.

"Your parents—your mom and stepdad."

I twisted the scrunchie around my wrist and nodded.

"And that's why you painted the living room white?" he asked.

I nodded.

The day after Mom brought in five cases of canned green beans, four gallons of water, and sixteen bags of soil and stashed them in the storage shed in the backyard, I decided to dig out my old clothes and hunt for painting brushes in the garage. When you were inspired by the fear that your mother has by her desire to horde away supplies like a survivalist, you would be amazed by how much you can get done on your own. I painted the living room and dining room, and I was about to start on the kitchen when I ran out of antiflash white paint.

"It looks good," he said, taking a big gulp of scalding hot coffee.

"You're patronizing me," I said.

"No, I wouldn't do that."

"Uh-huh."

"You know you can come to me about anything. I'm not blood, but we are related," he said.

I nodded but didn't look at him. It was embarrassing.

"Get your coat; we're going to McDonald's."

Suspension meant a Big Mac, fries, and a chocolate milkshake.

We sat in the corner booth and ate. Pops even dipped his fries in his milkshake. He liked them that way now.

We were mostly alone. The only other people were women with toddlers eating Happy Meals and pleading to go play outside on the playground.

"All they care about is being the first to get that damn mushroom cloud in the sky," I said. "Ready. Set. Die."

"The children?" he asked in his southern drawl.

"No, not the children."

"Good, I was worried for a second there. That one with the puppy dog tails looks a little guilty," he said with a chuckle.

"People say not to worry, that the government has this handled. That the government wouldn't do anything like ignite a nuclear war," I said. "It's like *Sesame Street* and their weekly stories about how we're all the same on the inside."

"Laura, listen to me—"

"I know what you're going to say, Pops. Write to my congressman—but we do, and they keep voting for missiles," I said.

"No, that's not what I was going to say. You should not trust the government. Look at me. The very first page of my life story is a warning sign that clearly states you should not trust the government. Don't take everything they say at face value. I like your distrust of the government. It gives me hope for your and Terrence's future. I don't want to see my grandkids living in some *Mad Max*[1] wasteland."

"You know *Mad Max*?" I asked.

"Your hip Pops knows *Mad Max*," he said with a laugh. "I've been to the movies."

I laughed too.

"Your dad mailed me this to give to you," he said, pulling out an envelope from his back pocket.

---

1 There's *Mad Max* (1979) and *Mad Max 2* (1981), and both movies take place in a not-so-distant future in a postapocalyptic Australia. Both movies were directed by George Miller. The story follows Max Rockatansky as he sets out on a path of revenge because his family was murdered by a biker gang. He's a total loner. It starred newcomer Mel Gibson.

Had everyone talked to my dad except for me?

"He was afraid you weren't getting his letters," he said. "But that's between your mom and him."

I stared at my name on the envelope: *Ms. Laura Ratliff*—so official. I was hoping for the best but expecting the worst.

"Go on," Pop said.

I nodded but took my time tearing it open. I read it out loud, pausing over the black marks.

> *Ladybug,*
>
> *I haven't been the best dad lately. I hope to work on that in the future. If there is a future, I mean. What I'm trying to say is that I'm sorry. And I hope to say this in person one day. But for now, I can't. And honestly, I don't know if I ever will be able to. There's been* ██████████ *here. We've been on* ████████ *for weeks.* ████████ *going off.* ████████████ *is routine. I'm afraid. I'm afraid for you. And I'm afraid for your mom. And I admit that was really hard to write. We screwed up everything—forever. Ladybug, I am sorry. Worst case scenario,* ████████████, *it will create* ████████ *throughout the area, and there will be* ████████████████. *I may never see you again, and that scares me. You are my daughter, my Ladybug.* ████████████████ *may be* ████████████. *I'm sorry, Ladybug.*
>
> > *Love,*
> > *Your dad*

"Ladybug," Pops said. "That's a cute nickname."

"It's so redacted. What was the government so afraid of little ol' me, a nobody, finding out?" I asked.

"Your dad wants to protect you because he loves you," Pops said. "We all do."

"I know."

"I wonder what's under the black marks," Pops said.

"Pops, Granny said there were men in suits with gas masks near the house the last time I talked to her. Do you think there's something wrong?"

"No, of course not. Your dad would let us know," he said.

"Could he?" I asked, pointing at the redacted letter.

"We shouldn't worry," he said.

"Really?" I asked.

"Really. When I start to worry, I'll let you know."

"Can I tell you a secret?" I asked Pops.

"You can tell me anything," he said.

"I don't want to die."

He nodded, scooted over in the booth, and wrapped me in his arms.

I cried. And he did too.

Then he bought me a box of Chocolaty Chip cookies to go. We had somewhere to be. The governor had never been to our town. Even when he was running for governor, he never made a campaign stop. I didn't blame him. But today he was accompanied by two black cars in Griffin Flat. Hollywood was making its appearance, and now so was the governor. Governor Clinton would not be playing himself; that role went to DJ Crazy Bob from 95.6. He'd be playing Governor Holt from the fake state of Whatsitsname, where fictional Pikesville was located. Governor Holt would be the one to announce the end of the world war here.

We used to be happy before we knew the future.

The sidewalks were cluttered with actual citizens and people who didn't live here but were pretending to live here in fictional Pikesville as extras.

And people were getting their picture taken with the governor. I did. I planned on having it framed.

"Don't tell your mom and my son," Pops said.

I locked my mouth and threw away the key.

Protestors showed up. They lined half the sidewalk in front of Dane's Ice Cream Shoppe and Dewayne's bookstore, which he probably loved, I said sarcastically.

END THE ARMS RACE—SAVE THE HUMAN RACE
NUCLEAR POWER IS NOT FOR HEALTHY CHILDREN AND OTHER
LIVING THINGS
NO NUKES IS GOOD NUKES
NO NUKES
NUCLEAR WEAPONS WOULD KILL MILLIONS—INDISCRIMINATELY
ATOM KILLS
LET PIKESVILLE LIVE
LET THERE BE A WORLD
PEACE

Not much had changed since my mom marched, braless with MAKE LOVE NOT WAR signs. They'd even brought red balloons, but the police shut that down real fast.

The governor was coming to town right when school was in session, but the administration made the executive decision to end school early. A civics lesson, so to speak. But Pops made the executive decision for me. I wasn't going to miss the governor here for a little suspension.

You could tell the director was annoyed at the mesmerizing control that the governor had over the crowd. All eyes were on him, and it was quiet. The director wished he had that influence.

"My fellow Arkansans," Governor Clinton said to the crowd, "I'm happy to see so many smiling faces this afternoon. Rumor has it there's going to be a nuclear war." The crowd erupted in laughter. "I want to reassure many of you that this is just a movie—a movie about average Americans going about their business as usual"—*until everyone gets fried*—"until the unthinkable happens. Though nuclear deterrence is on the forefront on all Americans' minds, it is"—And I tune him out. Political speech, blah blah blah—"Tonight, I ask all of you to stand with me for a future that will make us proud. God bless you all. Thank you."

Governor Clinton had a way about him. The way he talked

in a slow, deliberate, and comforting manner like nothing was wrong. He had a way about him that made me want to forget, at least for a moment, all the scenarios of nuclear devastation and the collapse of a working society that could occur: Cannibalism, famine, disease, death of the American dream, you know? Even though Arkansas had its very own nuclear warhead out on a cow pasture. But Governor Clinton was a politician, and he was just one man closer to the button.

The purpose of a nuclear war was to leave the entire planet devastated beyond recognition, and what if you were President Reagan, and you had to decide if you should push the button or not? What if you're Konstantin Chernenko, leader of the Soviet Union, and you had to decide if you should push the button or not?

Or not.

But this was fake. In reality the governor would be one of the politicians hiding in some bunker in Mount Weather (a nuclear fallout shelter that's at a top secret—I say top secret, but everyone knows—location for the president to be relocated when or if the unthinkable happens), waiting until this damn apocalypse passes by. We'd only hear a voice like his while we sat in smoldering ruins listening to a ham radio under candle-light while eating a can of Spam.

"Act natural," Tyson told DJ Crazy Bob from 95.6.

DJ Crazy Bob actually did a pretty good impression of Governor Clinton. It made the governor from the twenty-fifth state laugh.

"My fellow Americans, I am pleased to tell you today that I've signed legislation that will outlaw Russia forever. We begin bombing in five minutes," DJ Crazy Bob said (mimicking Governor Clinton) with a laugh (That was an actual thing that President Reagan said to lighten the mood; however, he was broadcast over the radio on August 11, 1984 and later leaked to the general public), which made us laugh but not the director, who was in a mood. He was even biting his nail and had sweat on his brow. He seemed nervous or worried. And since I was a constant worrier, I was now worried too.

There were a few practice takes with Tyson stepping in for the director and telling the radio host to "ham it up—embrace your southern drawl."

Once Tyson got the approval from the director, they decided to put it on film.

"Quiet on the set. Quiet on the set. And action!"

INT. RADIO STATION—MORNING

GOVERNOR HOLT's voice is heard over the radio.

Civil Defense sirens sound.

> GOVERNOR HOLT
> (somberly)
> In accordance with the authority vested in me, I hereby declare a Civil Defense emergency to exist in the state of Arkansas. This will put into effect emergency plans for your welfare. Arkansas Civil Defense organizations, including those of counties and assemblies, are directed to mobilize and act in accordance with approved plans, and I'm calling a special session with both houses of the legislature to convene at a place and time I will designate in a later announcement. I will ask that you cooperate with your Civil Defense officials. You will be advised of further developments by radio. Stay tuned for further information. This is Governor Jefferson Holt.

Civil Defense sirens continue to sound.

FADE TO BLACK.

Chapter Thirty

That would be the only take. Governor Clinton's security detail started talking to their wrists, and he was whisked away. No one said why. We asked too.

At least I did.

The director wasn't happy, and he voiced his displeasure. He said we were done for the day with a few expletives and headed off the set and to his car, where his driver burned rubber down Main Street. As did the state troopers with the governor. There was a cloud of dust in their way as they headed *not* in the direction of Little Rock.

Day before Obliteration

Well, if in fact a Red Warning occurs today, we certainly got a beautiful day for it.

The sunny skies and pleasant temperatures for this June day make standing in the middle of Main Street more agreeable while waiting for tensions to rise. If it happens, if the crisis does happen, then there's a slight possibility The Chronicle *will not publish tomorrow. But we will try.*

Eve of Destruction, *Book, page 50.*

Chapter Thirty-One

It was my day to die. It was cold, and the sun wasn't out yet. The only lights were the ones from the car and a few streetlamps. We pulled into the fairgrounds. Trailer lights were on, and people were running around in a frenzy. Off to the side was a semi with a couple of rides, and the Ferris wheel was being worked on by a crew. The Christmas Festival was to start a week after the movie crew departed. I couldn't wait to ride the Ferris wheel. It was the only ride I liked to ride.

Dennis was stopped at the gate and was asked his name by a man with a clipboard.

"Just dropping off my kids," he said.

"Names, sir?" the man asked. "We've been having a lot of people trying to get on set, and their names aren't on the list."

"Terrence Jennings and Laura Ratliff," Dennis said.

"Got them," the man said, checking Terrence's name and then checking mine with his pencil.

Dennis pulled up a little. He wasn't allowed to go past the gate.

"You two be good and shine," Mom said as I opened the door.

"We will, Edna," Terrence said.

"You two have a ride home?" Dennis asked.

"We'll find one," I said.

"The last day," Mom said. "I didn't think we'd make it."

"We love you both," Dennis said.

"We love you too," I said.

I closed the door and walked around the car.

BOOM.

The earth shook, and I grabbed Terrence's coat to keep my balance. His knees buckled and we almost went down.

"Just Skeet," Tyson said, meeting us at the gate. "He's going a little overboard with the pyrotechnics."

BOOM.

"Just you wait until this morning—he's going to rock this area," he said, looking at his watch.

Skeet's big explosion was going to be set off at exactly 10 A.M. Director Edman was a very method director. If the script said 10 A.M., it was going to be 10 A.M. when they said "action." Like it made any difference.

BOOM.

"And if you're wondering, yes, neighbors have complained, but we gave them money for their troubles. Who doesn't like money?"

"How much money?" Terrence asked.

"Ten bucks," Tyson said.

"That's all to be away from your house for a few hours?" I asked.

"The whole day," he said. "Most took our offer. Everyone on the mountain did."

"So there's not going to be anyone on the mountain besides us?" I asked.

"That's right."

BOOM.

"A lot of people decided to become extras, so they're getting paid extra if they decide to look like victims. The makeup crew is on hyperdrive."

Tyson started the engine to the golf cart.

BOOM.

"And people are actually shaving off their hair," he said. "Grown men and women, not just people your age. Seventy-five dollars must seem like a lot of money for you people."

"Hey," I said.

"I know, low blow, sorry."

"Yeah, sure you are."

"Yeah, I'm not. Soon I'll be out of these boondocks. 'Cause honestly, it's hell here. I needed to run an errand and had to drive thirty minutes to get to civilization, and they didn't even have what I was looking for. Could order it, but come on, the pony express was probably faster."

"Hey," Terrence said.

"What?" Tyson asked. "Come on. Being told to turn left after the fourth cow is not normal."

BOOM.

Tyson slammed on the brakes in front of Kitty's trailer.

"But I'll sure miss you guys," Tyson said.

I started laughing, but he was being serious.

"I thought you were telling one of those jokes that I don't get," I said. "Like your face." I smiled.

"Harharhar."

BOOM.

"If Skeet doesn't watch it, he's going to destroy the whole area," Terrence said.

"A bomb will only improve your little town," Tyson said.

"We can say it. You can't," I said.

"But you agree?" Tyson asked.

"I didn't say that."

Tyson smiled.

BOOM.

Chapter Thirty-Two

We were going to look like an American flag up on that mountain. Raymond had me in a blue dress while the boys were wearing red. Astrid would be dead. Exactly no one else wanted to be an extra up on the mountain. Everyone wanted to be part of the walking dead.

"Dylan will be filming you from behind, so I'm thinking a braid," Kitty said, brushing my hair. "And makeup light," she added, taking the pink eye shadow and dabbing it with a brush on my eyelid.

The door opened and then quickly shut. "Well, hello there, Laura," Astrid said, taking off her coat.

It was warm in there. Heaters with an *S*, plural. Those people from Cali (which they certainly did not call it and would roll their eyes if you did) could not handle the cold.

"I'm here to get my death look," she said. "Apparently, radiation has ravaged my body, eyes swollen, blood coming out of my nose. I'm going to look so pretty."

"Of course you will," said Kitty.

"You always do," added Raymond.

Kitty and Raymond looked at each other. You could cut the sarcasm with a knife.

"Aren't you both so sweet," Astrid said, smiling.

Kitty worked on my lips while Raymond was burning pieces of fabric for Astrid's costume. Yes, her character did get fire-blasted before.

"I've been in a firefight," Astrid said.

"And you lose," I said.

She laughed. "And I get paid for it."

"Well, when you go, I'll miss you," I said.

"Will you, now?" she said, more of a statement rather than a question.

"Yeah, that's why I said it."

"I'll be out of your hair soon enough."

"You're not going to stick around for the end-of-filming party?"

"It's called a wrap party," she said.

"Oh—"

"Besides, I'm up for the next John Hughes film. I'm playing the character named Sloane."

"Cool," I said.

"It is cool. I'm going to have to fall in love with the boy who almost nuked Seattle."

"That won't be hard," I said.

"Yeah, you don't exactly understand acting, but I get your point. He's cute," she said, smiling.

Kitty fixed the flyaways with a bit of hair spray and retouched my lipstick while Raymond helped me with my coat. The zipper got stuck on a snag. The coat was at least two sizes too big, but they assured me this was how all the actresses wore them.

"Are you all going to be alone up there without hair and makeup?" Astrid said, so distraught I thought she was going to cry for us.

"No, we're coming," said Kitty.

She shook her head. "I want to see what Skeet has in store. You know, the big bang."

I grabbed my *Nuke Me* tote bag, and out the door I went. I stood off to the side, waiting for the yellow school bus with Astrid, who was just getting in the way.

"You should be studying your line," she said.

I didn't want to overdo it with mine. It was like over-studying for a test. And anyway, I was just there to look pretty, as Astrid would have said.

Terrence was with Freddy in his trailer, probably playing video games. Owen was walking toward me. I haven't had much contact with him since filming began. And now we have to act together. I didn't know what I would say. Hey? Hello? Or just hi? But he walked right by me. Didn't say anything, like I wasn't even standing there.

"Owen, stop!" Tyson yelled as he ran right into him.

"I'm sorry," Owen said. "They dilated my eyes. I can't see a damn thing."

"Why didn't they wait until you got where you are going?" Astrid asked.

"Your guess is as good as mine."

I walked over to Owen, who was leaning up against a chain-link fence and staring down at the ground.

"I was going to say who goes there, but I smell your perfume," he said.

"I'm not wearing any," I said.

"Oh, Laura, I thought it was Astrid," he said.

"Seriously," Astrid said. "I'm offended by that."

"Wait—you're offended by that? I should be."

Astrid laughed.

"I'm sorry, Laura," Owen said.

"It's my own fault," Astrid said. "I sprayed a little of Opium by Yves Saint Laurent on her."

"Did I smell?" I asked.

"No, of course not," she said. "I was being nice." She shook her head. "I'll try better next time."

"Okay," I said slowly.

The school bus drove up, and the bus driver opened the door, and Tyson was the first on. Owen was blindly going along. I ran up to him and took his arm.

"Who's there?" he asked, but didn't give me a chance to answer. "Doesn't matter. I can do it myself."

"But—" I said.

"I can do it myself."

"You can do it yourself," I repeated.

I followed him on and took a seat three rows behind him.

The director and Dylan came walking up the steps of the bus. The director looked at Tyson. "I have an important job for you. You will communicate with this with Skeet down on Main Street." He handed him a walkie-talkie.

The director and Dylan sat behind the bus driver. Tyson found his seat opposite them. All we were waiting on were Freddy and Terrence.

"All here?" Tyson asked. "Nope, missing two."

"Here, we're here," said Freddy, breathing heavy, as was Terrence. Coach Flynn would be so proud. The first game of the season was soon. "Starting point guard out of breath equaled out of shape" didn't sound too good, did it?

"Ready?" the bus driver asked.

"We're ready," Tyson said.

"Let's get going," Owen said. "The faster we get this over with, the faster I can see."

"Why didn't you wait until we got to the mountain?" Freddy asked.

"Again, that's a very good question."

EXT. MAIN STREET—DAY

Zoom in on brick building covered in posters.

INSERT POSTER—CIVIL DEFENSE TEST IS AT 10 A.M. TODAY; NORMAL ACTIVITIES OF CITY TO SUSPEND FOR ONE HOUR

FADE TO:

INT. MARTHA'S HOME—MORNING

HER MOTHER is going through her closet. MARTHA is sitting on her bed playing with the ruffles on her pillow.

> MARTHA
> What do you wear for the end of the world?

HER MOTHER turns to her daughter and smiles.

> MOTHER
> Your best, as always.

FADE OUT.

Chapter Thirty-Three

"Come in, Yellow Bus. Come in, Yellow Bus," we heard over the walkie-talkie.

"This is Yellow Bus. Come in, Black Van," Tyson said, holding down the button on his walkie-talkie.

"Hold up; we have to turn around. Kitty forgot a chest we need," Raymond said over the walkie-talkie.

Tyson leaned across the aisle and told the director, who sighed, rubbed his forehead, and nodded. The director didn't look like he'd slept a wink.

"Ten-four?"

"Roger that."

It was only a thirty-minute drive, and traffic wasn't that bad. Only semis and a few cars with out-of-state tags traveling west. Our caravan was down to just us. One yellow school bus. The director kept looking at his watch. The sun was barely rising behind us. He was worried about the time. By my calculations we had plenty, but I'd only been in the movie business for a few weeks.

The bus driver veered off the interstate and turned right at the stop sign. And up the mountain road we went. I turned my head to look out the window but quickly closed my eyes when the sun blinded me.

When we arrived, Max was waiting with his hands stuck in his pockets near the mountain's edge.

It took a few maneuvers, but the bus driver finally parked the bus in a way that was easy for us to leave when filming was finished and without it being seen on camera. He opened the door.

"Good luck," he said.

"I don't need luck," Mr. Edman replied.

"All right, then."

The crew had come and set up the night before. Max and his dad had supervised, while his mom passed out hot chocolate.

"Dad's sleeping. He'll be back by the end of the day," Max said.

"Stay out of the way," Tyson said, looking at Max.

"Aye, aye, sir," Max said, saluting him.

Owen was standing next to the bus. I kept looking over at him, but he was staring at the ground.

"What's wrong with Owen?" Max asked.

"I'm not deaf," Owen said. "I just can't see."

"Need a hand?"

"Nope, I'm good," he said, leaning against the bus.

It was cold. Colder than usual. But even though it had snowed in Griffin Flat, there wasn't a touch of white powder on the mountain. We were wearing summer clothing under our heavy coats. Everyone was complaining in their own way.

Kitty and Raymond hadn't arrived yet. In fact, Tyson tried radioing for them using the walkie-talkie, but they weren't answering.

"It might not work. We're kind of in a dead zone," Max told Tyson.

"Ugh, I long for civilization," Tyson said.

"You're an asshole. You know that, right?" Max asked.

"I've been told that."

"Well, I'm glad that you've been told."

Tyson grabbed Owen's arm. "Laura?" he asked.

"No, it's Tyson."

"Seriously, first you think I'm Astrid and now Tyson? I'm officially offended," I said. "How much solution did they use to dilate your eyes?"

"Who knows—but I did hear an 'oops' and then 'oh shit,'" Owen said.

"Yikes," I said.

"We have to get this right the first time," Mr. Edman said after he gathered us around. "We only have one shot. Right when I say 'action,' we need to go. Skeet's going to set off the explosions, and we'll film it. Dylan's got this, right?"

Dylan nodded.

"I hate to be that person, but I can't see your nod, if you're nodding. Did Dylan nod?" Owen asked anyone who would listen.

"That's an affirmative," said Freddy.

It had been an hour, and Kitty and Raymond hadn't made it here. It shouldn't have taken them that long. But Tyson said they probably got distracted with the scene going on simultaneously on Main Street. Most businesses down on Main Street were delaying opening until after filming began. Some were going to be closed all day. Like, Dewayne's bookstore was going to be closed. He was going to be a victim. He got seventy-five dollars to shave his head—and beard. And if you knew him, you would know that was a major deal. A lot of my classmates were going to be victims today too. The director didn't want to use anyone under the age of twelve. I guessed he didn't want children to be traumatized, even though being traumatized was all the rage. The director, with the help of Dylan here and Eddie Payne, BC-AD Productions, and Economy Pictures, was planning to traumatize viewers with two disturbing hours of Hiroshima in the Ozarks.

"We'll do two practice takes and then one on film, got it?" the director asked.

Everyone nodded.

"Is everyone nodding?" Owen asked.

"Yes, they're all nodding," the director said, sounding annoyed. "Honestly, just assume they're all nodding to anything that is being asked."

"You don't have to be a jerk about it," Owen said, crossing his arms, but he kind of lost his footing, and without Freddy grabbing him, he would have fallen over.

"You all right, buddy?" Freddy asked.

"How close am I going to be to the edge of the mountain when we're looking at the bomb going off?" Owen asked.

"Not that close," Dylan said.

"Okay, good."

"Now everyone, rest. It's going to be a while. Tyson, I need the walkie-talkie," the director said.

Tyson ran over to hand the walkie-talkie to him.

"So what do we do now?" I asked anyone who would listen.

"Practice lines," said Tyson. "You don't want to look a fool."

I found a corner in the cave that Max was hiding out in and practiced.

"You're good at this acting thing," Max said to me.

"Really?" I asked.

"Sure. But it can't be that hard. Astrid does it."

"You do know how to lift one's spirits, don't you?"

Tyson came in the cave complaining that the walkie-talkies weren't working. He was shaking it, like that was going to get it to work.

"Service's not so good up here," Max said.

"That's just great," Tyson said, starting to walk out of the cave.

"Wait, Tyson," Freddy called.

"Yeah?"

"Are Kitty and Raymond here?"

He shook his head. "But don't worry. Norman says it's okay, you look good to go."

We practiced standing on the edge of Crow Mountain and pretended that we were watching Pikesville burn.

Tyson was trying to get the walkie-talkies to work. He walked clear across the mountaintop, or at least to where we were.

"Come in, anyone. Come in, anyone. This is Tyson. Does anyone copy?" Tyson would press the button, talk, and then release it, waiting for someone, anyone, to reply.

Seeing him so worried was making me worried.

"This is Pyrotechnic Extraordinaire. Copy?" Skeet said.

"Got him!" Tyson said, running to the director.

The director took the walkie-talkie and pressed the button.

Director: "Norman for Skeet. Copy that?"

Skeet: "Go for Skeet."

Director: "Are you ready? Copy?"

Skeet: "Ready to burn Pikesville. Hell, yeah."

Director: "You'll be on the walkie-talkie with Tyson. Copy?"

Tyson looked sick.

Skeet: "Ty Ty."

Director: "Yes, Ty Ty."

Skeet: "Totally stoked."

Director: "How about a countdown? Copy?"

Skeet: "Copy that."

Director: "Okay, stand by for Tyson."

Skeet: "Standing by for Ty Ty."

Tyson took the walkie-talkie from the director.

"Okay, we'll have one more run-through, and then we'll be ready to shoot," the director said through his bullhorn.

We scrambled back into place.

Terrence had one line. He was proud of that one line. Had worked on that one line for a long time.

Skeet: "Skeet for Ty Ty. Copy that?"

Tyson: "Go for Tyson."

Skeet: "We are ready to go. Copy?"

Tyson: "Copy that."

"Skeet's ready," Tyson yelled.

"Then so are we," the director said.

We got in position: "James," "Helen," "Hank," and "Jackson," aka Terrence.

Skeet: "Skeet for Ty Ty. Copy that?"

Tyson: "Go for Tyson."

Skeet: "Sirens are blaring. Copy?"

Tyson: "Copy that."

"The sirens are blaring," Tyson said.

"Yes, they're supposed to; we paid off the auxiliary," the director said. "Tell Skeet we're ready. Commence countdown."

Tyson: "Tyson for Skeet. Copy that?"

Skeet: "Go for Skeet."

Tyson: "Commence countdown. Copy that?"

Skeet: "Commencing countdown. Copy."

We didn't move. We were afraid to, actually. There was only one chance to get this right. Skeet had rigged the explosions to mimic a nuclear bomb. In the editing room, they would really make it look like a mushroom cloud.

Skeet: "Skeet to the survivors. Copy that?"

Tyson: "Copy."

Dylan filmed, and we watched the sky, ready to play the part we were meant to play.

Skeet: "Commencing countdown. Ten. Nine. Eight. Seven. Six. Five. Four. Three. Two. One—"

"Okay, remember, one shot. We're breaking ground here. Freddy and Terrence in one scene. Wow!" the director screamed. "And ACTION."

EXT. PIKESVILLE MOUNTAIN—MORNING

JAMES, HELEN, HANK, and JACKSON stand on
the mountaintop near the edge, watching the
town undergo a Civil Defense drill.
The Radio Station plays a message.

RADIO MESSAGE
A Civil Defense test, to test the vul-
nerability of the cities across the
continental United States, Alaska,
Hawaii, Puerto Rico, the Virgin Islands,
and Canada, will occur at 10 a.m. today;
normal activities of the city are to
be suspended for ten minutes while the
"bombing" takes place—

Sirens sound.

The Radio Station plays a message.

RADIO MESSAGE
Your attention, please. This is Neal Per-
kins, one of your official Civil Defense
broadcasters, with a special message.
Military authorities have advised us
that an enemy attack by air is imminent.
This is a Red Alert. You are advised to
go to the nearest shelter in your area
immediately. Find shelter. There is no
time to leave the city. Your state Civil
Defense director has just issued the following instructions: Please remain calm.
Every precaution will be taken for your

protection. Keep your radio turned to this place on the dial throughout the alert period for information. Telephone service to your home may be cut off to permit military and Civil Defense authorities to carry out vital operations. Do not attempt to join your family or your children if they are now separated from you. They will be cared for where they are. Obey your Civil Defense warden and find shelter now. Take shelter in your basement or in your nearest shelter area. If you can plug in your radio in a basement, take it with you. Use a portable radio set if you have one; otherwise turn up the volume on your radio so that you can hear it in the basement. Keep calm—don't lose your head. If you are at work, obey your Civil Defense authorities. Go quickly and calmly to your designated shelter. If your children are at school, they are being directed to shelter by their teachers. If you are in an automobile, pull over to the curb and then go immediately to the nearest shelter area. Do not leave your car where it will block traffic. This station will continue to stay on the air throughout the alert period to bring you all authentic information and official instructions. Stay tuned to AM 640 or 1240 on your radio for official information. Refuse to listen to unauthorized rumors or broadcasts. This is your official Civil Defense Broadcast.

JAMES, HELEN, HANK, and JACKSON grab hands.

> HANK
> Nothing is going to happen.

HANK squeezes HELEN's hand.

> HELEN
> I know.

> JAMES
> But what if it does?

JAMES turns to HELEN and looks at HANK.

> JAMES (CONT'D)
> This would be the perfect time for the
> Ruskies to attack.

> HELEN
> It would, wouldn't it?

> JAMES
> It would.

> HANK
> But they won't. No one will. It's just a
> test, practice in case of the real thing.

> JAMES
> But what if it's real? What if the
> government knows that the Ruskies are
> going to attack and this is one way to
> control panic?

                    HELEN
          That's a whole lot of what-ifs.

                    JAMES
                   I know.

HELEN shrugs and looks at HANK, biting
her bottom lip.

                    HELEN
          The government wouldn't do that. It
                wouldn't lie to us—

HELEN lets go of JAMES's and HANK's
hands.

                 HELEN (CONT'D)
                 Would they?

                    JAMES
      If it does happen, we have a front-row
            seat to Armageddon.

                    HANK
          That's a comforting thought.

                    JAMES
      Well, the very existence of the USSR is
            not part of America's plan—

                    HELEN
      The same could be said about America not
          being a part of the USSR's plan.

                    HANK
            The next atomic war—

                    JAMES
            When was the first one?

                    HANK
        You've heard of that there World War II,
                     eh?

                    JAMES
        Yes, but World War II was ended with two
        atomic bombs being dropped. It was not an
                  atomic war.

                    HELEN
            I have a bad feeling about this.

        HELEN takes JAMES's hand and then HANK's
        hand.

                    JAMES
        Just remember: if it does, look away from
                  the light.

                    HANK
                 The what?

                    JAMES
                 The flash.

                    HANK
                 The what?

A bright light flashes across the sky.

JAMES, HELEN, and JACKSON turn away. HANK looks right into the flash and instantly becomes blind.

HANK screams.

> HANK (CONT'D)
> My eyes.

> HELEN
> It was real. All of it was real.

> JAMES
> What have they done?

> HELEN
> My God, what have we done?

> JACKSON
> We're at war, and we're going to find out who did this, and we're going to kick their ass.

FADE TO BLACK.

Chapter Thirty-Four

"And cut!"

We cheered and jumped and celebrated. Sure, we were covered in dirt, and the sky was covered in ash and fire and dust, and it looked real—too real. But we celebrated.

"Skeet outdid himself," Mr. Edman said, clapping. "Bravo. Bravo."

Dylan kept filming. B-roll, or whatever it was called. The director went over to Tyson and took the walkie-talkie out of his hand.

Director: "Norman for Skeet. Copy?"

Silence.

Director: "Norman for Skeet. Copy?"

Silence.

Director: "Norman for Skeet. Copy? What's your twenty?"

Silence.

Nothing. "Absolutely nothing."

It was quiet. Really quiet. Too quiet. No animals were making noise. No vehicles were on the interstate, but the police had stopped them when Skeet set off the explosions for safety reasons.

Director: "Norman for Skeet. Copy?"

Skeet: "AHHHHHHHHHHHHHHHHHHH!!!!!"

Skeet: "Oh shit, oh shit, oh shit, oh shit, oh shit!"

Skeet: "AHHHHHHHHHHHHHHHHHHH!!!!!"

Skeet: "Run, run, run, run, go, go, go, go, go, go—"

Director: "Norman for Skeet. Copy?"

Nothing. Silence.

"Well, that was strange," the director said, handing the walkie-talkie back to Tyson. "I wonder if he thought the explosion was going to be that big."

The three of them witnessed the attacks on Pikes-ville. The citizens did not make it to their shelters in time. The planned government-issued Civil Defense drill across the nation failed. Unbeknownst to all, it was a surprise attack. "This might be a bomb" turned out to actually be one.

The sky to the northeast glowed brilliant in the midmorning sun. The damage was extensive, but the three who witnessed the atomic blast on the mountaintop did not know just how extensive.

Eve of Destruction, *Book, page 168.*

Chapter Thirty-Five

We stood on the side of Crow Mountain and stared out at the horizon. There was a lot of smoke, and it reached high into the atmosphere. Fires were raging. Lots of them.

"This doesn't look right," the bus driver said.

"What doesn't look right?" Tyson asked.

"Did your explosives guy just blow up half of Arkansas?"

"Nah," Tyson said, shaking his head.

Owen stood off to the side, his eyes giving him a lot of problems. He still couldn't see. How much solution had they given him to dilate his eyes? He had a handkerchief in his pocket and somehow twisted it and flipped it and wrapped it around his eyes and tied it behind his head. He leaned up against the bus and scooted himself down on the dirty, dusty ground.

The bus driver tried to get a better look. He stepped closer to the mountain's edge and leaned forward. But he lost his footing and started to fall. Tyson ran over there to help. I screamed. He grabbed the bus driver's waist, and they both fell back.

"What's going on?" Owen asked. I stood beside him. He reached out for my arm but found my boob instead. "Sorry, I didn't mean to touch that."

"The bus driver almost went over the mountain—with Tyson," I said.

"What?"

"The bus driver almost went over the mountain with Tyson," I said again.

"We need to radio for help," the bus driver said.

"Why?" Dylan asked.

"I dropped the keys."

"Shit. Shit. Shit. Shit. Shit," the director repeated. "We'll lose half the day, and we still have the girl's death scene."

Dylan grabbed the walkie-talkie out of the director's back pants pocket and pushed down the button.

Dylan: "Dylan for Skeet. Copy?"

Nothing.

Dylan: "Dylan for Skeet. Copy?"

Still nothing.

Dylan: "Dylan for Skeet. Copy?"

Again, still nothing.

"They're probably busy dealing with that," Freddy said, pointing to the smoke in the distance.

"Yeah, maybe."

"Maybe the explosives knocked out power," Terrence said.

"That's probably it," the director said. "It was a big explosion. I bet it looked great on film."

"Yeah, it looked great," Dylan said through the camera lens.

Tyson and the bus driver slowly walked back over to where we were. They were still visibly shaken.

"You guys okay?" I asked.

"I will be—eventually," Tyson said.

"I don't know about him, but I need a clean pair of britches," the bus driver said, and Tyson agreed.

"Well, Tyson, I'm glad you didn't go over. A good assistant is really hard to find," said the director as Tyson gave him a sidelong glance.

Communications were interrupted. The three did not know if the United States had counterattacked the Soviet Union. Was there time? And if so, did it have a similar devastating effect?

Eve of Destruction, *Book, page 170.*

Chapter Thirty-Six

We were stuck on Crow Mountain. We were cold, dirty, thirsty, and hungry.

"There's food on the bus," Tyson said.

Terrence ran onto the bus and went down the aisle, looking at each seat until he got to the back of the bus.

"No food," he said, crying. "There's no food."

"It's only been a couple of hours," Freddy said.

"Oh, the food's in the van with Kitty and Raymond," Tyson clarified.

"And where are they?" Freddy said, climbing off the bus.

"They have to be on their way," Tyson said, taking the walkie-talkie and changing the station.

Tyson: "Tyson for Kitty. Copy that?"

Nothing.

Tyson: "Tyson for Kitty. Copy that?"

Still nothing.

Tyson: "Tyson for Kitty. Copy that?"

Again, nothing.

"Dead zone, remember?" Max said.

Tyson stuck the walkie-talkie in his back pocket.

"I've got some food," Max said. "Crew left some last night, and I've got some left over from the party here a few weeks ago. Want some?"

"What kind of food?" Freddy asked.

"Junk."

We followed him into the cave.

"We have nothing to drink, except . . ." Max said, smiling and winking.

"You're freaking me out," Freddy said.

"Help me, Terrence," Max said.

Terrence followed him down into the cave where the moonshine was kept. So with the help of Terrence, Max brought up a wooden box with ten mason jars filled to the rim with hooch. I helped pass them out.

"Is this what I think it is?" the director asked.

"Wait, what do you think it is?" Max asked.

Dylan grabbed his, unscrewed the lid, and took a whiff. "Whoa, that will put hair on your chest."

"Who cares?" I said. "I'm already gross."

"No, you're not," Owen said.

"Funny, she's being complimented on her looks by a blind man," Freddy said, taking a swig of his drink.

"Hey, I'm not blind, I just can't see."

"That's the definition of a blind man."

We all drank—and drank, and ate, and ate. Laughed and told jokes. Max went back down with Freddy and carried up more mason jars full of moonshine.

"Do you want any?" I asked the bus driver.

"No, I'm driving," he said, shaking his head.

"More for us," Mr. Edman said, toasting to himself.

"This is good stuff," Dylan said, drinking and then crunching on a handful of Doritos.

"Yeah, it is," Max said, putting two crates down on the ground.

"Pass it over," Owen said, slurring his words.

Terrence grabbed one and brought it over to him. "Here you go, man," he said, unscrewing the lid.

"Thanks, man."

We were eating so much junk food that my mom would be disappointed. She didn't need to know about the alcohol. She would be so angry.

I was learning how everyone acted when drunk.

Me: sleepy drunk.

Terrence: stupid drunk.

Freddy: flirty drunk.

Owen: smart-ass drunk.

Max: happy drunk.

Bus driver: designated driver.

Tyson: gassy drunk.

Dylan: sick drunk.

Director Edman: angry drunk.

We were like Snow White and the Seven Dwarfs, except not—there were eight dwarfs.

I found a corner of the room and snuggled up with a blanket I found. It smelled of urine, but I didn't really care. It was cold.

"It's snowing," said Tyson as he made his way back into the cave after relieving himself behind a patch of bushes.

"Snowing. Snowing. Snowing," Freddy sang as he danced around the cave, spilling moonshine all over his shirt.

Dylan picked up his camera and filmed.

I got up and looked outside. Max and Terrence followed me and danced in the midst of the snow.

"Come on, guys, it's so fantastic," Freddy yelled.

Everyone went out. Even Owen, but he held on to the outside cave wall.

"Today we celebrate our Independence Day," Terrence yelled, raising his arm and his glass of moonshine.

"That's a great line. Remind me to use that line for a movie one day," the director said, clinking jars with his.

"Only if I can have credit."

"Of course."

The bus driver found a pair of binoculars on the bus and was using them to search for Griffin Flat. It was still smoky.

"Can I take a look?" Freddy asked.

"Sure," he said, handing them to him.

Freddy looked and moved closer to the edge.

"Watch your step," I said.

"Thanks," he said.

BOOM.

"What was that?" I asked, tripping on a rock and falling to the ground.

BOOM.

"Yeah, what was that?" he asked. "Oh, are you okay?"

"Yeah," I said.

Freddy offered his hand and helped me up off the ground. He smiled. I smiled. This would be the point in the movie where the hero and heroine kissed. Instead, this is the point in the story when I write, *The hero walks away, leaving the heroine with dirt on her butt.*

BOOM. BOOM. BOOM. BOOM. BOOM. BOOM.

"Fireworks?" Owen said.

"Well, it sure is pretty," I said, picking the tiny rocks out of my palm.

"But I wish they would have used different colors than red," Freddy said.

We all stood on the edge of Crow Mountain watching red fireworks light up the sky as it snowed.

"We need some music," Terrence said, dancing to the music in his head.

"I can make that happen," Max said, and ran back toward the cave.

We followed him and took the binoculars with us.

Max flipped through his collection of vinyl. He took a record out of its sleeve and placed it on the record player and set the needle: "I Don't Want to Set the World on Fire"[1] by the Ink Spots.

It was slow. Eerie. Matched perfectly with the constant fireworks rumbling in the distance.

Freddy and I danced in the middle of the room. Until we started making out, and Owen started to cry, and Dylan threw up, and the director grabbed his bullhorn and threw it at the record player, which knocked it off the table and stopped the music.

"What did we do? What did we do?" the director screamed at Dylan.

"What the hell," Max said, going after the director.

I had never seen Max that angry. He swung at the director, but the director met his fist and twisted. I swear he broke Max's hand. The scream that came out of Max's mouth was on par with a horror movie where the girl runs in the direction of the guy with the chain saw.

The "party" was over by then. Though the moonshine was still being consumed.

We stayed inside; it was still snowing, though the snow was gray and it smelled nasty, like something rotting. It had been over an hour since we filmed, and fireworks were still going off.

Everyone was in their own corner, like a boxing match. The high of being drunk was starting to fade a little. The director wasn't as angry and Dylan wasn't as sick, though it helped that he'd stopped drinking. We mostly had. We mostly wanted real food. A hot meal. The junk food was good in theory—not in execution. Terrence and Owen were discussing, really arguing over, sports.

---

1 "I Don't Want to Set the World on Fire" is a pop song written by Bennie Benjamin, Eddie Durham, Sol Marcus, and Eddie Seiler in 1938. First recorded by Harlan Leonard and His Rockets and later covered by many artists such as The Ink Spots, who are well-known for teaming up with Ella Fitzgerald. In 1941, The Ink Spots (Bill Kenny, Deek Watson, Charlie Fuqua, and Hoppy Jones) recorded the song and it hit #4 on the US pop chart.

"I've said it before, and I'll say it again. Any sport that can end in a zero-zero tie is not a sport—it's a playdate," Terrence said about the game of soccer.

"And the NFL is just stupid," Owen said.

"Oh, please, Lawrence Taylor could kick your ass."

"Yeah, he probably could."

They laughed. And that subject was done with.

Tyson and I were playing tic-tac-toe.

"This is just like that movie," he said, rubbing his eyes.

"Are you okay?" I asked.

"I have a headache."

"I'm sorry."

"Like they said, unwinnable," he said.

"They didn't say unwinnable. You can win at tic-tac-toe if you catch the other team off guard," I said.

"Do you have any aspirin?" Dylan asked, closing his eyes and rubbing his temples.

I shook my head. "I can ask Max. This is his cave, so he might."

"Uh-huh," he said, leaning over.

Max sat against the wall with Owen, who looked sick too. Max was coughing and coughing, like he'd smoked too many packs.

"Max, are you okay?" I asked.

"Screw you," he said.

"What's wrong with you?" I asked.

"What's wrong with me? What's wrong with *you*?"

"Whatever."

"Yeah, whatever," he said, coughing.

He was pale and looked like hell.

"We've got to get off this mountain," I said. "We need real food and water and probably a lot of coffee."

"Not before we film your death scene," the director said, looking at me. "You've got to die."

Chapter Thirty-Seven

This was what winning the contest was all about. My walk-on role. The role where I died. It's easy to pretend to be sick, but when you were really feeling sick, it was much harder. Tyson helped me with my makeup, actually messing it up with a little bit of moonshine. When he wasn't getting it in my eye and possibly burning my retinas, he was making me paler than I already was. He messed with my hair and threw dirt on my clothes. He was probably experiencing pleasure in all of this. He was no longer throwing up, and though he looked like death warmed over, he had a smile on his face.

"Kid, you made Laura look hideously good," the director said, looking at me.

"She does, doesn't she?" Max said.

"Watch it, or I'll go over there and knock out your teeth," I said, staring at him. I even did the whole two-fingers-pointed-at-my-eyes-and-then-pointed-at-his gesture, whatever that was called. My head hurt.

Thank God my death scene was soon, because I felt like dying.

"This will be easy," the director said. "Do you remember your lines?"

"Lines?" I asked.

"Lines, yes," he said, sighing.

"Sure," I said, lying. It was that awkward moment when the only thing that I knew was my name. Laura. Right? Honestly, you could have called me "hey, you," and I'd have been okay with that right about then. My head hurt like hell, if hell could hurt. Could it? I was delirious.

"You'll be fine," he said. "Dylan, we're ready."

Dylan staggered over and stood in front of us, and then fell to his knees and sat on his butt. He put the camera on his shoulder and looked through the viewfinder. "Ready," he said. "Is the light on? I can't see colors."

"It's on," I said, blinking.

"Good. My head's playing tricks," he said. "I haven't felt this bad since that time I did some mushrooms with—" He stopped talking.

The director dug into his pocket and pulled out a pill bottle. "Laura, when you get to your line about saving Owen's life for yours, you take your potassium iodide tablet and give it to him. Got it?"

"Got it," I said.

"And, Owen, you take it, okay?"

"Okay, wait. Do you want me to swallow it?" Owen asked.

"Of course, meta-acting. Anyway, it's just aspirin."

"It's what now?" Dylan asked, dropping the camera from his shoulder.

"Aspirin."

"I've been asking everyone for a pill, and you had them all along."

"Yeah, do you need one?" the director asked.

"You're an asshole," Dylan said, holding out his hand for the bottle.

"You can't say that to me," the director said.

"Why not?"

"You know who I am."

"Yeah, I don't care. I'm done. I'll do commercials for the rest of my life. I'm fine with that," Dylan said, grabbing the bottle of aspirin out of the director's hand and taking more than the recommended dose.

"Can we get this done so I can go and die now?" I asked, laying my head on Owen's shoulder.

"Okay?" the director said, holding out his hand for the aspirin bottle.

"Okay," Dylan said, chucking the bottle at the director's head.

"Well, wasn't that mature."

"Wasn't that mature," Dylan mimicked. He put the camera back on his shoulder and pointed it toward Owen and me.

"Action!"

"Are we not going to practice?" I asked.

"Cut! No, I'd thought we'd wing it. And action!"

"Really?" Owen asked. "Not one time?"

"Cut! Honestly, guys, I thought we wanted to get off this mountain for real food, and clean clothes, and a bath, because we all need a bath."

"Okay," Owen said.

"Okay," I said.

The bus driver was outside throwing up what sounded like his insides, but Freddy, Terrence, and Tyson went over to Max and sat and watched as I died.

"Okay, everyone, read. Okay, I'll take the silence as an affirmative. And action!"

INT. FALLOUT SHELTER—AFTERNOON

HANK is blind. HELEN sits beside him. She rubs her thumb against the back of his hand. They are the only ones in the room. The rest have decided to put on gas masks and go exploring into the new wasteland.

HELEN lays her head on HANK's shoulder.

HELEN wasn't supposed to come to this shelter. HANK invited her. There are only enough supplies for a certain number of people. HELEN doesn't even have a gas mask.

> HELEN
> I'm sixteen years old, and I'm going to die in an atomic war.

> HANK
> No, you're not.

HELEN fixes his bandages over his eyes.

> HELEN
> Yes, I am.

> HANK
> No, we all are going to live.

> HELEN
> Please.

There is only one potassium iodide tablet

left. It is supposed to help against radiation poisoning. HANK has given the pill to HELEN, but she is unwilling to take it. She loves him so much.

HELEN lifts the bandages off HANK's eyes and looks at his dead eyes. She moves his head to face hers.

> HELEN
> I love you.

HANK smiles.

> HELEN (CONT'D)
> I can't take the pill. It's meant for you.

HELEN kisses him. She holds the tablet between her fingers. They stop kissing.

HANK brushes the hair behind her ear with his fingers.

HELEN kisses him again, and when she stops for a second, she pops the tablet into his open mouth.

> HELEN (CONT'D)
> Swallow, please.

> HANK
> No.

HANK starts to spit the tablet out, but
she puts her hand over his mouth.
                    HELEN
        I love you. I want you to live.

                    HANK
                    But—

                    HELEN
                    Please.

HANK nods and swallows.

HELEN and HANK kiss.

HELEN fixes HANK's bandages over his eyes.

HELEN snuggles up against him, her breath
shallow. She closes her eyes and waits to
die.

                            FADE TO BLACK.

Chapter Thirty-Eight

"I'd like to say this is garbage. I really like you, Owen, but I would have taken the pill," I said.

He laughed.

"I'm not joking," I said. "When the apocalypse does come, I hope that you do realize, in life-threatening situations, we girls don't always think of the cute boy."

"Thank you, Gloria Steinem Junior," the director said, clapping. "I think that was the best dying scene I ever filmed."

"Thanks, I think."

"Now can we get off this damn mountain?" Dylan said.

"Yes," we said in unison.

We packed up the few belongings we had and exited the cave. The fireworks had stopped and it was eerily quiet. And dark, really dark. It was way too early for the sun to be setting.

"Let's get back to Griffin Flat before it gets dark. Have we been here that long?" Freddy asked, looking at his watch. "Ten-ten. My battery died."

The keys were in a whole lot of brush along the side of Crow Mountain. And no one was willing to risk their lives to go get them.

"I know the Wright family is down getting nuked on Sixth Street, I know they have an extra car, and I know where they keep the key," Max said.

"What kind of car?" Freddy asked.

"It goes *vroom-vroom beep-beep*. What more do you need to know?"

"How far?"

"A good mile and a half."

Everyone growled.

Dylan handed Tyson his camera. "I'll try to hot-wire the bus," Dylan said.

"Why did you wait until now to say something?" the director asked.

"We were about to hike it to the Wrights," Terrence said.

"Hike?" the director said.

"Ugh, do you want me to do it or not?" Dylan asked.

We nodded.

We watched him do what we'd all seen in movies or on TV shows. He removed the panel and tried manually turning the ignition switch with a screwdriver, and surprisingly it worked.

"Good, I don't have to strip wires to hot-wire," Dylan said, sitting in the driver's seat. "I'm guessing you want me to drive too."

"No, no, I've got it," the bus driver said, wiping his mouth on his sleeve. "I'm the only one sober to drive."

The bus didn't have quite the power it did when we'd arrived on the mountain, but we had the downward momentum and just coasted until we reached the bottom. We turned on the interstate and headed back to Griffin Flat.

Interstate 40 was deserted. There were no automobiles or semis. It was strange. It felt strange. The air was thick with dust, and the bus driver had to turn on the fog lights.

Everyone was quiet and looking out the windows. The trees had been stripped of their leaves and bark. And huge areas where trees once stood were now barren.

"Where's your camera, Dylan?" the director asked. "We need to get this on tape. It would be perfect as transition material."

"How did Skeet do this?" I asked.

"Don't you understand how this works?" Dylan asked.

"Apparently I don't. Because it looks like he blew up half the state."

"Well, of course it does. He's the best in the business," the director said.

The bus driver used the windshield wipers to clear away the black soot.

Dylan grabbed his camera and went to the bus steps. He pried open the door as we drove down the interstate—the only one—and filmed the desolate wasteland that was known as Central Arkansas. The smell of rotting trash filled the bus. We covered our noses with our jackets. Like that did any good.

"Guys, my eyes," Owen said, leaning his head up against the seat in front of him.

"Can you please stop your complaining? I've lost three teeth. Do you understand how much time that is going to take to get fixed?" Freddy asked, climbing on his seat to turn to stare at him.

"Wow," Max mouthed, looking at me from across the aisle. "You made out with him." He smiled. "Yeah, you did." He held out his hand for a high five. "Don't leave me hanging."

I slapped his hand away.

A bloodcurdling scream echoed throughout the bus and made the bus driver swerve. It knocked me against the window and made Terrence hit his chin on the seat back. And Dylan almost went splat on the concrete highway as we zoomed at a respectable seventy miles per hour.

"What the hell?" Tyson said, looking at Owen.

I made my way up the aisle and almost lost my lunch. Terrence did. He had a weak stomach.

"My eyeball just fell into my lap," Owen got out, whimpering.

"That's not normal," Freddy said.

"We need to get him to a doctor," I said. "Keep going to Conway. Don't stop in Russellville. For the love of God, don't stop in Russellville."

The bus driver pressed on the gas, and he topped the max speed for a yellow school bus, which was eighty.

"Going to die, we are, hmmmmmmmm," Max said in his Yoda voice.

"I'm fine," Owen said. "I'm fine."

"You're not fine," I said.

"That's not an eyeball," Freddy said, picking up the so-called eyeball. "It's just a bloody, balled-up bandage."

Max went up to Owen's seat, lifted the bandage, and poked him in both eyes.

Owen screamed.

"I'm not a doctor, but I can say with certainty that you still have both eyes," Max said.

"That hurt, asshole."

"Yeah, but it's better to know, right?"

Owen closed his eyes and leaned his head back on his seat.

"False alarm. We don't need to go to the hospital," Freddy said. "He's still got both eyes."

"I still can't see a damn thing," Owen whispered.

"Well, don't worry, neither can I," the bus driver said, turning into the right lane.

We were almost home.

"Insane how it spread this far," Dylan said, still filming the outside.

"This is going to cost us a hell of a lot of money," the director replied.

Griffin Flat was the next exit.

"The first thing I'm going to do is get out of these awful clothes and into something—" Freddy stared out the window. "Clean," he said, finishing his thought.

We got off the interstate and turned right at the stop sign, and around the sharp corner that nearly knocked Dylan out of the bus again. The bus driver had to dodge abandoned cars as he swerved onto Sixth Street.

There was smoke everywhere. The crew had set fire to a couple of old buildings on Sixth Street, and the blaze had spread. There was glass everywhere from broken windows. Citizens of Pikesville, aka Griffin Flat, were walking around in a daze with shaved bald heads, prosthetic latex scar tissue, and burn marks affixed to their faces, plastered with coats of artificial mud and dressed in tattered clothes and coughing up movie blood and their oatmeal-coated guts due to their faking radiation sickness.

Dylan kept filming, but the director looked a little sick. "Like I said, this is going to cost us a hell of a lot of money."

Hours after the atomic bomb falls on Pikesville, rescue squads are dispatched to scour the area for stragglers to get them to shelters. Danger is imminent. The deadly cloud of radioactive particles, invisible to the naked eye, will soon blanket the town.

Eve of Destruction, *Book, page 175.*

Chapter Thirty-Nine

The road to the fairgrounds was blocked. A huge sign, written in capital letters—THE END IS HERE—was crudely spray-painted with an X.

"What's going on?" I asked, sitting up straight.

"I think the explosion was worse than we thought," Dylan said, shutting the bus door with one hand and then grabbing the handle to help him up. He went back to his seat.

"Bet it looks great on film, though," the director said. "I bet Popeye got great footage."

Popeye was the other camera guy. Not his real name. They called him that because he smelled like spinach. He was the one who got all the footage from Main Street.

While the director talked Oscar nominations and award speeches, I was wondering when and how and, more importantly, who was going to rebuild our town.

I bet Mayor Hershott was angry. But I also bet he already had a plan. He always had plans. They just were never really executed well.

The bus driver put the bus in park and pulled the lever to open the door. He was the first one off the bus. The director followed him, along with Dylan and Freddy. Terrence helped Owen off, then Max, Tyson, and me. But I turned around and grabbed the screwdriver from the ignition. Protection. Just in case. I hid it in my coat pocket and ran to catch up with the group. The smell was intoxicating. And that wasn't a good thing.

The gate that used to be there was gone, like it had disintegrated. Same went for the fence and the golf carts, and the trailers.

"What the hell happened?" Freddy asked the director, who was just as dumbfounded.

The explosion took out everything.

We did a walk-through. Nothing was there. We spent most of the time going, "That was there, and that was there, and that was there." Even the Ferris wheel was now gone too. The shell of a minivan was left standing, though. It was Kitty's and Raymond's van. They made it back here. But where were they?

"Kitty? Raymond?" I yelled.

We searched all over, but there wasn't a soul here. The director looked for a place to sit, but there was no place to sit except the ground. And no one wanted to sit on the ground.

I held the screwdriver out in front of me for protection.

"Is anyone here? Anyone at all?" Tyson yelled.

No one responded. It was strange. I thought I saw a cockroach as big as my head—but on further thinking about it, it probably was just a shadow—but anyway, I wasn't paying attention, and I tripped on debris and almost face-planted.

I screamed and nearly fainted. Max grabbed a stick, and we all ran over to where they were.

Max pointed.

I screamed.

Freddy too.

The bus driver passed out.

Terrence and Tyson threw up.

Dylan filmed it all.

"Is that—a body?" I asked. "Was that a person?"

Max nudged it with a stick, and then he walked over to it. It was hard and made a hollow noise. A human being wouldn't make that noise.

The director bent over and touched the crusted black thing with his hand. "I think it's a mannequin."

Everyone took a deep breath and laughed.

These explosions that Skeet built had done more damage than anyone thought.

We got back on the bus. I handed the screwdriver to the bus driver, and he started the engine. There was nothing left for us here. Freddy was crying. He lost all those video games and his console in the explosion. But I didn't know who was more distraught, him or Terrence.

We went back to Sixth Street.

The director ran up to a few people who were out, trying to ask them what happened. Where Skeet was. Where the rest of his cast was at. But they just stared at him. Black eyes. Like all the life was sucked out. Or a gag order had been put in place.

"Ma'am," the director called, "can you tell me if you've seen any of my crew?"

She looked up at him and burst into tears and ran down the sidewalk.

"Well, that can't be good."

Dylan was filming all of this.

"Wait!" the director yelled, and we stopped dead in our tracks. "How stupid are we? Filming has to be going on. We better get out of the shot."

He moved across the street and we followed. Stood underneath an awning waiting to hear "cut." But "cut" never came.

"It was supposed to be a long sequence," the director said.

Dewayne's store was just down the way. Next to Dane's Ice Cream Shoppe. The windows were broken out and trashed.

Comic books were torn, wet, or burned. I dug through the pile and found one that was in okay condition. I stuffed it in my bag.

Terrence came out from the café and passed out candy bars. One for each of us.

We ate and went searching for more. This time we found Cokes, which we drank with our second candy bar. And a pair of sunglasses for Owen. We waited for a while until Max said we could go to school, and according to the clock above the cash register, school was in session, but closer inspection revealed the clock had died at exactly 10:05. There had to be a logical explanation. We climbed onto the bus and went to school.

There would be no miracle. An atomic bomb had hit the city. A blast wave had crumbled buildings and buried its citizens. A dark mushroom cloud had spread over the sky. Much of the country had been devastated by massive atomic attacks. The small town of Pikesville had not escaped unharmed.

Eve of Destruction, *Book, page 180.*

Chapter Forty

Being at school when we didn't have to be at school was a new experience. Unique. And I could tell Terrence especially didn't like it. But then we saw light—specifically candlelight coming from the chemistry classroom—that told us there had to be other people here too. As in alive and possibly able to tell us what the hell had happened while we were on the mountain.

Terrence and I went down the hall while the rest of them went searching for food in the cafeteria.

We found Rodney in a fetal position underneath the lab table where he and Max, just days before, had been doing science experiments. (Or Max had been, and Rodney had been on the verge of burning the school down with a spark from the Bunsen burner.) Rodney was shaking. He had a cut on his forehead, and both arms were bloody.

"Damn, man, what happened?" Terrence asked, kneeling down beside him.

Rodney shook his head.

"Where is everyone?" I asked, grabbing Terrence's shoulder as I knelt beside him.

"Come on, man, you're safe now," Terrence said, trying to reassure him.

But all Rodney did was give one short laugh.

"Where's everyone? Where's Mr. Truitt?" I asked, grabbing his face with both hands.

He sat there, legs stretched out, hands on his knees, staring at me.

"Laura, did you die?" he asked, his voice shaky.

"Yeah, I died."

"It's just a movie," he said, and then repeated, "It's just a movie. It's just a movie."

"Come on, man," Terrence said, slapping him across the face.

"What the hell, man," Rodney screamed, rubbing his cheeks.

"Is everything okay?" Freddy asked, standing in the doorway with Owen, the director, and Dylan, who had tons of food in their arms.

"Let's eat," Owen said, his hand on Freddy's coat.

Rodney joined us around two lab tables, surrounded by candlelight, eating bread and peanut butter, and drinking water out of a jug.

"Boy, are you in here? Bollocks, you all are alive," Astrid screamed, her arms open, her eyes bloodshot, and her hair a mess, which the director pointed out. She gladly showed him the bird.

"Why wouldn't we be?" the director asked.

"Ugh, the explosion kind of got out of hand," she said, peering over our shoulders and seeing the food. "I'm so hungry. He went looking for food and I guess found all of you."

"Here," I said, spreading some peanut butter on a piece of bread, folding it in half, and handing it to her.

"Thanks," she said, chewing with her mouth full. "So good."

She sat between me and Max and told us a fantastic tale that had to be exaggerated, because it couldn't be true.

"I'm going to set the scene: It was a sunny June day. We stood outside in our summer dresses on Main Street as Mayor Forte was telling us that we shouldn't freak out when we hear sirens, that it's only a test for a possible Red Warning," she said.

"Are you giving us a synopsis of the script?" I asked.

"No."

"Are you giving us a synopsis of the novella?"

"No."

"Are you—"

"Shhhhhh."

I zipped my lips.

"There were a lot of people waiting for Skeet to do his thing, which he did, and it was, like, so awesome. The sirens blared, and he counted down to one, and then the strangest thing happened. I've experienced nothing like that in all my life. He started screaming 'Oh shit' over and over again and telling us to run. The sirens were blaring and things were exploding. The next thing I know, my arm is being grabbed, and some chap is pulling me toward the school."

"Huh?" Max asked.

"Yeah, I found this chap Rodney, right? We went into the basement and through this huge door. There were cots and blankets and smelled—so much potpourri. There were shelves and shelves of canned food. Rodney went searching for a can opener. But there was water and a few cartons full of Cokes. There're books and medical supplies."

"Medical supplies?" Freddy asked. "Owen needs some medical supplies."

"So does Rodney," Terrence said.

"The fallout shelter. You found the fallout shelter in the basement," I said.

"Yeah, want to go?" she asked, standing up. "But bring the bread and peanut butter. We can't find the can opener."

"I think I can help with that," the bus driver said, pulling out his Swiss Army knife.

"Go, you," Astrid said, smiling, without a tinge of sarcasm.

Before we went downstairs to the fallout shelter, Max took Dylan to the A.V. Club closet to get a few unopened videotapes, and I stopped at my locker to grab a composition notebook. In case Dylan couldn't get the tapes to work, I decided I would write everything down for posterity. Heck, it might make a great comic one day.

During the day, when the sun was shining and the power was on, the stairs were really scary, but I could contest they were much scarier now.

The vault door was made of some type of thick metal. I had no idea what kind. You had to watch that you didn't slam your hand in the door because it would close fast and hard. They had it propped open with a chair and desk and a bookcase.

History:

The fallout shelter was built in 1962 but last year was remodeled. It was practically the entire basement. It was large enough to fit all of us students (remember Griffin Flat wasn't that big of a town, so there wasn't a lot of procreation), plus teachers and staff. It also had nonperishable items, medical supplies, cots, blankets, flashlights, candles, and radios. Everything that Astrid had said and more.

"Where's everyone else?" Terrence asked.

"What do you mean?" Astrid asked. "There's no one else, at least not here."

Rodney wouldn't look anyone in the eye. He held his flashlight up to the ceiling. It was painted blue, I guessed to remind everyone who had to be in here when the bombs went off that the sky was blue.

We lit more candles around the room. Though it was dark and smelled of mothballs, it was dry.

"Don't you think we should close the door?" Astrid asked.

"Why?" Tyson asked.

"Because—"

"Are you afraid of the riffraff?" Terrence asked.

"No, it's just already crowded in here and—"

"Stop talking," Max said.

But Astrid didn't listen, and with all the strength she had in her body, she moved the chair and desk and the bookcase, closing the vault door with a slam.

We, all ten of us, were stuck.

Owen sat in the corner with a flashlight on his eyes. You could see the reflection of the light on his sunglasses. He still couldn't see. It was scaring him. To be honest, it was scaring me too. His eyesight should have been back by now.

Dylan was working with Max and the bus driver, trying to see which tapes were salvageable, while the director supervised. Astrid was supposed to be fixing their makeup, but she was focused on her chipped nail polish instead. Terrence, Freddy, and Tyson were in the corner discussing basketball, like boys did . . . or maybe like boys were supposed to do? I could tell this wasn't a normal conversation. Of course it wasn't. They were as scared as I was. But their pretend topic was the NBA draft in June. All three were talking over one another in a rapid stream-of-consciousness word-barf, arguing about who would have the greatest career: Hakeem Olajuwon,[1] Michael Jordan,[2] Charles Barkley.[3] Terrence's money was on the white boy, John Stockton.[4] Only Rodney was sitting under the makeshift

---

1 He played center for the University of Houston and was the overall first pick in the 1984 NBA draft. He plays for the Houston Rockets.

2 He's a professional basketball player. He's a shooting guard. He played for the University of North Carolina. He was drafted in the first round but the third pick for the Chicago Bulls.

3 He's a professional basketball player. He played for Auburn University. He's a power forward who was drafted in the first round and the fifth pick for the Philadelphia 76ers.

4 He's a professional basketball player. He's a point guard who played for Gonzaga University. He was drafted in the first round and was the 16th overall pick by the Utah Jazz.

window that had been painted yellow, like the sun was glistening in.

"Rodney, are you okay?" I asked, sitting beside him.

He didn't answer. He looked at me and shook his head.

"Rodney—"

He shook his head. "You won't believe me if I told you."

"Tell me."

He handed me a Polaroid. It was of a cloud—a mushroom cloud.

"This is a fake, right?" I asked.

He shook his head. "No, it's real."

"Astrid, did you see it too?" I called out from across the room.

"Oh, the cloud," she said with a giggle. "It's just from the bomb that Skeet did."

Dylan walked over to us and I handed him the Polaroid.

"Skeet's good, but not that good," he said.

"It's part of the film," the director said, taking his turn looking at the Polaroid.

"It's fake, as in—like, not real," Astrid said, picking at her nails.

"But the sirens," Rodney finally spoke.

"Were part of the film," the director said.

"But the Polaroid."

"Come on, don't be so naive," Astrid said.

"You're some dumb rich white girl from London, England, who's never encountered a real problem in your life. You're freaking out over your damn nails—" I stopped myself before I snapped.

"Are you insulting me?" she asked. "How dare you?"

Rodney took the Polaroid back. "This is real. This explosion wasn't just put on—it wasn't fake. I saw it with my own two eyes."

Everyone sat around him.

"I was standing on the sidewalk when the sirens went off."

Rodney was shaking and crying, wiping his nose with his shirt-sleeve. "But explosions were going off. I had taken my Polaroid camera. It was like the Fourth of July out there. But then it got quiet. A flash of light and then the loudest sound I've ever heard. I looked up into the sky and took one photo and ran. I grabbed her arm and ran into the school, down the hall, and down the stairs to here." He looked at the Polaroid.

"Where's everyone, then?" Tyson asked.

"Vaporized."

Chapter Forty-One

Everyone was in agreement.

This was real. The bomb was really a nuke. Hollywood wasn't playing some kind of prank. The cameras weren't filming, and the lines didn't call for this to happen.

"Unless—" Freddy said.

Strike that. We weren't in agreement.

Chapter Forty-Two

We had been debating how long we had to stay in this fallout shelter, if in fact that explosion wasn't just regular pyrotechnics, but a genuine nuclear detonation. Yes, as in a nuclear bomb exploding in our backyard. Fallout was radioactive. And we'd been outside. We'd breathed. And drunk. And were covered in radiation.

We were walking time bombs. Maybe it was just a test that went horribly, horribly wrong. Or maybe we were hit. Maybe Russia finally did it. Or maybe *we* finally did it, and Russia countered. A preemptive strike, to use technical jargon. I imagined missiles in the sky, carrying deadly payloads to their targets. X marked the spot. It was sure to end in thirty minutes or less. Just like Domino's Pizza.

The FEMA pamphlet said that we were to stay inside for two weeks—but the sign beside the vault door said five days, tops. We decided to make it six just to be safe.

We were probably out of our minds, but we didn't even know if this was really a nuclear missile exploding, or if Skeet had outdone himself. Skeet was talented. He said so himself. We had no idea if this was war. All we had was a Polaroid of a mushroom cloud in the distance of Main Street.

I think someone would have said something if we were under a nuclear attack. But maybe there wasn't time. It could have all been movie magic. The makeup department sure did a great job making us look like we were on the brink of death. The makeup on Astrid's cheeks was peeling.

If Country A launches an atomic bomb at Country B, and Country B counters with an atomic bomb, and Country C inadvertently sets off an atomic bomb at Country D, and Country E becomes collateral damage, what are the chances that citizens of the world realize that the leaders of the world are doing this war scare for propaganda purposes?

Eve of Destruction, *Book, page 2.*

Chapter Forty-Three

Day One
December 6
Who knows the time?
• • • • • • •

Freddy found the potassium iodide tablets tucked in the back of a drawer while we were looking for toilet paper. Let's just not talk about the bathroom situation. They didn't mention the bathroom situation smell in the FEMA pamphlet. Thankfully, whoever remodeled this place had the decency to put up a shower curtain, and not one of those clear ones but one of those decorative ones, so we couldn't see the person do their business, though the sounds were on another level. Radiation didn't stop bodily functions. In fact, it kind of made them worse, especially when we started adding blood to the equation. So we were happy when Freddy found the potassium iodide bottle.

Unlike the scene in the movie where I died—Helen

sacrificed her life for Hank to live—I wasn't going to make the mistake like Helen did. I was taking the pill.

"Everyone needs to take one," Freddy said, frowning. "Sadly, there are only nine pills for ten people. Someone will have to sacrifice their life for ours."

"Dude," Rodney said, "are you serious?"

We looked at one another and then at the bottle in Freddy's hand. He shook the pill bottle at us and smiled.

"Should we take a vote?" Astrid asked.

"Are you serious?" I asked.

"I say we let the crippled . . ." Astrid said, her voice trailing off while looking at Owen.

We all turned to him.

"Even though I can't see, I can feel all your eyes on me. Am I right?" he asked.

"No," we said in unison, lying.

"Liars," he said, crossing his arms.

Someone found a banana and tossed it at Terrence. It was dark, so I couldn't tell who.

"Okay, that's racist, and hell, no," Terrence said.

"Bananas have potassium," someone said, disguising their voice. "That's not racist."

Terrence peeled the banana and ate it. "Oh, that's racist, but I still want my damn pill."

"Since you all obviously want a pill, maybe we should—"

"Hell, no, no games, nothing," Max said, walking up and snatching the pill bottle out of Freddy's hand. He shook the bottle. It was full. "You are a bastard. A bastard that is most definitely going to hell."

"Dude, it's a joke," Freddy said, laughing.

Terrence grabbed the bottle out of Max's hand and started handing out pills. When he got to Freddy, even though they were friends, he considered not giving him one, but he did because it was the right thing to do.

Potassium iodide side effects include: stomach or

gastrointestinal problems, rashes, inflammation of the salivary glands.

We all had the side effects.

Also to note: there were no plans for what to do with the buckets after they were full.

RADIATION SICKNESS SYMPTOMS

- nausea and vomiting

- diarrhea

- headache

- fever

- dizziness and disorientation

- weakness, fatigue

- hair loss

- sloughing off of skin

- mouth ulcers

- infections

- low blood pressure

- skin burns

- dehydration

- bleeding from nose, mouth, gums, and/or rectum

Chapter Forty-Four

Day One (later)
December 6
Who knows the time?
• • • • • • •

We were digging through drawers and found some supplies that made us question our teachers' extracurricular activities. The condoms were a bit worrisome.

"What if we need to repopulate the earth?" Tyson asked.

"We won't need these, then," I said.

"But we might."

"Dude, did you pay attention in biology? You. Don't. Wear. Condoms. If. You. Want. To. Make. A. Baby."

"Classy," Astrid said, nodding.

I went back to digging in the drawers. Battery-powered radios. But we tried and kept trying to get a signal.

It had only been one day in here, and we were bleeding from

orifices that we hadn't thought could bleed, and the boys were still thinking with their penises.

Ugh.

"Oh, crap, crap, crap, crap, crap," Max said over and over again, pulling out a heavy green metal box. It had a handle and knobs and switches.

"Just say 'shit,' boy," Dylan said, curling up on his cot with a blanket. He had just spent a lot of time on the bucket.

"Okay, shit, shit, shit, shit, shit, better?"

"Much."

"That's a Geiger counter," I said.

"That's, like, from the old movies. That's not real," Astrid said.

"It's real."

"Like this?" she said, waving her arms about.

"If it goes off, then yes, it's real," I said.

"Turn it on," she said. "Turn it on."

Max didn't want to be the one who confirmed our worst nightmare. None of us did. I think we enjoyed the little oblivion that we were living in at the moment. Dylan finally gave up, threw his hands in the air, and told us to shut the hell up. He grabbed the Geiger counter, which had been put on the floor. He flicked the switch, and it buzzed. There was no denying it. Radiation. He moved around the room, placing the Geiger counter in front of each of us, and then himself. We were all radioactive. He turned it off.

For a while no one said a word. What was there to say? Our worst fears were realized. Whatever had happened out there had emitted radiation. And we'd gotten a high dose of it.

It was a leap from radiation poisoning to *X-Men*. But it was made. At least Rodney was optimistic.

Dead parents. Check.

A dose of radiation. Check.

Like the greats (Batman, Superman, Spider-Man, the Flash, Firestorm), we have our tragic backstory.

"We're the children of the atom," Rodney said, tearing a Razorback basketball T-shirt in half to cover his face from the fallout that he was convinced he was breathing in.

"No. I think that's our children," I said, picking at the dead skin on my thumb.

"This isn't fucking *X-Men*," Terrence said, slamming his empty water jug on the ground.

"Well, fuuuuuuck!" Rodney said.

"Fuck is right," Freddy said, grabbing a chunk of hair that had fallen from his head and stuffing it deep in his back pocket. "Was this supposed to happen?" he asked.

"Maybe they're messing with us. Maybe this is just good makeup," Astrid said, taking out her lipstick from her now brown-pink jeans.

"Damn," Freddy said, sticking his right index finger into a sore on Astrid's right cheek. "I can touch bone."

"Don't touch me!"

"Kitty is good but not that good." Freddy wiped his finger on his pant leg.

"But we were on the mountain, and we didn't get the seventy-five-dollar treatment," I said.

"Yeah, Laura's right," Terrence said.

"It doesn't matter now," Freddy said, tightening his ponytail, but all that did was cause his hair to break and fall to the floor.

"I'm one step closer to becoming Professor X," Rodney said.

For several days, Pikesville remained immobile. It was unclear what had happened. There was no message from the president. Was he alive? Did he make it to Mount Weather? Was there a cease-fire?

Eve of Destruction, *Book, page 185.*

Chapter Forty-Five

Day Two
December 7
Who knows the time?
• • • • • • •

Dylan, Tyson, and I were working on the shortwave radio that we found in the back of a closet. Dylan messed with the antenna. Max and the bus driver were working on the walkie-talkies. And the director was asking the same question over and over again: "This is Griffin Flat High School. This is Griffin Flat, Arkansas. Is there anybody there? Anybody at all?"

The walkie-talkies weren't working just like the radios weren't, but that didn't stop us from trying. We were trying anything. We didn't have anything to lose. When those six days were up, we didn't know what or who would be out there when we opened those doors.

We spent most hours in the day sleeping. Then reading. I read *Eve of Destruction* by Boudreaux Beauchamp to the group. When my voice got tired or I started coughing up blood, someone else took over. When we weren't reading or talking about TV shows or movies, we were forcing food down and trying to keep it down.

"Ugh," Astrid said, touching her armpits. She smelled her fingers, shook her head, and went back for another swipe. "I need a razor."

"Don't look at your legs," I said, looking at mine.

"I didn't even think about that. Kill me. I'm losing my hair on the top of my head but nowhere else."

"We're going to have to use Nair when we get home."

"And tweezers. My eyebrows are out of control."

Dylan hit the shortwave radio with his fist. It left his knuckles bloody, but we heard a little less static, and then we heard a man's voice.

"Broken Arrow," said a man.

"Copy that," said another man.

"Do they know that we can hear them?" Terrence asked.

"Doubtful," Dylan said, trying to make out what they were saying by messing with the signals.

The signal was kind of clear. Clear enough to let us eavesdrop on a conversation between two men.

Man 1: "Devastation?"

Man 2: "Affirmative."

Man 1: "Survivors?"

Man 2: "Negative."

Chapter Forty-Six

Day Two (night)
December 7
Who knows the time?
. . . .

"Nuclear war? There goes my sex life," Freddy said. Though we didn't say it out loud, we all agreed.

Tyson, Dylan, the director, and the bus driver were asleep, so they didn't hear us talking about sex. I was glad for that. That would have been awkward.

"I'm going to die a virgin," Astrid said.

"Wait—you're a virgin, really?" Max asked.

"Why would I lie about that?"

"But you're a movie star. You can do anyone you would like."

"I have standards—" Astrid started.

"What about Drake Cooper?" I asked.

"Ugh. Publicity. We barely held hands."

"Sex is good. Sex is fun. That's what Judy Blume says," I said.

"Who's a virgin? Raise your hand," Freddy said.

Only a few of us raised our hands. Sometimes it's easier to say you weren't even if you really were. So I didn't raise my hand.

"You're not a virgin?" I asked Terrence, who didn't raise his hand.

He shook his head.

"He's had sex with quite a few girls. Your friend Dana was one," Rodney said.

"Dana?" I said. "She never said. When?"

"At prom," Terrence said.

"Prom?" I went to prom with the boy who barfed on me in the second grade. There was no sex.

"And Kathy," Rodney said.

"Kathy? 'Jesus is my boyfriend' Kathy?" I asked.

Terrence nodded.

"That promiscuous whore."

"They're not whores," he said.

"I wasn't talking about them."

"It doesn't matter now. Impotence is a symptom of radiation. We won't have to worry about our sex lives," I said.

"Is that why it won't—never mind," Rodney said, sitting down on the cot next to Terrence, who scooted closer to the wall.

Chapter Forty-Seven

Day Three
December 8
Who knows the time?
• • • • • • •

What We Miss:

Laura: breathable air
Terrence: basketball
Max: homework
Astrid: teeth
Owen: sight
Freddy: two-ply toilet paper
Rodney: girls
Dylan: hair
Tyson: deodorant
Bus driver: television
Mr. Edman: giving orders

I'd like to point out that no one mentioned a person.

"Who wrote homework?" Freddy asked, looking over my shoulder. "Because honestly, of everything in the world, you miss homework?"

"It was me," Max said, raising his hand. "I miss a routine."

"Routine I get, but homework?"

"Yeah, that's a little insane," Terrence said.

Max walked toward me and tried to take the composition notebook out of my hands.

"No, you can't change it. So it is written. So it shall be done," I said.

Chapter Forty-Eight

Day Four
December 9
Who knows the time?
• • • • • • •

Famous Last Words:

"I remember this one time at camp, we would sit around the campfire and sing songs," Max said. "I'll start—"

Hi, my name is Joe
And I work in a button factory
I got a wife and two kids
One day, my boss, says, "Joe, are you busy?"
I said, "No."

MAKE IT STOP!!

Terrence found the tape player, batteries, and a tape rack. He didn't even look at the title or the artist. He just stuffed the tape into the slot, closed the door, and pressed PLAY.

We sat in silence, humming, and eventually singing along with Levon Helm and The Band to their hit "The Weight."[1]

We rewound the tape and sang again. And again. The Band was home. We eventually put in another tape and sang to that. You could tell a teacher put this fallout shelter together. It was full of '60s and '70s music.

For five minutes and fifty-five seconds, we forgot we were in whatever mess we were in and sang, matching pitch with Freddie Mercury.[2]

Was Beelzebub punishing us? We were probably reading too much into a song. Into all of this. We weren't at war. We weren't dying of anything. Maybe we all had the same bug. We were sick, that was it. Nothing bad happened, minus the explosion that made everyone . . .

Skeet outdid himself. That was it. That was all. Skeet was a master at the pyrotechnics. He was a master of the over-the-top game. We were fine.

We belted out "Bohemian Rhapsody"[3] like life depended on it. We even air guitared. And danced until we all puked from dizziness. Because we had a bug. That was all. A bug.

We dug for more and more music. It was hard to find something from this decade. But when we did, we rocked it hard. "Thriller" was appropriate. Even if we weren't exactly zombies, we were as close as we could get to the walking dead.

---

1 The Band, *Music from Big Pink*, Capitol Records, 1968. The Band is a staple around my house. The group formed in Canada, but Levon Helm is from Turkey Scratch, so yeah, we claim them.

2 One of the greatest singers of all time. He's the lead singer of Queen. And the greatest showman ever.

3 Queen, *A Night at the Opera*, Elektra, 1975.

Chapter Forty-Nine

Day Five
December 10
Who knows the time?
. . . .

No one could stop complaining. Everyone was bitching and bitching about anything and everything. It smelled in here. The food was awful. Why didn't we risk it and open the door? What was the point? We were all probably going to die anyway. That was the consensus. Apathy. I had heard of it when it came to the Hogs, but to life? But we had it. We were apathetic.

We talked about whether or not government officials had been whisked away to Mount Weather. If there was a designated survivor in place. It was funny thinking about that. We spent so much time practicing for drills under our desks. Making bomb shelters under the ground. Making sure we had supplies to last us days, months, years, until it was safe to go outside after the fallout. But how do we know it's safe? We don't test thermonuclear weapons on each other. We do it in the sea— or underground. We don't know the effects. How do we know Mount Weather will even work? They could all die.

We weren't talking. We were sitting on our own cots, staring at everyone but not saying a word. We were going to snap. We didn't have that much longer in here.

What the hell would we find after that?

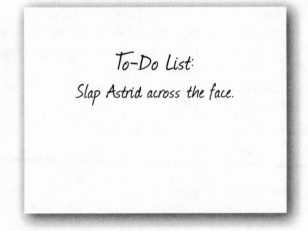

To-Do List:
Slap Astrid across the face.

To-Do List:

~~Slap Astrid across the face.~~

Chapter Fifty

Day Five (later)
December 10
Who knows the time?
• • • • • • •

"Shut the hell up, you wanker. Your voice is, like, so bloody annoying," she said. Her British accent was like a caricature at that point.

Everybody was getting on everybody else's nerves.

I was glad I slapped her across the face. But after I did, I noticed that her beauty mark was gone. I didn't mention it. I didn't want my head chewed off. I rubbed my palm. I slapped her harder than I'd been aiming to. But I did notice a brown mass on my middle finger. It wasn't there before I slapped her.

She coughed again in her hand, and blood smeared on her palm.

"Astrid," I said, getting down on my knees in front of her.

She spat on me, and a tooth flew out of her mouth and onto my dress.

"Oh, I don't feel so good," she said, leaning on Max.

I picked up her tooth and held it in front of her.

She laughed, taking it from me. "Did you know the tooth fairy teaches us to sell our body parts for money?" she said, throwing the tooth across the room.

"What happened to your mole?" I asked, straining to point out her flawless face.

She touched the spot where her mole once was. "It fell off," she said.

"Is that normal? Because that doesn't sound normal."

She sighed, kicked at my legs, and sat beside me and whispered, "It wasn't real."

"What?"

"It wasn't real, okay?"

"Again, what?" I asked.

"I was discovered in a department store—"

"By one of those you-can-be-a-supermodel-if-you-pay-me-a-hundred-bucks people?" I asked.

"No," she said, shaking her head.

"Sure."

"Hey, Cindy Crawford was discovered picking corn, so anything's possible."

"So the mole was fake?" I ask, poking at her face with my finger where the mole once was.

"Yeah, it was fake, and I prefer the term 'beauty mark.'"

"Call it what you want; it's still a mole. Witches have moles. Are you a witch?" I asked, laughing.

"Not a witch, but you're one with a *B*."

"Nice comeback," I said. "So why the mole?"

"It was chocolate."

"What?"

"I was eating a chocolate bar, and a piece of chocolate got stuck to my upper lip. My mum was with me, and she didn't tell me until it was over, but the damage was already done. The talent scout was super into Cindy and wanted another one just like her, beauty mark—"

"Mole."

"Beauty mark and all."

My stomach hurt from laughing so hard. "So you had to keep up the charade?"

"Every day since I was discovered in that department store."

"Every day you get up and put on a fake . . . beauty mark?"

"Every day."

"Tedious."

She nodded.

My mind was blown. To go that far for "beauty." I mean, I got it; it was a trademark look. Cindy Crawford wouldn't be Cindy Crawford without her mole. Madonna wouldn't be Madonna either.

"Now it won't be so tedious," I said. "Be you. Embrace the demolition."

She laughed. "I can't. It's my trademark."

"You're a good actress," I said.

She shook her head.

"Yeah, I'm being honest. I've seen everything that you've been in."

"That's sweet," she said.

"Why are you such a bitch?" I asked, something in me snapping.

"What? You can't talk to me like that."

"Oh, please forgive me for speaking the truth to you. I forgot that you live in a different world where people sugarcoat everything for you," I said. "Wait, didn't I already say this to you? No, no, even if I did, it still applies."

"Words cannot describe how unfathomably little I care about this—or you," she said, rolling her eyes.

"I'm not saying I hate you, but if you were on fire and I had water, I would drink it."

"Go to hell, you ingrate hick from Arkansas," she said, pronouncing Arkansas like "Ar-Can-Saw" in a southern twang that was so overly exaggerated that only a two-bit actor from Hollywood by way of London, England, could have mustered it.

I screamed at her. And she screamed back at me.

"Go to Arkansas, they said. It will be fun, they said. Well, they lied," she said, crossing her arms.

"I know aid workers who don't take their lives as seriously as you do," I said, glaring at her.

"Ugh, you are—"

"I am what?"

"Why are you two fighting? You were getting along so well," Freddy said, sitting down beside me on the cot next to Astrid's.

"She started it," I said, remembering a solid elementary school comeback.

"Oh, how lovely," she said, snapping her fingers at Max for help getting up off the cot.

"Leave my sister alone," Terrence said, leaving out the word *step*.

"And," she said, looking at Terrence and Freddy, who was standing right beside him, "stay away from me, you mean vigilante justice squad."

"What?" Terrence said, taking off his jacket. "Is it hot in here, or is it just me?"

"No, it is hot in here," Freddy said.

They started removing their clothes. So did Astrid. And so did I.

"Watch out, Owen, she's probably signing her name 'Mrs. Laura Douglas' on her secretly ordered stationery with her married monogram, like good southern girls do," Astrid said, holding on to Max.

"What the hell are you talking about?" I asked.

"I don't know. My head hurts."

Max led her to the other side of the room, but that didn't stop us from arguing.

"Laura, you've already gone to second base with Freddy," she said.

"How do you know that?" I asked.

"I'm Astrid Ogilvie. I know everything," she said.

"But she made out with Freddy up on the mountain," Max said.

"Shut it," I said, glaring at him.

Astrid started laughing. "Who haven't you made out with?" she asked in between breaths.

"I was drunk," I said.

"Yeah, we were drunk," Freddy said.

Max nodded. "His lips touched yours." He smiled.

"It was a drunken moment—"

"Of passion," Max finished for him.

"No, of stupidity."

"Hey—" I started.

"We've all been there," Owen said.

"But it was nice, and Laura, of course I would do it again," Freddy said with a wink.

"What just happened?" I asked.

"A love connection," Max said.

"No," Freddy and I said in unison.

"Okay, not a love connection," Max said.

"But I do blame Max," Freddy said.

"Excuses, excuses," she said.

"Hey!" Max screamed. "I didn't force you to drink it."

After that, we were quiet.

I was still angry with Astrid for bringing up Freddy. It was my own damn fault for drinking Max's family moonshine and making out with him. But that didn't mean that I didn't like kissing Freddy—because I did. He was a good kisser. Ugh. What was wrong with me?

"I think I found your mole," Max said, picking it up from the floor. He tried handing it back to Astrid but she swiped his hand away.

"It's a beauty mark," she said. "It's a bloody beauty mark."

Chapter Fifty-One

Day Five (later than that)
December 10
Who knows the time?
• • • • • • •

Max sat on a cot, picking at his teeth. He was crying so hard that snot was coming out of his nose. He had just realized that he was going to be stuck with braces for the so-called apocalypse.

The joke was on us, though.

Astrid and I got our periods. Thank God for the teachers who remembered to put tampons in the fallout shelter.

"How can you tell?" Freddy asked. "We're all bleeding from down there."

"But they're hemorrhaging from the vagina," Max clarified.

"I'll cut off your dick, and you won't have anything to beat on during the night. Yeah, we hear you, all night long," Astrid said.

Freddy retreated to the corner.

"No. She's got her period." Terrence nodded.

Once upon a time there was a scientist who wanted to kill millions of people. And the only way for the scientist to accomplish his plan was to come up with a capable invention.

Eve of Destruction, *Book, page 1.*

Chapter Fifty-Two

Day 6
December 11
Who knows the time?
· · · · · · ·

Everyone took another dose of potassium iodide. We couldn't tell if it was working or not. But did it matter? Everyone drank a Coke, and we toasted to our last night here—our last meal. We thought it was night. But for all we knew, it could be day. We picked out a can of food for each of us and took turns using the can opener that we'd found on the second day. And while we ate, we finished *Eve of Destruction*. The ones who had never read it wanted to know how it ended. It was bleak. Boudreaux Beauchamp did not write uplifting inspirational stories. The ending, though it gave hope, wasn't exactly a happily-ever-after tale. Rodney wanted a sequel.

We wanted to believe that there would be one for us—a sequel. Though it was undeniable that it would be different.

Dylan talked about the footage and how no matter what, he was going to put it together in some edit room and make it a movie. Even though it wasn't his job. He was a cinematographer, not a film editor. But we all would have to adjust.

Astrid wouldn't be on the cover of any magazine, unless it was for a medical journal. Freddy and Owen wouldn't be the leading men they hoped to be. Rodney, Max, Terrence, and I probably were *the* graduating class of 1986. All four of us. But Director Edman was the one who was adamant that his future wouldn't be so much different from what he had always lived. He was so sure that he would have a little gold statuette, an Oscar, in his future.

"We will be at the Academy Awards," he said. "Our names will be read."

"Yeah," Freddy said. "In the 'in memoriam' part of the show. They'll put our pictures and our profession."

I hoped that they wouldn't use my Jostens school picture.

Chapter Fifty-Three

Day Six (late)
December 11
Who knows the time?
. . . .

It was quiet. Most were passed out. The director and Dylan were going over final scene shots like this movie was going to get an ending. I sat by myself on a cot writing a letter to my future self. Mrs. Martin brought it up in the meeting when I got suspended—the second time in the last couple of weeks. She thought it would be therapeutic to put down all my feelings about what I thought would be the forthcoming apocalypse, but I hadn't gotten around to it. Now seemed like as good a time as any.

"Laura, you awake?" Terrence asked.

"Yes," I said above a whisper.

He stepped over legs and buckets and fell onto the cot next to me. "Sorry," he said.

"It's okay," I said, rubbing my head. He didn't give me this headache, but it still throbbed just the same.

"What do you think it will be like?" he asked.

"What do you mean?"

"I mean, out there?"

I shrugged. "But studies have said and then movies have shown that—"

"We don't know, is what you're saying," he said, interrupting me.

"Yeah."

"But it will probably be hell."

"Yeah, hell."

We sat there for a while in silence by candlelight. Then he grabbed my hand and squeezed.

"You know our parents are probably dead," he said.

"I know."

"We are probably the only family we have left."

I squeezed his hand. "You'll always be my brother."

"And you're my nerd of a sister."

I laid my head on his shoulder and closed my eyes. We'd need our sleep. We had no idea what was waiting for us on the outside of this fallout shelter.

"Terrence, I don't want to die," I said finally.

"Me either."

Chapter Fifty-Four

Day 7 (We Rest)
December 12
Who knows the time?
• • • • • • •

We didn't want to go outside, but we didn't want to stay in here.

They said cockroaches were the only thing that would survive. That didn't give us much hope. Staying put in here, even if it smelled like shit and vomit and urine, meant safety. We didn't know if safety would be guaranteed if we went outside.

"In the first issue of *Teenage Mutant* we meet Destiny with powers so great from a nuclear bomb that she can do anything. We could be like her. We were all touched by radiation. But to fulfill our potential, we need to leave this fallout shelter," I said.

"Are you trying to rah-rah us up about opening the vault door?" Astrid asked.

"Well, I was trying. Is it working?"

"No."

"I can quote another," I said, thinking.

"Stop. I'm embarrassed for you," she said.

"Did you just quote a comic book?" Terrence asked.

"Yes, I did," I said. "Mine—one of the best superheroes ever."

We gathered what we wanted to take with us. My *Nuke Me* tote bag was full of first aid supplies, food, and other necessary items.

"We might have to hoof it to find civilization," I said.

"Find civilization?" Terrence asked. "You're making this sound like some stupid science fiction plot to some bad movie."

"Wait—hoof?" Astrid asked.

"Walk," Max defined for her.

"Why didn't you just say that?"

"It's a saying," I said.

"Again, your American idioms," she said, shaking her head.

"We don't know what's outside. It could be fine or—" Tyson said.

"It's fine," the director said.

"But the radio said—" I started to say, but was cut off by the director going on a tirade about the government and propaganda.

"It was touch-and-go through the first two periods, but I knew that everything would be okay when Mike Eruzione scored his famous third-period goal to put the Americans ahead. Do you believe in miracles?" Rodney asked.

"Hockey?" Freddy asked.

"It was the Olympics—against the Russians. USA . . . USA . . . USA!"

We chanted "USA" like some insane glorified patriotic crazy person. But it helped. Did we believe in miracles? Yes, of course we did. Everything could have been fine outside. Everything could have been normal outside. Like some crazy adventure. A Hollywood joke.

"It doesn't matter—we've got to go," the bus driver said.

"What he said. I've got to find a bathroom with privacy."

"Privacy." Max sounded it out for Astrid the proper American way. Like all Americans do with tact and understanding. (That was sarcasm.)

"Let's get the hell outta Dodge," Dylan said.

Terrence, with the help of Rodney, grabbed the handle on the vault door and waited until it was time. We had a moment planned. Dylan turned on the camera and filmed our exit. The director stood behind him, giving direction. One of the last scenes for the movie that might never be.

Tyson stuffed the tape that he chose for the moment the vault door opened into the tape player.

"And action!"

At the moment the vault door opened, the director pressed PLAY. The volume was turned to full blast, and "We Are the Champions"[1] echoed throughout the hall.

We stepped outside the fallout shelter.

Astrid walked out first. Freddy helped Owen; he was Owen's eyes. Rodney, Terrence, Max, and I followed behind. The bus driver and Tyson were in the rear, but the director was the last one to leave. He didn't want to be in the shot. It was our moment. The eleven of us. What started as a novella about four people turned into a story about eleven. Eleven different people all on a journey of destruction. That sounds cheesy and sappy, and for that I am sorry.

It was quiet. The air smelled of burning flesh and, surprisingly, burnt popcorn. But once we got upstairs and to the front door, we saw we weren't alone. There had been an invasion—by the United States Air Force.

We stopped on the stairs that led to the charred ground where the flagpole once stood. A man in a protective suit, including gloves and a gas mask, was raising an American flag. Dylan was filming it all, including the helicopters that flew in the sky. A perfect backdrop. The director patted Dylan on the back, probably

---

1 Queen, *News of the World*, Elektra, 1977.

thanking him for thinking of the perfect visual ending to this horrific story.

The men, probably soldiers, carried guns, and they were pointed at us. The soldiers were also wearing protective gear. But we kept walking toward them. We were dirty. We smelled. We probably didn't look like human beings.

Rodney was walking with a limp and leaning over in pain. He was moaning. He had been for a while. Stomach problems. We all had them.

"Shit," I heard a soldier yell.

"Copy," yelled another before he shot Rodney twice in the head. "Confirmed kill."

Rodney fell to the ground.

"What the hell?" someone yelled, and we ran toward Rodney. We could have been shot too, for all we knew.

The soldier who shot Rodney was getting screamed at by a superior officer. The soldier had yelled "shit," not "shoot," like the soldier had thought he heard. The word *zombie* was thrown around. We didn't look human—but we were still alive. We weren't the walking dead. But Rodney was dead.

The ten of us circled around his lifeless body. To survive a fake but real whatever-the-hell-happened, only to be killed by a gun? What were the odds?

In the summer of the Year of the Horse, meaning 1954, three individuals did the unthinkable: they ventured onto the streets of Pikesville in search of the truth—and to find food.

The following is all that remains of the ordeal. What you are about to read is real and may not be suitable for those who suffer from nucleomituphobia.

Eve of Destruction, *Book, page 1.*

In the fall of the Year of the Rat, meaning 1984, ten individuals did the unthinkable: they ventured onto the streets of Griffin Flat in search of the truth—and to find food.

The following is all that remains of the ordeal. What you are about to read is real and may not be suitable for those who suffer from nucleomituphobia.

—Paraphrased by Laura Ratliff

Chapter Fifty-Five

"Now we are all sons of bitches," I said, holding Terrence's hand.

"That's a good line," the director said. "Can I use that? I'll credit you."

"Sure, but Kenneth Bainbridge, an American physicist, said that to Robert Oppenheimer after the Trinity test. You should probably credit him."

The director patted me on the shoulder.

Dylan had been filming but was ordered to stop by the United States Air Force. They took away the camera and confiscated the tape that Dylan had on him.

"Ugh to literally everything about this," he said. "I say we flood the world and start over."

"I think we did," I said.

"That's a wrap," Mr. Edman said, wiping his eyes. What would have been his greatest feature was being taken away from him, and all he could do was cry.

I hid my composition notebook in my bag, along with the

tapes that belonged to Dylan. I wrapped them in dirty radiated socks. I had a feeling that the soldiers would freak out when they saw the camera. They wouldn't look. I hoped they wouldn't look. They would confiscate them and my composition notebook over my dead body. I could just imagine all the black marks. They would have sanitized, classified, redacted, all meaning the same thing—erased. There wouldn't be anything left. Though it would have been hard for them to put a black mark over the state of Arkansas.

We asked what happened. All they said was, "We can neither confirm nor deny." We asked them if we all could have a mask. A soldier said, "You don't need them."

"Well, give me yours, then, if we don't need them," Freddy said.

But the soldier wouldn't.

Two soldiers took Rodney's body away. They wrapped it in a white tarp. His hand was sticking out. We didn't have to ask where they were taking it. We saw. A huge dump truck. It was full of bodies.

"How to dig your own grave in three easy steps," Max said.

We laughed. We shouldn't have. But everything was just so surreal.

"Gallows humor indeed," Mr. Edman said.

We stood in a circle, being doused with water from a truck. It was cold but kind of comforting. It had been a while since we had felt the touch of water on our bodies.

"Undress," a soldier said.

"What happened?" Terrence asked.

"Classified."

"Bullshit," I said, then screamed.

We started to undress. There were no partitions. We left our underwear on.

"Where are you from?" I asked.

"Texas," the soldier said.

"Texas? Why did they bring in Texas?" Terrence asked.

"Well, those there are from Oklahoma, and those over there are from Kansas, and those back there are from New Mexico. So we're not all from Texas."

"You can't tell us what happened at all?" I asked. "We are the ones who lived through it."

"We have a Polaroid of a mushroom cloud," Max said, and I gave him a death glare.

The soldier kept on doing his job, but the word *mushroom* did get him to lower his guard a little while a superior of his came and took away my bag

"We nuked ourselves," the soldier whispered.

"We did what to ourselves?" I asked.

"It was an accident." That was all he said.

Dylan and the director looked at each other like they were speaking telepathically. Lots of shaking of heads and nodding.

Bombs accidentally being dropped on our soil? Not that it'd be any less tragic to bomb someone else, of course, but it was so much more embarrassing to have done it to ourselves. Now everything that my dad wrote in that letter that was redacted made sense. It was a warning.

"Is the base still in Little Rock?" I asked the soldier.

At first I thought he was confused by my question, but then he shook his head.

Terrence walked through the puddles and mud and hugged me.

I got dizzy. The thought of no one surviving was logical, but it didn't mean that it was believable. Mom, Dennis, and Dad—*gone?* Granny, Pops, Ms. Wilcox, all my teachers, and Kevin, Chuck, Kathy, and Dana too? My knees buckled and I slowly dropped to my knees. The soldier grabbed one of my arms and Terrence grabbed the other, but still my butt touched the radiated ground. My eyes closed.

I didn't remember anything after that.

• • •

I came to in the back of an ambulance with an oxygen mask on my face and an IV in my arm. I looked to my left and saw Terrence staring at me. He had an IV in his arm too.

"Fluids," he said, lifting his arm. "You okay?" he asked.

I nodded, taking off the oxygen mask and laying it beside me. "Is it true?" I asked. "I mean, our parents—are they really dead?"

"Yes," he whispered, nodding. "There are not a lot of survivors."

I wanted to cry. I was supposed to cry. But I couldn't. I was still in shock. I sat up on the gurney and stared at him.

"We're the only family we've got now," Terrence said, taking my hand, tears running down his cheeks.

When I saw him cry I started to cry.

Freddy, Max, Astrid, Dylan, Mr. Edman, and the bus driver filed into the ambulance and sat beside Terrence and me on the two gurneys.

"Through all the darkness and tribulations, the hopelessness and lack of remorse—the trumpeting sound of the apocalypse that fills throughout the heavens, remember . . . we as a race will persevere. We will find a way, a way to make things worse. We will persevere," I said.

"Is that from another one of your comic books?" Astrid asked.

"Yes."

"Well, it's kind of comforting."

I think that was when we all realized that all of us, at least the ones who lived here, probably didn't have any family left.

"Do we seriously want to survive this? Like, seriously?" Astrid asked, shaking.

It didn't matter if we wanted to or not. We did, at least for a moment, but we were in a *Mad Max* wasteland now.

"Now what?" she asked.

"Well, haven't you seen *Planet of the Apes?*"[1] Max said. "Exactly like that."

"Honestly," she said, slapping Max on the arm.

"You finally, really did it. You maniacs! You blew it up! God damn you! God damn you all to hell!" Freddy said, raising a fist in the air.

"Nice," Terrence said, nodding.

"I thought we needed a great closing line for a movie that we didn't get to finish."

"Oh, we'll finish it," said the director. "If it's the last thing I do."

Eve of Destruction was just a movie about average people going about their day as usual until the unthinkable happened on the day they accidentally nuked Arkansas.

---

1 A 1968 science fiction film directed by Franklin J. Schaffner and starring Charlton Heston, Roddy McDowall, Maurice Evans, Kim Hunter, James Whitmore, James Daly, and Linda Harrison. Astronauts wake up from a deep hibernation and discover that it's no longer 1972 but instead the year 3978—and they haven't aged a day, well, except for Stewart. She's dead and decayed due to a crack in her sleep pod. The remaining crew departs the spaceship and wanders around the planet where they crash landed, encountering talking apes and humans being imprisoned. At the end they discover that the strange planet was home all along. Damn y'all to hell!

The best they could do was to hope that the apocalypse and post-apocalypse wouldn't be as bad as anyone imagined. But if they were, the human race would adapt—as it always had—and survive.

Eve of Destruction, *Book, page 199.*

And with a big, loud bang, everything is gone. A bright white light flashes over the landscape of Griffin City. A mushroom cloud fills up the atmosphere. A firestorm sweeps across the land. Buildings explode, burn, and crumble. People are vaporized—their skin melts and their skeleton disintegrates into dust. After, there are human monsters, scarred with radiation burns and charred skin. As time passes, people lose their hair. Blackened bodies litter the rubble where buildings once stood. Animal carcasses flood farms. A white ash covers every inch of the city. Society crumbles much like the concrete and steel. Vandalism and murder are the norm. There is no electrical power; medical care, food, and water are almost nonexistent. But Destiny got lucky, as she was locked in the cellar below Old Barnaby's Farm with a few of her friends.

For seven days Destiny and her new ragtag group of mutants lived, argued, and tried to survive. But not everyone made it out alive. Fallout was too strong for some immune systems. And the one shining light in the cellar, the one who was nice to everyone, the one who had a wicked layup, was found drooling blood. Rodney died in Destiny's arms. A single tear rolled down her cheek as Rodney's body shook from the radioactive particles as they took hold in his bloodstream. Sadly, he didn't get his mutant powers.

Destiny knew that Rodney would not die in vain. She would make it her life's mission to avenge his death. Though she wouldn't know the extent of her powers until she was called to save the city from unknown forces that seek to destroy what is left. She is a mutated child of a new revolution called to protect the future—and the future is now.

Max Randall and Laura Ratliff. "Origin Story," Teenage Mutant #1 (December 1984).

The End Is Here.

ECONOMY PICTURES

ALBERT BURG FILMS PRESENTS
in Association with ECONOMY PICTURES

A Norman Edman Film

Astrid Ogilvie • Owen Douglas
EVE OF DESTRUCTION
with Freddy White

Music by	Wanda and Dale Fisher
Costume Designer	Raymond Sinclair
Film Editor	Melvin Meyers
Production Designer	Dolores Granger
Director of Photography	Dylan Paige
Executive Producers	David Seed and Robert Burton
Produced by	Bruce Coleman and Anthony Dillard
Based on the Novella by	Boudreaux Beauchamp
Screenplay by	Eddie Payne
Directed by	Norman Edman

We are grateful to the people of Griffin Flat, Arkansas, for
their participation and help in the making of this film.
—BC-AD Productions

Don't Hesitate—Evacuate!
December 6, 1984
Griffin Flat, AR
Home of the Big Bang!

Epilogue

It's been thirty years since half the state of Arkansas was nuked by an accidental intercontinental thermonuclear bomb detonation. It was a Broken Arrow accident. It was Hollywood's fault.

Mad Max was right all along. Hollywood would do something idiotic and the government would cover it up.

It's the sixtieth anniversary of the novella *Eve of Destruction*, and it's the thirtieth anniversary of the movie that never quite was. Documentaries have been made and I've been interviewed many times by many a magazine, newspaper, and tabloid. I am the girl who survived. I am the girl who lived to tell the tale. My book, *The Incredible True Story of the Making of Eve of Destruction*, went on to be a bestseller that was shelved in the fiction section, all because no one wanted to believe what happened, happened.

But it did.

Even if it took *decades* for the truth to finally come out.

Not many believe it. How could they? It sounds farfetched. The United States of America nuked themselves in a Broken

Arrow event. Not even Hollywood could make up a story that fantastic. It wasn't some evil power that did us in. We did it to ourselves.

Speaking of Hollywood, they're now making a movie about my book—the making of the making of the movie that resulted in the state of Arkansas being decimated and the fallout extending to the lower eastern seaboard.

Hundreds of thousands of people were affected by that day on Crow Mountain. And it was covered up by the powers that be. When we walked out of that fallout shelter that day into what Max would later claim to be a truly *Mad Max* wasteland—it was our new reality. We were never the same. It was dark, cold, and silent. No one ever truly understood the silence. Only a few survived living so close to ground zero. Only when FEMA arrived and took charge of the situation did everyone fully realize it wasn't the Russians who attacked us. However, it wasn't until ten years later that it become public knowledge.

It was a man with a camera and his powerful lens cap that caused a chain reaction that caused the ICBM to explode.

Cinematographer Dylan Paige was the scapegoat. Sadly, he was the first to be silenced. Conspiracy theories ran wild. But then he went to work for the government. He was responsible for the propaganda films that you see today, like *Fallout Bad*. In a way, Mr. Paige went to work rewriting history.

The rest of us weren't so lucky.

Everyone wants to know what happened to the Griffin Flat Ten.

I'll tell you.

Here's how we ended up:

Terrence and I received confirmation from the people in charge that everyone close to us was dead. There were no bodies, so we didn't get visual confirmation. But they waited the appropriate time and decided to make it official in written form. Not a lot of people survived. It took me and Terrence forever to grieve. We were in shock and disbelief over the fact that we witnessed a fireball in the sky. We waited forever for the bomb to drop and then it did, sort of. Terrence and I wouldn't let each other out of sight for the longest time. We were family. We stayed strong because Mom and Dennis would want us to. Dad too. Pops would be happy for how close Terrence and I are. Ms. Wilcox would have probably made a snide remark but been glad her son didn't have to go on living alone.

We were relocated to a small town in Colorado. The air was crisp. It was perfect for our damaged respiratory systems. Once the fallout from the actual fallout happened we were able to live our lives, though the government liked to keep tabs on us.

Terrence and I remained close. We even share a driveway. He is the best brother ever. He works at a radio station, where he plays the music of his youth.

Max has finally let me and others see his drawings. He's also a published writer of science fiction romance novels. He writes under the pen name Axm Griffin.

Freddy has become my best friend. We talk almost every day. His acting career has flourished. He's producing the movie version of my book, and his son—who may or may not have a tail—is going to be playing him in the movie. Freddy is also Max and I's backer for our venture into television. A network channel is bringing comic books to the screen, and we think *Teenage Mutant* will have appeal. Just as long as they don't whitewash our stories.

Astrid became one of those recluse celebrities, though she's rumored to have a tell-all book coming out. I doubt it. The government didn't look too kindly upon my version of events.

Sadly, Owen never regained his sight. He has, however, found his calling in science-fiction stories told through different lenses. His new work is a spin-off of a *Star Wars* kind of series. It's full of humor and heart. He's been trying to get Astrid to star in one of the walk-on roles, but she keeps declining his offer.

Once it became public knowledge that Director Norman

Edman let Dylan take the fall for the "accident," it was hard for the director to find work in Hollywood. Eventually he moved back to the small town in Colorado and became the community director of the local theater.

The bus driver, whose name I can't remember, died in 2004. He spent his remaining years working as a bus driver for a local retirement home. He seemed happy but had a lot of flashbacks due to his PTSD.

Tyson eventually became a director himself and has signed on to direct the movie version of my story. Hopefully, he doesn't turn into the kind of director Norman Edman was and, from what I hear from the actors at the local theater, still is. Get the footage no matter the cost.

And me? Whatever happened to Laura Ratliff? Well, you just read my version of events, and hundreds of thousands of millions of people did too. My comic books with Max are a huge success. *Teenage Mutant* is even getting action figures. People of all ages want to be Destiny when they grow up, kicking butt and taking names.

Sometimes it's hard to realize what we went through those seven days back in the Griffin Flat High School bomb shelter. Not everyone believes us. Though the evidence is there. Maybe one day everyone will finally believe the Griffin Flat Ten.

Well, my name is Laura Ratliff. And this is my story. Let no one tell it differently than me.[1]

---

1 All of this may or may not be true. Big Brother is still watching.

Acknowledgments

Thank you so much to editor extraordinaire Dan Ehrenhaft. Honestly, not a day goes by that I don't stop and think how lucky I am to work with you.

And thanks to Bronwen Hruska, Janine Agro, Rachel Kowal, and everyone at Soho for championing *The Incredible True Story of the Making of the Eve of Destruction*.

To my family. Thank you for always being there and letting me follow my writing dream. Thank you Mom, Dad, and my brother, Alex. I love y'all.

And thank you for joining me in the Fallout Shelter and reading, *The Incredible True Story of the Making of the Eve of Destruction*.

Go Hogs!!!